Praise for Layne Harper's
Falling Into Infinity

"I am completely blown away by Falling Into Infinity by Layne Harper. I was not expecting to fall head over in heels in love with both Colin and Caroline (Charlie). I devoured this book in one long sitting without putting it down. I was completely captivated with the romance of Colin and Charlie and what would become of their relationship, each wanting to succeed at their dreams that are also tearing them apart."

— Jessica's Book Review

"Falling Into Infinity is a very nice debut from new author Layne Harper! This story has drama and just the right amount of light-hearted humor, and it should appeal well to those who enjoy both."

— Sinfully Sexy Book Review

"Let me start out by saying that I thoroughly enjoyed this debut novel from author Layne Harper! Colin and Caroline (Charlie) were amazing characters and it was absolutely a joy to get lost in their story. I was captivated in every way by this book and spent a number of pages in tears, laughter and finally holding my breath a few times."

— A Love Affair With Books

"Brilliant, brilliant book. I was holding my breath the whole way. I couldn't breathe. Just awaiting what happens next was sucking out all the air from me."

— Elaine's Book Reads

Falling Into Infinity

Layne Harper

Falling Into Infinity is a work of fiction. Names, characters, places and incidents either are the product of the author's imagination or are used fictitiously. Any resemblance to actual persons, living or dead, events or locales is entirely coincidental.

Falling Into Infinity
All rights reserved

Cover Design: Michelle Preast
Formatting: Polgarus Studio

Other Works By Layne Harper:

Infinity Series:

Falling Into Infinity
From Now Until Infinity
Finding Infinity
Infinity.

Infinity Series Short Story:

Aiden's Broken Heart

The World Series:

The World: According to Rachael (publishing November 2014)
The World: According to Graham (publishing in 2015)

This book is dedicated to my father-in-law, who passed away this year. One of the last days that I spent with him, he checked out my e-reader and saw the romance books that I had loaded on it. He told me to quit reading trash and suggested a few books that he liked (they were all biographies). Even though he would shake his head at Colin and Charlie's story, he would be very proud of me for finally writing it. Colin drinks a scotch in his honor.

CONTENTS

January, Senior Year 1

January, Sophomore Year 13

February, Senior Year 34

Summer after Sophomore Year 39

February, Senior Year 60

September, Junior Year 77

February, Senior Year 83

September, Junior Year 87

February, Senior Year 97

February, Senior Year 104

September, Junior Year 109

October, Junior Year 125

February, Senior Year 138

The Present 141

Chapter One 143

Chapter Two 152

Chapter Three 163

Chapter Four 172

Chapter Five 188

Chapter Six 196

Chapter Seven 208

Chapter Eight 215

Chapter Nine 228

Chapter Ten 238

Epilogue 244

Acknowledgements: 251

About Layne: 253

January, Senior Year

I TURNED my Porsche Cayenne onto University Drive and headed toward Café Eccel. The new Lady Antebellum song was blaring on the radio, and I found myself tapping to the beat on the steering wheel while I sang along to the chorus. I was meeting my best friend and roommate for our last ever first-day-of-class supper.

Rachael and I began the tradition in the ninth grade. Tonight, we were celebrating our fifteenth first-day-of-class supper, if you count summer school which, of course, we do. We're both seniors at Texas A&M University and will graduate in May.

Here's the ritual: We choose a restaurant that serves great desserts. We order our dessert first and share it. Then, if we're still hungry, we order an entrée. So far, we've never needed to see the appetizer menu.

As the song ended, I parked my car in a good spot near the door. Before I unbuckled my seatbelt, I dug my phone out of my purse and sent Rachael a text letting her know that I had arrived. Then, I sent Colin—boyfriend and expensive car purchaser—a quick message letting him know about dinner, and that we would probably need a ride home if he made it to College Station in time. Rach and I tend to drink one too many glasses of wine at our first-day-of-class suppers. Knowing the two of us, we'll need my chauffeur.

Before I could put my phone back in my Louis Vuitton purse, I received a text from Colin (boyfriend, expensive car purchaser, and ridiculous purse giver).

> *Colin: Absolutely! I would like nothing more than to drunk cab you and Rach back to our apartment. I should be in College Station in about an hour. I'll let you work off the fare.*
> *Me: It's my apartment that I am letting you crash in, and I'm sure that you can think of some way for me to pay you back. Love you.*
> *Colin: ;-) Love you, too.*

The waitress showed me to a table in the corner and handed me a menu. I began drooling over the dessert descriptions when Rachael rushed in excitedly.

"Charlie, I can't believe that this is our last supper," she said with a look of silly giddiness on her face. "We did it, girl. We managed to not get uninvited from Texas A&M."

I laughed at her joke. We were both graduating with near perfect GPAs. There wasn't a chance of us getting kicked out, but I guess graduating from college is an accomplishment nonetheless.

"I'm so proud of us, but I'm a little sad that this is our last first-day-of-class supper. Do you think we can make a pact to meet every year for at least one of these dinners?" I didn't want to be a downer, but I had a feeling that I was going to depend on Rachael's friendship even more after we graduated than I did now.

"I'm sure Mr. Quarterback will fly you wherever I am in the world if you flip your caramel-colored hair his way," she half-jokingly replied while rolling her eyes.

Rachael's an international business major who has been accepted into the Wharton School of Business for her MBA. She's ridiculously beautiful with her platinum-blond hair, bright green eyes and fair skin that would make Nicole Kidman jealous. She's got a killer body, and she is fluent in five languages. Rachael could very well become the ruler of the known world.

"Rachael, stop it. I'll use my airline miles to come and see you." This is such a sore spot for me. I wish it weren't. My mom has told me time and time again that you can't help whom you fall in love with. It's her polite way of saying *get over the fact that Colin likes to spoil you.*

Just then, the waitress greeted us and asked us for our drink order. We ordered a bottle of red wine and both reached for our driver's licenses knowing that it would be her next question. Once assured that we really were over twenty-one, she asked if we were ready to order.

Just like the silly fourteen-year-olds we were when we started this tradition, we both said the dessert that we wanted at the same time. So far, we've always said the same thing.

"Ready? One, two, three."

We both squealed, "Crème brulee cheesecake!"

We laughed with delight that our tradition had made it eight years. The waitress gave us a look of disapproval and left, shaking her head and mumbling about our poor dinner choice.

I wanted to get my uncomfortable conversation with Rachael out of the way before our dessert arrived. Once our wine glasses were filled, and we both had a sip, I started. "How do you feel about Colin staying with us on and off for the next three months? He has some time off before he has to be back in Dallas. He offered to get an apartment in our complex, but I hate to see him waste the money."

She rolled her eyes at me and said, "Charlie, you know that I like Colin. It's fine. I'll tell him to pick up my part of the rent and bills and he's welcome."

I gave her a friendly kick under the table. We both knew that Colin would find a way to pay more than his share.

Soon our very yummy dessert arrived. We indulged ourselves for the rest of the evening by eating too much dessert and drinking too much wine. We laughed until our sides hurt. I missed spending alone time with Rachael. She was always with Aiden, her boyfriend, and I'd been busy with school and traveling every weekend for Colin's career. I sincerely hoped that we would keep in touch even after we stopped living together.

Around nine o'clock, the waitress gave us a dirty look so I asked for our bill. We were informed that it had been taken care of by a gentleman at the bar. I let out a sigh, knowing exactly who had picked up our tab.

Colin McKinney. His name is a statement, and in College Station, Texas, he's a god. I guess Dallas also has him on a godlike pedestal because he'd led them to their first football playoff win in a long time. He's the starting quarterback for Dallas. He's six-feet, five-inches of sculpted muscle with wavy light brown/dirty-blond hair, depending on the amount of time that he spends in the sun. His eyes are the clearest green with just a few flecks of yellow. His half-smile makes women swoon. The man has blogs and Facebook pages dedicated to his appearance. The strangest part about it is that he is crazy in love with me, and completely oblivious to all the hot models and actresses that he could be banging. I've given him plenty of outs in our relationship and I all but begged him to dump me when he was drafted to Dallas. I told him that he needed to be single and free. How did he respond? He asked me to marry him. I replied with, "Not today."

That has been our inside joke since we began dating. Every day, he asks me to marry him, and he always gets the same answer: "Not today." One day, he's going to wake up and realize that future doctors and starting quarterbacks will never last. Until then, I relish the fact that the smart girl, who wasn't a cheerleader in high school, has landed the quarterback.

I started calling him my Mission Statement, or Statement, for short, when we began dating. He's like a company's mission statement. Colin McKinney was the complete package: charismatic, great looking, incredible athlete, funny, charming, loyal, and he has the biggest heart of anyone I know. Even when he's not feeling well or in a bad mood, he signs autographs and talks to his fans. The downside to the Mission Statement is that he's one of the most well-known men in the country.

Colin's eyes sparkled and his half-smile raised his left cheek when he saw me. "Charlie, are you and Rachael letting strange men buy you dinner again?"

I threw my arms around his neck, and he gave me a big kiss. It had been a week since I had last seen him. I glanced around to see everyone in the restaurant looking at us. Colin is a local hero here in College Station. Ignoring the stares, "we only let really hot guys buy us dinner," I teased. "You shouldn't have."

We've been together for two years, and he still gives me butterflies. His level of devotion to me can be overwhelming at times. I mean, I'm a great girl and all, but he tells me often that I'm the perfect woman. I worry that one day he will open his eyes and see that I'm far, far from ideal.

I grabbed his hand and led him to our table. He stole a chair from a nearby restaurant patron and sat down so close to me that our legs were touching. He grabbed my hand again as soon as he was situated. There was no doubt in the minds of the fifty or so people in the restaurant that I belonged to him.

"I was just about to text you to come drunk cab us home. We just have a little bit left in our bottle," I explained, trying to turn so I could see his face, but he wouldn't let any air in between us.

"How many bottles is this, ladies?" he asked, giving us a raised eyebrow.

Rachael and I looked at each other, and she sheepishly replied, "Two."

"Not bad. I see that you've shown restraint," he laughed, pulling me closer to him.

It took exactly two minutes for one of his fans to engage him in a conversation about football. I wished that we could go out in public just once without being interrupted.

Colin is great. He signs autographs and talks to everyone. Seriously, we've had grocery shopping trips that lasted two hours because he was mobbed. I've been known to leave him in public. I don't have the patience to stand there while people gush over him. My favorite, though, is when women hand me their phones and ask me to take a picture of the two of them together. He always smiles apologetically at me, but it doesn't make me feel any better. It's just plain rude.

I turned to Rachael and finished our conversation, completely ignoring his biggest fans that were now surrounding us. This is part of the baggage that comes with my Statement, Colin McKinney.

When our wine was gone, I was ready to take him back. So, I did what any twenty-one-year-old girlfriend to the hottest man on the planet who's obsessed with her safety does. I grabbed my $3,500 purse, keys to my $85,000 car, my best friend, and threatened to drive home. Attention was now successfully diverted back to me.

He jumped to his feet and chased after us while I giggled to myself, and Rachael gave me a dirty look. She whispered, "Part of the package."

Colin lightly hitting my behind rewarded my bad behavior. "You know better than to mess with me." He pulled me to him and wrapped his long arm around my waist and kissed me on my head. I love when he does this. It makes me feel so wanted.

So here's the deal: I drive the ridiculously over-the-top car that he said I had to have to keep me safe. He, on the other hand, still drives the biggest, ugliest truck on the road. I nicknamed it Big Bertha. It's a fifteen-year-old diesel Dually truck that I need a stepladder to get into. I hate it. It stinks. The amount of pollution that it puts in the atmosphere is enough to kill the ozone layer.

Colin teases me that Bertha is his soul mate. Every time she breaks down, I secretly hope that he can't repair her. Unfortunately, he's now richer than Scrooge McDuck, so he keeps pouring more money into her.

"We'll leave Bertha here and take your car, Charlie," he said as he took the keys out of my hand.

I smiled sweetly at him and batted my eyelashes. "I sure hope no one steals her."

He flashed me his patented Colin McKinney half-smile and smirked at my sarcasm as he climbed into the driver's seat of the Porsche.

"This is a great car," he said while the Porsche automatically adjusted to driver number two.

Buying this car was hell. Before, I had a ten-year-old Honda that my dad had given me. It was in bad shape. As soon as Colin was drafted, the endorsement deals came rolling in. Colin took one of the first checks that he received and dragged me to every car dealership in Dallas, insisting that if I was going to be running the roads between Dallas and College Station that I was going to have a safe car. He had me drive every SUV on the market. Then, we went back to his fortress-in-the-sky of an apartment while he researched the safety statistics. I didn't argue with him that I needed a new car. However, I just about had a heart attack when the next morning he announced that I was getting the Porsche Cayenne. I pleaded with him that there were perfectly good choices for me that were priced under $30,000. I tried reasoning with him that I would look like a gold digger if I let him drop $85,000 on a car for me. He, of course, didn't care what anyone thought. I almost had him talked into the Ford when I reasoned that the Porsche would make me a target for carjackers. His face grew pale, and he pulled me into his arms. He went back to the computer to see what he could find about the rate of theft.

Then, to my horror, the Porsche salesman said that they would throw in free roadside assistance as long as I owned the car and some sort of GPS location system. Colin was so pleased with himself. "See, Charlie, I am buying you the safest car on the road. What color would you like?"

He put the car in my name to further drive home the fact that the car was mine. I've learned that there are times that I can fight him and there are times that I have to ride out the storm that is Colin McKinney. The car has been one of many storms.

Our drive home from dinner was uneventful. As usual, Rachael and I got a case of the giggles. Being happy-drunk with your best friend is fun!

Colin and I headed up to the apartment while Rach went and checked the mail.

Rachael and I live in the oldest apartment complex in College Station. It's not particularly nice, but there is nothing wrong with it. It's cheap, on the Aggie bus line, across the street from the mall, and electricity is included in the rent. That means that even in the heart of August, we can still keep the air conditioner on seventy degrees—I know, that is bad for the environment. However, THIS IS TEXAS!

The big advantage to this complex is that the apartments are huge. Our place is more than one thousand square feet. We each have our own big bedroom, walk-in closet and own private bathrooms attached to our bedroom. For a girl who shared a room and a closet with her sister, and one bathroom with three other sisters her whole life, this place is a palace. We just pretend that the mismatched avocado green and harvest yellow appliances are retro and will be back in style any day now.

Rachael's parents were not particularly pleased with our choice of address. Her mom insisted that we look at the high-rise private dorms that have sprung up around the perimeter of campus. They were out of my pay scale, and they came with a maid service. Ummm … I have been doing my own laundry and cleaning up after myself since the fateful day Mom discovered that Aunt/Step-Mom Carmen (Daddy's head nurse) was pregnant with Daddy's fifth daughter. I can use a Laundromat.

Fortunately, Rachael's parents decided that our apartment would teach her character.

Colin stopped by the kitchen and fixed me a glass of water while I changed into my sleep uniform, which was Colin's boxer shorts and a tank top. Just as I was about to put my toothbrush in my mouth, Rachael yelled that I had mail. I nearly killed myself to intercept it before Colin saw it. I was waiting on acceptance letters to medical school. I'd had to apply before we knew what team would draft Colin, so I had applications in all over the country. The thought had been that I would go to medical school in whatever city drafted him. We would get married. He'd play football while I went to medical school. We'd purchase a McMansion, have two-point-five children and adopt a dog from the animal shelter.

I walked into the living room.

"Oh God!" I gasped to myself. There was a thick letter from Harvard lying on the counter. "Shit! Shit! Shit!" I cussed. Thick letters only mean one thing. I'd gotten in.

I was hoping that I wouldn't be accepted. Harvard is the number one school in the world. No one turns down Harvard. I mentally yelled at myself, *Why did you have to apply?* I should be doing back-flips and excitedly calling my family, but I knew that now I actually had to decide which medical school to attend.

My heart began to race, and I broke out into a cold sweat. I'd been blessed with the hottest, kindest, most perfect boyfriend in the world and all he'd asked of me was to marry him, come to football games every Sunday and pursue my dream of becoming a doctor while he paid for it and showered me with mind-blowing sex, unconditional love, and support. Yet, there I stood, contemplating going to Harvard and breaking his heart.

I'm such a horrible person for not walking over to the garbage can and tossing the letter in. Instead, I shoved the letter in a drawer. I needed to read it when the Statement wasn't waiting to give me his undivided attention.

I walked back into my room. He immediately noticed that something was wrong. "Hey baby," he said. "Is everything okay?"

He had already unpacked his duffle bags and made room in my walk-in closet for his clothes. That made my heart beat even faster. I loved being with him, but seeing his personal things in my space made me feel claustrophobic. I mentally gave myself a pep talk. *This is Colin, Charlie. You are going to marry him one day. The least that you can do is share a closet with him for a few months.*

I flopped down on my bed. "Yes. I'm just a little sad that Rachael and I had our last first-day-of-class supper. You know we've been doing it since ninth grade." I rationalized that this wasn't exactly a lie.

He stopped what he was doing and walked over to me, flashing his half-smile. "I know, Charlie, but you are moving on, or in, with bigger and better things," he said, taking my hand and placing it on his very hard erection.

I smiled and licked my lips. I really did appreciate where he was coming from—pun intended. "Yes. I definitely like bigger things, but it doesn't mean that I am not going to miss her."

I watched him walk back into my closet as I admired his perfect ass. It was firm and round, and awesome to squeeze. He must have sensed that I was staring at him because he gave me a little wiggle. Sometimes it was hard for me to believe that he was really mine.

He's also a mind reader. "Look, sweetheart. I'm yours, for the most part, until April first. Tell me what I can do to make your last semester in college perfect, and I'll do it," he said, while folding his last pair of jeans.

That is why this relationship was so hard on me. Essentially, from mid-January through to the beginning of April, Colin McKinney was the perfect boyfriend. Besides the whole mobbed in public thing, we were like any other normal couple. It was the other seven and a half months that we struggled.

At this time last year, we were in crazy-panic mode trying to determine where he would be drafted. We sat with his parents, agent and advisors, running scenarios. By the time that draft day came, I had lost five pounds that I didn't need to lose. He had a calm appearance in front of the cameras, but behind the scenes he was a mess of nerves. There was a strong rumor that Dallas was looking for a new quarterback. It just so happened that Dallas had hired one of the offensive coaches from A&M. Colin and the coach had a great relationship.

Colin had wanted Dallas so bad that he ached. He knew that he would have to earn the starting job, but it meant staying in Texas and close to me.

We were in New York the night before the draft. God bless his parents. They just accepted the fact that we were a couple and sharing a hotel room. We lay awake all night, holding each other, praying that it would work out like it should.

And it did. I nearly collapsed when Dallas announced that they were drafting Colin. The Texas boy didn't have to leave the state, and I was a mere three hours away from him by car. Then, to finish off Colin's perfect plan, I got early accepted into the University of Texas at Dallas Medical School two weeks later.

Almost immediately, Colin was flooded with endorsement deals. America's team had drafted the all-American boy. Then, to my surprise, we got offered endorsement deals together. Someone wanted to pay us to get married on TV. I thought Colin was going to stroke out on me. However, when *Playboy* called and asked if I would be interested in posing nude in their magazine, he went into a blind rage.

I'd thought that it was flattering. I suggested that I could be nude with just a stethoscope around my neck. I believe his exact words were "Over my dead body. The only person that will see you naked is me, Caroline."

Caroline is my real name and Colin only uses it when he is majorly upset with me, or something having to do with me. I didn't even consider accepting the offer, but pushing his buttons was a favorite pastime of mine.

I had neglected to mention to him that I hadn't formally accepted my offer to UT Dallas Medical School. I wanted to see what other schools accepted me, and go from there. Truth be told, there was a little part of me that resented him planning my life. I loved him. I wanted to spend the rest of my life with him, but I wanted some control over my future.

Once he had unpacked his toiletries, he came over and flopped down on the bed. "Penny for your thoughts?" he asked.

"I'm so happy to have you back in College Station," I said while I snuggled into his side. "I've missed you like crazy."

He pulled me to him and kissed my head. "You weren't the one making night drives to College Station during the week because you couldn't keep your hands off me."

"You did that because you have an unhealthy addiction to me," I clarified for him while I ran my hands over his chest, twirling his soft hair. I was teasing him, but we both knew that there was some truth in my statement.

"Maybe if more couples had this unhealthy of an addiction to each other the divorce rate would be zero," he said with a slight laugh, but I knew that he was making his point.

I pounced on top of him and captured his mouth. I kissed him with everything that I had. Colin confirming just how much he loved me was such a huge turn-on. He responded to me immediately. We made mad, passionate, crazy love all night, enjoying the idea that he didn't have to rush back to Dallas for practice and we were going to get to wake up together in the morning.

As I fell asleep, wrapped in his arms, an ugly thought popped to the forefront of my brain. I tried to dismiss it, but it lingered in my head and on my heart.

I wish that I felt as sure about our future as he does.

January, Sophomore Year

"CAROLINE, CAN you come to my office?" my dad asked when I answered my phone.

"Sure. I'm just finishing up with a patient. I'll be there in five," I said as I hung up. My dad's a very well respected sports medicine doctor. He has an entire floor of the Smith Tower in the Houston Medical Center. Athletes come from all over the world to consult with him because his specialty is helping them extend their professional careers.

I've dreamed of being a doctor since I was kid. Even though I was a sophomore at Texas A&M, I still drove the two hours one-way once a week to Houston to work for my dad. I knew that the experience would look great on my medical school applications, and the things that I was learning were beyond valuable.

My former Aunt Carmen, now step-mom Carmen, is the business manager for the practice. Even though I hate to admit it, Daddy and Aunt/Step-Mom Carmen seem to have a great relationship. They have two daughters, which makes six female children for my father.

I finished up the physical therapy appointment with a local gymnastics legend who'd had knee-replacement surgery. It was great to see her making such progress each week.

I walked her to the reception area and gave her a hug, letting her know that I'd see her at the same time next week.

As I headed to my dad's office, Aunt/Step-Mom Carmen gave me a wink. I smiled back. I wondered to myself what was going on.

I knocked carefully on my dad's oak door and waited patiently for him to acknowledge me.

After a couple of seconds, my dad called, "Come in Caroline."

I opened his door and was shocked by who I saw in his office: Colin McKinney, Texas A&M's star quarterback, was lounging comfortably in one of Dad's plush silk chairs. I was immediately taken aback by just how good looking he really was in person. He had a maroon plaster cast on his right ankle. I'm not a diehard Aggie football fan, but you would have to be blind and deaf not to know who Colin McKinney was. A&M is not known for producing great quarterbacks, however, he had single-handedly led the Aggies to winning seasons and top-ten rankings. The word around campus was that he would go professional.

"Colin, this is my daughter, Caroline Collins." My dad made the introduction and motioned for me to take a seat in his office. I noticed that Colin's parents were also in my dad's palatial office. He forgot to introduce me to them.

"It's nice to meet you, Colin. I go by Charlie." I somehow managed to get the words out of my mouth without sounding like an idiot. I decided to keep standing, because I knew that this introduction would not take long. My dad is a man of few words.

My heart was about to beat out of my chest. For some reason, I felt nervous. I stared at his face. His cheekbones and jaw looked like they had been carved out of marble. The only flaw was a slightly crooked nose, however, it almost added to his overall appearance. No wonder the girls on campus threw themselves at him. Probably the fact that he would be stupidly rich one day didn't hurt either.

"Colin, Caroline is a sophomore at A&M and works for me on Tuesdays. You can catch a ride with her every week. I absolutely will not clear you to drive until I am confident that your ankle has healed completely. I would like to see you at least once a week for twelve weeks to check your progress. I'll give your trainers at A&M the rehab protocol that I want you to follow." When he finished, my dad looked at me and gave me the Collins family nod in dismissal.

See, I knew that I made the right decision by standing, I congratulated myself.

"Um … excuse me, Doctor Collins, but I am going to need Charlie's phone number," Colin said. His voice was sexy. It was deep, but jovial, and I found myself longing to hear him talk more. My cheeks flushed that he took the hint about my name and called me Charlie.

"She'll leave it at checkout. I need to start the exam," my father stated, ignoring that I was still in the room. He had a habit of doing this to everyone but Aunt/Step-Mom Carmen.

"Colin, it was a pleasure to meet you. If you hand me your phone, I'll put in my number," I said, ignoring my father. Two could play at that game.

He fished his phone out of his pocket, and I swear Colin's hand lingered on mine a heartbeat longer than necessary when I handed him back his phone.

"Charlie, I'll see you next Tuesday. I'm looking forward it," he said. My heart did a triple flip. Colin McKinney just said that he was looking forward to spending almost four hours in the car with me.

***

Sure enough, the following Monday, I received a text from Colin giving me the address to his private dorm and confirming his pick-up time.

Monday night, I cleaned out my eight-year-old piece of junk Honda. My father believed that being poor builds character. Therefore, I drove an old Honda and lived below the poverty line. As part of the divorce agreement, Dad paid for my college and very basic expenses, so at least I wasn't in debt.

Cleaning the Honda didn't improve it much, but I was mentally reassured that there weren't any sport bras or deodorant containers for Colin to stumble across.

I was born and raised in Houston, Texas. More specifically, I grew up in West University. It's an affluent area of Houston built around Rice University. My dad chose this neighborhood because it is very near the

Houston Medical Center, which is where some of the most prestigious hospitals in the world are located. We moved there when my dad completed medical school and started his residency. I was three. Chelsea was five. My other sister, Amy, was almost one. Have you heard of buying the crappiest house on the nicest street? Well, that's what my parents did.

Soon after we moved into our house, my mom got pregnant with my fourth sister, Julie. As my mom tells the story, Dad was sure that Julie would be a boy. Um … not so much! My dad had four girls in eight years.

When you get us alone, ask the four of us the same story about our childhood, and we will tell you four different versions. I shared a room with Chelsea. Amy and Julie took the other room in our three-bedroom home.

I'd known my little family was in big trouble when I heard my mom yell my "Aunt" Carmen's name while I was in the living room watching cartoons on TV. Aunt Carmen was my dad's head nurse in his very booming practice. I was ten years old when Mom sat us girls down to explain that Daddy was moving out. It turned out that our Aunt Carmen was not exactly our aunt. She was sleeping with Dad, and had been for some time. They were expecting a baby together—another girl. Sarah was born about three months later. Tiffany—named after the fine department store—came along one year to the day later. Guess what? The divorce was still not finalized.

My mom decided to keep our "bungalow," as she called it, in West U. Apparently, Dad had made a lot of extra payments so it was cheaper to live in it than to move us. Although, if Mom had decided to sell the bungalow and go ten miles up Highway 59, she could have paid cash for a house where we all had our own rooms. I'm sure my life would be completely different if she hadn't fought so hard to stay in our affluent enclave. I also would not have met Rachael, whose family home was a refuge for me.

My mom got interested in real estate and has worked her way up to be a very successful agent. After my dad left, she was a very unhappy person. Imagine it from her point of view: she put Dad through medical school while we ate Ramen noodles. She joked that she'd had to breast-feed my two sisters and me because there was no money for formula. Then, we ate ground chuck while Daddy was in residency. He was finally in private practice, and we were seeing the rewards of our/her sacrifices when he left us.

Mom was determined that my dad's wandering eye was not going to deny her girls a single thing that we were entitled to. That meant that Mom played hardball in court. She made sure that my dad was still going to pay for our elite private schooling, college with the bare minimum of living expenses, and a healthy child-support payment. My dad refused to pay for a single thing extra.

One time, I asked for my monthly living stipend a little early. My dad said that he didn't mind at all. He would just have his attorney draw up the papers and have my mom sign them.

A car was part of the negotiations. Mom didn't have the attorney specify that the car at least had to have power steering, which was why I drove a Honda that was an absolute piece of junk.

After I was done cleaning my car, I pulled out my cutest pair of scrubs (if that's possible). They were lavender, and the color looked great with my caramel-colored hair, light olive complexion, and purple/blue eyes. I even tried them on for Rachael to get her seal of approval.

"Charlie, this is hysterical," Rachael teased. "I've never seen you put so much effort into your appearance."

It made me feel defensive. "Just because I want to look nice and have a clean car doesn't mean anything except that I have self-pride. Right?" I asked her.

After my shower, I actually pulled out and dusted off my blow-dryer and blew my hair straight. I put a light spritz of expensive perfume on and double-checked my appearance before walking out of my apartment. I literally didn't put this much effort in even for a date.

On the drive to Colin's, I pondered why I cared so much about how I looked. Was it because he was Colin McKinney? Was it because he was drop-dead gorgeous? Was it because I wanted to impress him? The answer became clear. There was something about Colin that I liked. I thought about how he'd touched my hand for an extra second when we were exchanging phones. I hated to admit it, but he gave me butterflies.

He was waiting outside for me when I arrived at his dorm. Dear God, even in a cast and crutches he was fine. He was wearing a long-sleeved, fitted green T-shirt that skimmed his chest perfectly. His khaki cargo shorts rested comfortably on his hips. My mind wondered for a second what his abs looked like under that shirt. The green made his eyes even greener, if that were possible.

When he smiled and winked at me and my heart fluttered, I reminded myself quickly that Mr. McKinney had a reputation of being a ladies' man, but at least now I knew why. Any girl would consider herself lucky to get used by Colin McKinney.

I pulled into the circle drive, and he hobbled to the car on his crutches. His face was red with frustration. I got out of the car and rushed to help him. The look he gave me when I placed my hand on his back and helped him into the car let me know that this was not a position that he was comfortable with.

He was so bloody tall that I really had to work to get his crutches into the back seat. I finally decided to angle them and pray that my door would shut.

I climbed back in the driver's seat, and said in a cheery voice, trying to lighten his dismal mood, "At least my dad didn't buy me a Volkswagen Bug."

He laughed and smirked. "You sure know how to see the bright side of life, Charlie."

"So here's the scoop," I said as I reached for my case of CDs. "This car is old enough that my iPod doesn't connect. We actually have to go old-school and listen to CDs. Feel free to choose something."

He turned toward me and, with lightness in his voice that I wasn't expecting, said, "I think that I would like to get to know you better. We'll save music for when we run out of conversation."

Did he just say that? Wow! Colin McKinney wanted to get to know me better.

I turned the radio on to an old country station for background music. After all, this was College Station, Texas. Liking old country music is a prerequisite for entry.

"Okay, but don't ask me hard questions," I warned him, raising my eyebrow.

As I turned onto Highway 6, Colin said, "I've wondered all week why your dad calls you Caroline, but you go by Charlie. It's not a typical nickname."

Thank goodness he gave me an easy question. I loosened my grip on the steering wheel. "Well, I have five sisters. My oldest sister, Chelsea, started calling me Charlie. If you knew Chelsea, you would know that she was most likely calling herself Charlie, but the name stuck. My younger sister was just learning to talk and she jumped on it. Therefore, my birth name is Caroline Jane Collins, but the only person that calls me that is my dad. He thinks nicknames are ridiculous." I drop my voice mimicking his. "You name a child what you want them to be called. Anyway, I like Charlie. However, I plan to drop it for medical school."

"You're going to medical school?" he asked with a hint of surprise in his voice.

"That's the plan. I want to be an orthopedic surgeon, like my dad. He has great dreams of us going into practice together. I think that would be great later on, but I want to do Doctors Without Borders for a little while." This was the most that I have talked about myself in … well, forever. He was so relaxed and quiet filling up the seat next to me. There was just something about him that made me want to tell him all my stories.

He shifted in his seat. He was so tall that I didn't think there could be a more comfortable position for him, but what did I know. "Are your grades good enough?"

I would normally be offended by the question. However, I found that I wanted to impress him. Had I ever cared about impressing a guy? I couldn't think of a time. "I have a perfect GPA."

He didn't comment. I liked that. He changed the subject. "You are obviously very fit. What sports do you play?"

Oh! He noticed my body. I tried hard to not blush. "I run, bike, and swim."

That launched us into a conversation about working out and fitness that lasted until I exited Highway 59 and onto Fannin.

"Charlie, thanks for the lift. This has been the most enjoyable two hours in a car that I've spent. I don't think that we need CDs yet," he said in a jovial tone while giving me a wink.

I would like to say that I said something equally amazing back, but instead I just exhaled the breath that I didn't know that I was holding.

His frustrated scowl was back when I pulled up to the patient drop-off area. He apologized at least ten times for asking me to get his crutches and help him out of my car. He really looked ridiculous, folded into my tiny Honda.

I told him to go up to the thirty-fourth floor, and I would be up shortly.

He hobbled into the building reminding me of a toddler just learning to walk.

After I left the Honda in its assigned spot, I took the elevator up to my dad's practice. I checked in with Aunt/Step-Mom Carmen. Colin was already in an exam room. She sent me to monitor rehab patients who were using the rowing machines and treadmills.

Forty-five minutes later, I heard him before I saw him. Poor Colin was a disaster on crutches. How could someone be so physically talented and yet look like Bambi on ice when you took his right foot away from him? I walked over and helped him get situated on a machine that worked his shoulders.

"How did your appointment with my dad go?" I asked, expecting a flippant answer like fine. That's the way that most patients respond.

Instead, he said, "My ankle looks great. Your dad is very pleased with how it's healing. I need to rub vitamin E on the scar to help diminish its appearance, but I've heard that chicks dig scars." He winked at me. "He promised me that if I keep up the good work I can lose these damn things in two more weeks." He shot his crutches a very dirty look.

"Do you mind me asking how you hurt your ankle?" I asked him as I adjusted the tension on the machine.

"I broke it in high school and it didn't heal correctly. I spent the whole last season playing with a taped swollen ankle. Your dad said that I needed to have it fixed because it was only going to get worse."

"You know, it happens more often than you think. You'll not regret having the surgery and doing the rehab. I promise," I said, with a reassuring smile. What did I know? But, for some reason I wanted to make him feel better.

"I already don't regret it because I've met you," He flashed me a half-smile.

Why did my words fail me now? I didn't know how to respond, except with perhaps, "Would you like to go to lunch? You can do your rehab after."

We fell into a pattern over the next eleven weeks. I picked Colin up on Tuesday morning. I offered him my antiquated CD case. He refused to choose music and told me that we hadn't run out of conversation yet. He made obvious flirtatious statements. I ignored them or changed the subject. We didn't talk during the rest of the week, except for the obligatory text on Monday to confirm the pick-up time. I was so confused. He seemed to like me, but he showed no interest in me except on Tuesdays.

Tuesdays soon became my favorite day of the week. Our conversation flowed nicely. We laughed at each other's jokes, and we even had serious talks about my parents' divorce and the pressures that he felt to play professional football. I came to think of him as a trusted friend. I spent many nights trying to fall asleep but instead wondering why he didn't ask to see me any other day of the week. I was so desperate that I even got on Google to see if he had a girlfriend that he had conveniently forgotten to mention. Nothing. If there was a College Station girlfriend, she had not made it to the Internet.

I also wondered why he hadn't tried to kiss me. We seemed to have great chemistry. Sometime in the early hours one morning, I reasoned that I was obviously a friend to him, and not a girlfriend. I talked myself into learning to live with it. I would rather be like his kid sister than not have him at all. That's how much I had grown to like him.

When week twelve came around, I picked him up as usual for our last car trip to Houston. He had been off his crutches for eight weeks now and was in a walking boot. I knew that he was aching to drive. He said that he missed the ability to run, but he missed not being able to drive the most. I promised him that if he got a clean bill of health from my dad that he could drive us back to College Station. He looked like a kid in a candy store.

We had learned a lot about each other over the course of the last three months. He probably knew as much about me as Rachael did. He'd shared a lot about his family with me, too. He's an only child with two adoring, still-married parents—score one for them. He grew up and played football in a small town outside of Austin. His childhood couldn't have been more fairytale if Disney had written it.

As we got close to my dad's office, Colin said, "So, as a celebration of my soon-to-be release from medical captivity, I would like to take you out to dinner. I am not familiar with Houston, so pick a nice restaurant, and we'll stop on our way out of town."

"That sounds great. You've worked really hard. You deserve to celebrate," I said.

My mind started racing. Was this a date celebration or just a celebration? I was wearing scrubs. I couldn't go anywhere too nice. Did I want this to be a date? No, and yes. I couldn't date him. I couldn't have a boyfriend until I graduated from medical school. I also knew that it wouldn't last. See exhibit A: My parents.

But I liked him. I liked the person that he was. I realized that even if he were a math major I would still like him. Also, if I really admitted it to myself, my ego was a little bruised that he hadn't asked me out.

Sure enough, Colin got his release papers. Apparently, my dad lectured him up one side and down the other about not going crazy, but I don't think Colin heard him. I understood. I tended to tune my dad out when he lectured me, too.

I was helping a patient get adjusted with the right settings on a treadmill when all of a sudden my feet left the ground, and I was twirled around in the air. "Guess what, Charlie?" Colin laughed. "I got my walking papers."

He was so lighthearted and fun. I hadn't realized just how depressed the surgery had made him. There was a sparkle in his eye that I hadn't known was missing and he flashed me a half-smile that shown in his eyes. "Give me your car keys. I'm going for a drive!"

How could I resist? I walked to my locker and handed them over. "I'll be back to pick you up in two hours. Don't stand me up," he said with a wink.

The next couple of hours dragged by painfully slowly. Finally, my shift was over. When I walked over to get my purse, I noticed a clothing bag hanging on the outside of my locker. I thought someone had made a mistake. Just as I was about to bring it to Carmen, Colin appeared.

"I bought you something to wear for our celebration dinner. I hope it fits. Carmen said that you wear a size four," he said with a hint of nervousness in his voice. His pleading eyes told me that I needed to accept whatever he had purchased and play along, no matter what the dress looked like. I didn't want to rain on his parade. No one had ever done something so thoughtful for me before. I mean he was a guy that was considerate enough to realize that I didn't want to wear scrubs to dinner.

"Thank you. I'm sure that it's lovely. Give me a minute to change," I said as I walked into the female locker room, expecting to find something hideous inside the plastic. I slipped the dress out of the bag and it took my breath away. It was a lavender wrap dress that did wonders for my natural curves. Also in the bag was a pair of silver ballet flats that fit like a charm. I made a mental note to thank Carmen for helping him. I quickly ran a brush through my hair and pinched my cheeks. My heart beat wildly in my chest as I looked at myself in the mirror and said, "Congrats, Caroline. You got what you wanted. Remember: don't fall in love until after medical school."

I walked out of the locker room and he gave me a low whistle. "Turn around for me Charlie. I want to see all of you."

I did as I was told.

"That looks even prettier than I had imagined," he said in a deep voice.

Either I'm imagining things, or he might be in to me.

He led me to the car without so much as a limp. He opened the Honda's passenger door and offered me his hand while I sat down. He shut my door and walked over to the driver's side.

"Can I just tell you how much I have missed driving," he said, his half-smile matching the twinkle in his eye as he slammed the door.

I sat back and let the only other man who had ever driven my car besides my father chauffeur me to dinner. Apparently, Carmen had helped Colin choose a restaurant. We went to one of my favorites, Mi Luna in Rice Village. Once again, Colin opened my car door for me. He was being the perfect southern gentleman.

As we walked toward the restaurant, he reached down and took my hand, squeezing it gently. I felt a small jolt of electricity flow between us. Instinctively, I gasped.

He looked at me in surprise. *Did he feel it too, or is he concerned that I gasped?*

I had always thought of myself as a feminist, but I really liked how he took charge and seemed so careful with me. It made me feel important to him – a feeling that I was not used to.

Once we were seated, he leaned in close to me over the table. With a sparkle in his eye he said, "Everyone is looking at how gorgeous you are. I'm just glad that you're here with me or I would be jealous of the guy with you." He opens the menu without missing a beat. "What's good here?"

No Colin. They aren't checking me out. They are wondering who the plain girl is with the man that is so beautiful that he looks like a mission statement.

Instead, I said nervously twisting the napkin in my lap, "Thank you. I really love the dress. You have great taste." Then I changed the subject. "I like the cheese plate and steak with saffron rice."

I purposely avoided wine with dinner for two reasons. One, I didn't want to drink too much and do something with Colin that I might regret.

Two, I was afraid that I might have to drive if his ankle started bothering him.

Neither happened. I dropped Colin off at his private dorm without so much as a kiss goodbye, nor a promise of anything more. Our conversation on the way back to College Station was nothing more than friendly banter. I watched him walk into his dorm like the would-be doctor that I was, and he did great. His gait was very strong. He was going to be just fine.

After I pulled away from his dorm, I decided to rid my life of Colin McKinney. No more Tuesdays with him. I could now just wash my hair and put it in a twist. I didn't have to worry about what scrubs I was wearing. My life was going back to the simple and uncomplicated way it had been before. I deleted his number from my phone and washed my hands of Colin McKinney.

I chalked this experience up to a big reminder as to why I shouldn't get close to guys. I would worry about boys after I graduated from medical school.

**

By Sunday, I was a bit depressed. He hadn't called. Not that he had given me any reason to think that he might. I guess there was a small part of me that had hoped that he would text or call. Maybe I got what I wished for. Maybe I should have flirted more with Colin.

Rachael decided to cheer me up. She persuaded me to go country dancing at Hurricane Harry's. She knew how much I loved to dance, and I am damn good, if I can brag on myself. I put on my cute blue jean skirt with the frayed hemline, brown leather cowgirl boots that were worn but not gross, and a white sleeveless button-up blouse. I had gotten a little sun during an afternoon run so I didn't need makeup, except for mascara and lip-gloss.

Rachael had on her tightest jeans. The two of us really made a stunning pair.

"Charlie, let's go find us some cowboys," she said.

We paid our cover and made our way to the bar. I bought the first round using my fake I.D. and carefully carried our beers to the table.

The place was just starting to get busy. There were a few people dancing, but no one that particularly caught my eye.

We were on our third round when suddenly Rachael's eyes grew as wide as saucers. "Charlie, you will never believe who just walked in."

I looked around and spotted him. Colin. Fucking. McKinney. Damn! He looked fine. His jeans were faded, and seemed to have been painted on. I couldn't help but notice that he had a bulge in his pants. My mind drifted to how big he must be to have that kind of package. I quickly coaxed my eyes up to his white button-up shirt. I noted that we matched, both in our denim and white shirts. I wondered how nice I would look in that shirt tomorrow morning ...

"Shit!" I squealed. "Maybe he won't see me. We can squeeze through the crowd and escape. Come on. Let's go."

She reached out and grabbed my arm. "No. He's spotted you and is headed this way. Put your big girl panties on and get this boy out of your system," Rachael ordered.

What were the odds of the two of us being at the same bar? Not good. Maybe this was fate.

I let out a huge breath of air when his arm wrapped around my shoulders. "Long time, no speak, Charlie. Is your phone broken?"

"What do you mean, Colin? I never said that I would call you," I said, confused and a little offended.

"Ah ... but you never said that you wouldn't," he countered arrogantly. "Let's see," he said as he grabbed my phone from the table. "I bet my phone number has already been deleted." I had never seen this side of Colin before. He was being cocky and a little mean. I only knew sweet Colin, who held doors open for me, and talked about his family.

Damn! He knows me so well, I thought.

I just sat there and let him scroll through my contacts. "Yup! I'm pretty sure that my name should be right here. I'm hurt that my number has already been deleted. I'll add it back for you." He banged a little too hard on my phone's keyboard for my taste.

Rachael looked at me like, *say something, you idiot.* I sat there stunned. For the first time in my life I was in uncharted waters.

Colin kept right on. "Now, I think that you should dance with me as your way of apologizing for not calling me and deleting my number."

Mentally, I was screaming, *you could have called me also, asshole.* For some reason, though, I had lost the ability to speak.

Before I knew it, he was holding my hand and dragging me to the dance floor. Someone tried to get his attention but he waved her off. I'm sure that I looked like a deer caught in headlights. Overwhelmed didn't come close to describing how I felt. Colin McKinney was a man on a mission. That mission seemed to be dancing with me.

He left me standing in the middle of the dance floor while he walked over to the DJ to request a song I assumed. I stood there uncomfortably pondering if I should bolt for the restroom. For just a split second it looked like that he might leave me standing there and I almost melted in embarrassment. Fortunately or unfortunately, he stalked back to me. There was no one else dancing yet, so all eyes were on us.

The perfect two-stepping song began to play, and Colin put his arm around my waist. He then positioned my arm around him. I realized quickly that he thought that I had never danced before. What I had neglected to tell him during the hours that we drove back and forth from College Station was that I had been country dancing since I could walk. It was the one activity that all my sisters were good at and could do without fighting.

I let him try to teach me. It was cute. About halfway through the song, he leaned in and said, "This isn't your first time to two-step, is it?"

I shook my head no, and peeked through my lashes giving him a sheepish smile.

"Alright then, show me what you can do," he whispered in my ear, his warm breath sending shivers down my spine. He pulled me to him a little tighter.

He started twirling me around the floor. I kept up with him and enjoyed the huge smile on his face immensely.

When the song was over, he leaned me back in a very deep dip. For half a second, I thought that he was going to kiss me. But then confusion clouded his eyes and at the last minute he seemed to change his mind.

He looked at me and shook his head in confusion. "Is there anything that you don't do well, Charlie?"

I just smiled at him. "I am not a very good singer."

The next song began to play. It was fast and made for jitterbugging. Colin swung me around his back, threw me up in the air and in between his legs. People actually stopped talking to watch us. I'm sure they thought that we had been dancing together like this for years. When the song was over, we got a standing ovation from a group of about thirty people near the dance floor.

I noticed that Rachael had joined the group and was standing next to a cute guy with very dark hair and skin. They looked like yin and yang.

"Charlie, I'd like to introduce you to my friends. Come with me," he said, barely out of breath. He grabbed my hand. The spark was back again and jumped between us. He looked at me with big green eyes.

"Did you feel it?" I nodded my head yes.

"Then why did you delete my number?" he whispered in dismay running his free hand through his hair.

Before I could answer, the yang handed me a fresh beer.

"Charlie, this is my best friend from high school, Aiden," Colin said, gesturing toward Yang. He sounded annoyed that we had been interrupted. "I see he's already met your roommate. Rachael, is it?"

Before I could speak, I was bombarded by a feisty, tiny girl with crazy-beautiful, naturally curly hair that seemed to have come out of nowhere. "Hi! I'm Jennifer. I've heard so much about you. Colin is my fiancé's best friend. We've been dying to meet the girl that fucked with his head so much. Who knew that you would be here? It's really nice to see you. Hey! Can I buy you a drink? The way you were dancing, you must be thirsty."

I'm not sure that she stopped to breathe at all. I wondered what "fucked with his head" meant?

"I, um, I'm Charlie," was the best that I could mumble out. I took an extra-long swig of my beer and shot pleading eyes at Rachael to help me.

I felt two very large hands grip my shoulders. I looked up and saw Colin standing behind me. Those hands touching me called for another big gulp.

"Charlie, don't let Jennifer intimidate you. She's Quinn's fiancée and always in everyone's business, but that's why we love her," Colin said to Jennifer in a patronizing voice.

Jennifer playfully reached up and hit Colin's arm, giving him a pouty face. The guy who I assumed was Quinn gave Jennifer a kiss on the check and pulled her close. "She can't help it. She feels like she has to take care of the boys."

Before I knew it, my empty beer was being replaced with a full one. I noticed that Colin only drank water. A fleeting thought passed through my head, but my foggy brain wasn't able to grasp it.

Jennifer filled Rachael and me in on everyone's business, while another group pulled Colin away to talk football. He was still right by my side, just slightly turned away from me. I learned that Quinn was a starting running back. Jennifer and Quinn were engaged, and lived in a house in Bryan. Aiden had gone to high school with Colin, and the three guys became best friends their freshman year at A&M.

Aiden and Rachael seemed to be hitting it off. They were standing very close to each other and, they kept finding excuses to touch each other. He was quiet and sweet. I liked him immediately. Apparently, so did she.

After countless bottomless beers, I started to feel sleepy, and I obviously couldn't drive home. Colin hadn't left my side all night. It felt like he was staking his claim, but he hadn't done more than hold my hand or touch my shoulders.

He must have sensed that I was getting tired because he wrapped his long arm around me and pulled me against his side. "How about one more slow dance and then I'll drive you and Rachael home?"

I nodded in agreement.

He walked to the DJ booth and requested a song. Then, he grabbed my hand and pulled me on to the dance floor with him. I noticed that Aiden and Rachael had also made their way out here.

I instantly recognized the song. It was George Strait's "The Chair."

The electricity was back and our bodies were humming as we moved gracefully across the floor. He leaned down and sang the words softly in my ear giving me goose bumps. "Yeah, I like the song too, it reminds me of you and me. Baby, do you think there's a chance, that later on I could drive you home? No! I don't mind at all."

His soft breaths against my ear made electricity shoot straight to my lower stomach. I felt flushed and buzzed from too much beer and Colin. *I must remember that alcohol and Colin do not mix well.*

When the song was over, he dipped me back. As I came up, he gave me a kiss on the cheek. His soft lips took me by surprise. It was a kiss that was no more romantic than how one would kiss their mother, but it made my face tingle. I felt the presence of his lips on my skin long after they had left.

"Thank you for the dance," he said, with smoldering eyes.

"No. Thank you," I said with a smile. "Does Aggie football require that you take dance lessons?"

"No. Growing up in a small town in Texas does." He led me off of the dance floor.

"Colin, this has been an evening filled with surprises. Thank you."

"The biggest surprise was running into you here. Now, let's get you and that roommate of yours home before Aiden starts pulling out his dance moves and really embarrassing himself," he teased as we walked hand in hand to retrieve my purse.

Rachael and Aiden traded phone numbers while I said goodbye to everyone that I'd met. I was rewarded with a wink from Jennifer and a "Hope to see you around."

We made our way into the parking lot and towards the biggest and ugliest truck that I had ever seen. *Surely, this is not Colin's vehicle,* I thought.

When he went to unlock the door, I burst into laughter. I laughed so hard that I had tears rolling down my cheeks. He just stood there, looking at me like I had two heads. Finally, I was able to spit out, "To think I was embarrassed for you to see my eight-year-old Honda." Then I started laughing hysterically again.

Colin looked affronted. "I love this truck. What's wrong with her?"

"She looks like a Big Bertha," I said through my giggles.

"You know, Charlie, I always thought that she needed a name. I guess Big Bertha it is. Now, let me help you up," he said, flashing me his half-smile.

Thank God that I hadn't offended him.

The next day, I texted Colin and thanked him for the ride home. He had complained that I didn't call or text, so I figured that I would just put the ball firmly in his court. Now he knew that I didn't delete his number for a second time.

I didn't hear from him until the following Sunday when I got a text asking if Rachael and I would be going dancing that night.

Frustrating boy! If he seemed to like me as Jennifer indicated, then why hadn't he called or texted all week? Rachael and Aiden had already been on two dates.

Ugh! I said to myself and waited until Rachael got home to get advice on what to do. We decided to go dancing. Once again, Colin acted as if we were a couple. He only danced with me, drank water, and drove me home.

When I was climbing out of the beast that was Big Bertha, I asked him, "Care to run with me in the morning?"

"Sure. I guess. When and where?" he asked.

"Meet me at the park in front of my apartment at six thirty. We'll run my route," I said.

I don't think that I told him bye or thanked him for the ride home. He had me so confused; I actually hadn't expected him to say yes. This meant that we would see each other more than once this week.

When my alarm went off at six fifteen, I can honestly say that I didn't think that he would be waiting for me.

I threw on my sports bra and running shorts. I shoved my hair into a ponytail and grabbed my music and headphones.

I'll be damned if he wasn't stretching next to a park bench. Colin had on a maroon Aggie Under Armor shirt and running shorts. I had never seen his thighs before. I paused a half second to admire them. My God, he was an Adonis.

"Morning, sunshine," he called to me. "Let's see what you got."

My goal was to embarrass him. He kept my pace until mile seven. As soon as I saw him start to pant, I sped my pace up by fifteen seconds. It wasn't a lot, but it was enough when he was already winded. He hung on until mile eleven.

He grabbed my arm. "Charlie, I've got to slow down," he said while doubled over, his hands on his thighs, breathing in huge gulps of air.

I smiled at him. "Did you get outrun by a girl?" I was so proud of myself. I'm not sure why I felt the need to be better than him, but I did.

"Not any girl," he said while panting. "I got my ass kicked by Caroline Jane Collins, who is fucking perfect."

I laughed and said, "We're only about a mile from my apartment. I'll let you walk home."

I invited Colin inside for a glass of water and a stretch before I sent him on his way.

"So Caroline, when did you become a marathon runner?" he asked with a raised eyebrow and a smirk while he stretched his hamstrings.

"Actually, not until college. I swam from elementary through my senior year of high school. When I came to A&M, I had a really crummy roommate in the dorms. I started running to get away from her and found that I enjoyed it. Did I forget to mention while we were driving back and forth from College Station that I run about four marathons a year?" I asked, while giving him my innocent smile.

He picked up one of the couch pillows and tossed it at me. "I have a feeling that there is a lot that you've forgotten to tell me."

About three times a week, I found Colin outside my apartment stretching by a park bench and waiting to run with me. I would not let him run more than thirteen miles, because the doctor in me didn't think that it was good for his feet, but his pace improved dramatically. Our running banter was kept lighthearted and fun. He danced like a fool the day that he kept with my pace perfectly and wasn't very winded at the end of the run.

I then challenged him to swim laps with me ...

February, Senior Year

THE HARVARD envelope sat in the drawer like a grenade. I was scared Colin would see it. I was afraid to open it. Colin had told me last night that he had to go back to Dallas for a few personal appearances that one of his sponsors had asked him to do. He said that he would be gone for two nights, but he might have to stay longer. My heart fell into my stomach at the thought of him being gone.

He had only been staying with me for three weeks, but we already had fallen into an easy pattern with each other. He woke me up every morning with a marriage proposal, which I declined. We got up and ran. I showered and went to class. He headed straight for the gym. We met somewhere on campus for lunch. Most of the time it was the athletic complex so other students wouldn't mob us. He spent the rest of the afternoon working on his business deals, endorsements, and all the other stuff that comes with being Colin McKinney, Professional Quarterback in a football-crazy state. I went to study groups, worked on homework, or whatever pertained to school. I tried to work in a swim, but I usually preferred to go home and have Colin work me out. To say that we were making up for lost time was an understatement. We couldn't get enough of each other.

When he dropped the trip to Dallas on me, I was sad to see him go, but I also knew that I needed some time away from the Statement to think about medical school.

When I was sure that Big Bertha was gone, I went into the drawer and found the envelope. I took it into my room and opened it. Sure enough, in

34

big black print on Harvard stationery it read, *Congratulations Caroline Collins on your admittance to Harvard Medical School.*

Here, in front of me, were the words that every future medical student dreams of reading, and I wanted to die. My initial thought was that I would just decline. It would be easier for me to do what Colin wanted me to do. I would finally agree to marry him. We'd move into a McMansion. I'd go to medical school in Dallas. I'd hopefully avoid getting knocked up until I was out, and then I'd practice some place local. That way, I would get medical school and Colin.

But, as I kept telling myself, it's Harvard … It's FUCKING Harvard! No one turns down Harvard. You graduate from Harvard and you pick where you want to practice.

I knew that Colin would lose his mind if I chose Harvard. There are two things in this world that Colin McKinney cares about: that's me, and football, in no particular order. Big Bertha might be a close third. I honestly didn't know that he wouldn't quit football if I chose to go to Boston. So far, he'd never been in a position of having to choose between his loves.

I threw my running clothes on and went for a long jog to sort out my head. Around mile twenty, I realized that I deserved to have it all. I wanted to go to Harvard. I wanted Colin to play football. I wanted us to date, or hell, even get married, but we could live relatively separate lives until I graduated. If our relationship was as strong as he seemed to think it was, then why wouldn't it last through that? I finally felt happy thinking that I could have it all.

At mile twenty-two, I had a moment of clarity. I'd lived with him for three weeks, and for the past six months I'd missed him like crazy. We made ourselves crazy.

Colin had moved to Dallas in May. He'd fought incredibly hard and worked his ass off to earn the starting quarterback position. That meant I spent a lot of time sitting at his fortress-in-the-sky, waiting for him to be done with practice or watching tape, or whatever he was doing. He would drag himself in the door, and we would crawl into his giant egg-shaped tub.

We did very little dancing and lots of movie watching. I played domestic goddess. I fixed him dinner, bought bath mats, and kitchen hand towels. I organized his closet and folded socks. It wasn't the way that I had planned on spending the summer before my senior year in college, but I spent the nights with him. No matter how tired or sore he was, he made sure that I was always happy and knew how much he loved me.

He tried his hardest to make my summer awesome. We took a couple of long weekend trips to Cabo, and he spared no expense. He even flew Aiden and Rachael down to Mexico so I could spend time with her.

The media was relentless last summer. Some idiot blogger had started a CharCol—the name the media gave us—wedding watch. A rumor spread like wildfire that I was pregnant so we had paparazzi camped outside the fortress. I purposely wore skintight pants every day to make sure that they saw no bump.

Then, to Colin's horror, fan websites started posting pictures of me, and digging into my background. I had no past worth posting about, but apparently, there were freaks who decided that I was attractive enough to masturbate to. He absolutely lost his mind when someone put up a poll. "Who would you rather fuck: Charlie, or some other quarterback's girlfriend?"

I took it all in stride. Colin called his agent, Mark, and demanded that the poll be taken down.

I had more issues with Colin trying to go shopping at a mall with me. I'd just needed a stupid bathing suit for one of our trips to Cabo. I was willing to go by myself while he was at practice, but he wanted to watch me try them on and model for him. I indulged his fantasy. I walked out of the dressing room in a string bikini to see my Statement surrounded by people wanting his autograph. I'd turned around and walked back in the dressing room. That ended our mall trip.

Once the preseason began and school started for me, we were back in separation hell. I saw Colin the Friday before home games through Sunday afternoon. If it were an away game weekend, he flew me to wherever his game might be. We saw each other during stolen moments.

I missed him, but he was losing his mind. One night during a Skype session, I decided to introduce Colin to my friend B.O.B. (Battery Operated Boyfriend). I thought he would think that it was really hot to watch me use it. He nearly lost his mind when I slid my vibrator into myself. Three hours later, Colin was in my bed ravaging me. He left four hours later and drove back to Dallas. I'm sure that he had tons of energy for practice that day.

By the time Colin led his team to the playoffs with a very exciting and unexpected win, he was mentally drained. He was texting me incessantly. When I saw him back in the fortress after his win, he took me in his arms and for the first time in a long time, we didn't make love. He cocooned me to him and held on for dear life.

I was able to spend the week with him while he prepared for the next playoff game, which was out of town. I tried to be as supportive as possible without distracting him. I made him a good luck meal the night before he left. We watched *Any Given Sunday*. By the time my plane landed, I had ten texts from him, begging me to see him. I was his balm, his drug of choice. All he wanted to do was find different ways to be inside me. I should have forced him to focus, but I wanted him just as much as he wanted me. The game did not go well, but fortunately, it wasn't a total meltdown on Colin's part. The boys licked their wounds and headed back to Dallas.

I realized during my run that I couldn't do four years without him. He couldn't do four years of me in Boston without him. We couldn't do a long-distance relationship. We needed the constant reassurance of each other to function.

I was spent, mentally and physically when I finished my run. I needed a hot soak in the tub, a glass of wine, and a magic eight-ball. Maybe it would guide me through my personal hell.

When I walked into our apartment, Rachael was sitting on the couch. She did not look pleased. "How many miles?"

"I ran a little longer than I normally do," I admitted while I grabbed some water from the kitchen.

Rachael knew me too well. "I am not going to tell Colin how long you just ran, but if you do it again, I will. I will not have you slip back into bad habits, Charlie. Want to tell me what's going on?"

I tried giving her a reassuring smile. "I'm fine. I'm just a little freaked out about graduating." I was going to have to come up with a better excuse. This one was not going to last for much longer.

"I think you're full of shit, Charlie. But, whatever. When you're ready to talk, I'm ready to listen," she said while she walked into her room.

I was going to have to find a better way to deal with my anxiety besides exercising. I didn't want my past struggles with feeling out of control to upset Rachael or Colin. I entertained calling my old therapist for just a second, but decided that I would work hard to get it under control myself before I took that step. Colin would want to know why I was so upset, and I wasn't ready to discuss Harvard just yet.

Summer after Sophomore Year

"HEY, CHARLIE," Rachael yelled from her room while I was unloading the dishwasher. "Has Colin mentioned anything about going to the lake house for the fourth of July?"

I walked into her room and plopped down cross-legged on the foot of her bed. "Yes. He mentioned something about it. I'm not sure if I'm going. It's going to be all couples. I'm afraid that it will be awkward."

I watched Rachael pulling outfits out of her closet, admiring them, and either hanging them back up or tossing them on a suitcase in the corner.

She paused her packing and turned towards me putting her hands on her hips. "For God's sake, Charlie, will the two of you just go ahead and fuck? If you don't do it for each other, do it for the rest of us, who have to witness this absurdity," she said, rolling her eyes.

I should have been mad at her, but I wasn't. Colin and I hadn't even so much as kissed on the lips, yet, we ran together at least three mornings a week, went dancing every Sunday and had a standing date each Thursday to visit the children's wing of a local hospital and then go eat barbeque at a gas station about five miles out of town. It's one of the few restaurants that Colin could go to where the people just let us eat in peace.

I hadn't so much as looked at another boy since I met Colin. From what Rachael—who was now attached at the hip to Aiden—and Jennifer said, Colin hadn't accepted another girl's phone number since he met me in January.

I wasn't sure what our status was. I knew that if I agreed to go with Jennifer and Quinn (whose names might as well be one word), Rachael and Aiden (who had crazy monkey sex all the time) that Colin and I would feel pressure to act as a couple. If that wasn't what he wanted, then I'd run the risk of losing him as my best friend, which he had become, and it wasn't worth taking the chance.

"Please, Charlie. Just go. It will be so much fun. Apparently the house is quite nice. It's on a cliff overlooking Lake Travis. It has an infinity pool and a hot tub. If you don't want to share a room with Colin, then sleep on the couch. It's two nights away from here, with great friends, and all we have to pay for are groceries," Rachael said, making one hell of a great case.

"I'll text Colin and let him know that I'm in," I said in a resigned voice.

Two days later, I was dropping a duffle bag in Aiden's trunk, hoping that I would quickly develop malaria so I could stay at home. I was so nervous about the Colin situation. If he just liked me as a friend, I would know it this weekend. This was going to the most amount of time that we'd spent together at one time. I really liked him. I wasn't sure if I wanted a boyfriend, but I knew in my heart that if he started dating someone else I would be very jealous. *Why did relationships have to be so complicated?*

The three-hour drive with Aiden and Rachael was torture. They couldn't get enough of each other. It was "Sure, baby" this and "Ha! Ha! Ha! Honey" that. Thank goodness I'd brought a book.

Colin was meeting us at the house. He had gone home to spend a few days with his parents before football season became crazy.

The house was everything that Jennifer had promised. It was a one-story with the entire back lined with windows that overlooked Lake Travis. The kitchen was gourmet quality and, most importantly, the refrigerator was big enough to hold all the booze.

Colin arrived just as we finished putting the groceries away. Everyone greeted him like he was some kind of rock star, however, he ignored them and walked straight to me and gave me a hug and a kiss on the forehead. "Thanks for coming, Charlie," he whispered in my ear.

"No problem," I muttered.

The house had three bedrooms. Jennifer and Quinn took the master suite, complete with a sauna and Jacuzzi tub. Aiden and Rachael thankfully took the smaller of the other two rooms.

When I went into the room Colin and I were supposed to be sharing, I almost had a panic attack. It was a queen-size bed. Colin is like the size of two normal people. There was no way we were going to keep from touching. I dropped my bag in the corner and took out my bikini. *Maybe I can get drunk enough to pass out on the couch.*

I was the last one to join everyone around the pool. Rachael took one look at my face and handed me her homemade Piña Colada. "Here, friend. You look like you need this more than me."

I noticed that Aiden and Quinn were both drinking beer. Jennifer, Rachael and I were all making mixed drinks. Colin had a bottle of water.

He spotted me hanging with the girls after only a few moments. The look on his face confirmed what Jennifer and Rachael had been telling me all along: Colin looked at me like a thirsty man looks at glass of ice-cold water. He started at my feet and made his way up to my aqua bathing suit bottoms. He licked his lips when his eyes passed over my flat, tan stomach. I didn't have big boobs, but the aqua bikini top really did a nice job of making them look fabulous. Our eyes locked together, and when he made the *come hither* gesture with his finger, I didn't hesitate. *I guess he really does like me as more than just a friend.*

As much as he wanted me in that moment, I wanted him, because Colin, shirtless in swim trunks, made my heart flutter. He really was so gorgeous that he looked like a mission statement. No. Not a mission statement. He was my mission statement.

I walked to where he was leaning against a post, feeling like a goddess. He reached his hand out when I was close enough and pulled me to him. He leaned down and whispered in my ear, "Caroline, you are the most beautiful girl in the world. Marry me."

I looked up with my eyes wide with shock. I stood on my tiptoes and whispered in his ear, "Not today."

He picked me up, laughing like a crazy person, and threw me over his shoulder. Before I knew it we were both in the pool.

The rest of the day couldn't have been more perfect. We swam in the infinity pool until the sun went down. Aiden, who was quite the chef, did burgers for us on the outdoor grill. We ate too much, laughed too much and drank just a smidgen too much … everyone except for Colin. He stuck to his bottled water.

Around ten o'clock, Aiden and Rachael, who had been all over each other the entire day, were surprisingly tired. About thirty minutes later, Jennifer developed a mysterious headache and she needed Quinn to rub her temples.

That left Colin and I alone. Thankfully, there was a great movie selection in the house so Colin and I cuddled on the couch and watched the very romantic movie *Die Hard*.

When it was over, Colin asked me to go lie outside with him and look at the stars. I ran into the room that we were sharing and grabbed us a blanket. By the time that I got outside, Colin had his MP3 player playing old country and two sun loungers pushed together. He patted the lounger next to his, inviting me to lie down.

"Have we run out of conversation? Is that why I get music?" I said with a smirk as I crawled next to him.

He pulled me closer and said, "I think that I could spend a lifetime with you and not run out of conversation. You are an enigma."

"Oh really, Colin? I always know exactly what you are thinking," I replied, sounding snottier than I meant. Apparently that was a conversation ender. We lay in silence, listening to the music, watching the stars and cuddling under the blanket that he spread over us. He didn't try to kiss me or move his hands accidentally over my breasts. We were the definition of PG.

Just as I was about to excuse myself and go inside, Garth Brook's song "The Dance" began to play.

"Will you dance with me?" Colin asked.

"Sure," I replied still so confused as to what his intentions were towards me.

We slow-danced under the Texas stars, next to the infinity pool, with my head resting against his bare sculpted chest.

"Charlie, please don't ever say goodbye. Don't make me like the guy in the song that says that he could have missed the pain, but he would have had to miss the dance. I want to keep dancing with you forever," he said into my hair as we swayed to the music.

I stopped dancing and looked up at him. "What are you saying?" That sounded like a declaration of love to me. This man kept me constantly second guessing his feelings. I mean did he like me as more than a friend or not.

"I'm saying that I want to marry you one day. I'm crazy about you," he said as we stopped dancing. He stared into my eyes with intensity and passion. His green eyes looked lovingly into mine.

"Don't you think that we should date first?" I asked. *Is this guy nuts?*

He stepped back, drilling me with his eyes. His face morphed from lustful to hurt. "What have we been doing for the last six months, Charlie?" He dropped his head towards the deck and ran his fingers through his hair. "Have you gone out with anyone else? Dear God, you better not have slept with anyone else. You don't even spend as much time with your roommate as you do with me. If this isn't dating and falling in love, then I don't know what is!" He raised his head crossed his arms over his chest staring at me with such a deep intensity that it made me shudder.

I threw my arms up in frustration. "Colin, I am so confused. You've never even kissed me on the lips. You've shown no interest in me sexually until I walk out in a bikini and then you completely eye-fuck me. I need clues that you are in to me, and you don't think of me as your sister," I raised my voice.

In the same tone, he said, "Let's see. You've kissed me on the lips. No wait. You haven't. You've shown interest in wanting to fuck me. No wait. You haven't. I need clues you are in to me too, Caroline!" His fists balled tightly by his thighs and he leaned towards me as if that would better make his point.

Okay. Now, I was yelling. "You're Colin. Fucking. McKinney, football god. You're a walking fucking mission statement. Every girl in the state of Texas, and a few of the guys want to fuck you!

"I'm a pre-med nerd who spends eight hours a day on campus studying. I need a clue you want me. You're a given. If you want me as more than just your dance partner, running buddy, and Thursday lunch date, you need to tell me. Even better yet, show me. Try kissing me. Try grabbing my ass. I don't know. Maybe show some sort of interest in me other than what you would show your kid sister." With that, I turned and walked inside leaving his stunned face in my dust. I would be damned if I was going to sleep on the couch. He was the presumptuous one. He could figure it out.

I walked into the bedroom and locked the door. I put on my pajamas and proceeded to cry myself to sleep.

I woke up early the next morning after a very restless night, but I was scared to leave the room until I heard other people. Colin and I needed a buffer after last night. So I laid there watching the blades of the fan spin in circles. Then I heard Quinn say in a raised, anxious voice, "Oh my God! Colin, what have you done? Colin?"

I jumped out of bed, still in my pajamas and threw open the bedroom door and found Colin sitting on the couch with a half empty bottle of Jack Daniels on the coffee table in front of him and Quinn standing over him shaking him back and forth. Aiden just stood there staring at him with a look of despair on his face.

Aiden and Quinn looked at me with pleading eyes when I entered the living room.

My eyes darted between Quinn and Aiden begging them to give me a clue as to what was going on. All I got back were shocked expressions. I looked at the bottle of Jack. *That's not that much alcohol to drink, but then again, Colin doesn't drink. Does he?*

Colin was the most wretched sight that I had ever seen. He was sitting on the couch with his forearms resting on his legs. His head was dropped.

The half-drunk bottle of Jack Daniel was in front of him, as if reminding him of his bad deeds.

Rachael yelled from behind me, "Charlie, do something!"

When he heard my name he picked his head up, and with glazed eyes started looking around for me. When he finally spotted me, he attempted to point at me and said, "You. You made me regret the dance."

I inwardly rolled my eyes. *Could he be any more dramatic? "I made him regret the dance." Seriously! That's something that a drunken sorority girl would say.* Instead of me making fun, I yelled at Aiden and Quinn. "I thought he didn't drink."

Jennifer answered for them. "Honey, he doesn't drink until he does."

"What the fuck is that supposed to mean?" I growled. I wasn't in the mood for riddles.

I collapsed on the floor in front of him. "Colin, look at me. Why didn't you come and talk to me? Let's get you up, and I'll take care of you."

He looked like a beaten dog. His beautiful, wavy hair was matted and hanging limply around his face. His usually bright green eyes were cloudy and his eyelids heavy. His face was so red that I was concerned that he had sunburn. I rubbed his back. "Come on, Colin, come with me. I'll make you feel better."

I think that I finally got through to him, because he started to try to stand up. I put my arms around his chest and helped him to his feet.

"Charlie, I don't feel good," he confirmed.

"I know. You drank too much. I'm going to take care of you," I whispered to him.

I started barking orders. "Rachael, go find me aspirin. Jennifer, bring me a stack of towels. Aiden, go get him a glass of water. Quinn, help me get him into the bathroom."

Thankfully, between Quinn and me we got him into the bathroom attached to the room that we were supposed to be sharing. Quinn helped me maneuver Colin in front of the toilet.

Quinn said very quietly, and just to me, "Charlie, he has so much pride. Leave him be."

"He's in this position because of me. I'm not leaving him. I'll let you know if I need help," I stated very bluntly.

I closed the door behind him and locked it. I knew that Colin was prideful, but apparently I was the love of his life, and this was what loved ones do.

Pathetic was the only way to describe his appearance. His head was resting on his arms, which were folded on top of the toilet seat. "Colin, listen to me. I know that you just want to go to sleep, but I can't let you. We've got to get all of this out of your stomach. Even though you're a big guy, you have no alcohol tolerance. You never drink. You feel bad because your body isn't reacting well to the Jack. You're going to need to make yourself sick."

I shake him, and he doesn't respond – his body limply flopped back and forth. "Look, you're worrying me. If you can't make yourself sick, then I'm going to take you to the E.R. Do you understand me?"

He mumbled something that sounded like an agreement. Then he picked up his head and looked at me with eyes filled with hurt. "Do you love me like I love you?"

I stroked his beautiful face and said, "Colin, I know that there is no one else that I would rather nurse through a hangover than you. I look forward to the time that I spend with you. If that's how you feel about me, then yeah, I guess I love you like you love me."

"I'm going to keep asking you to marry me until you say yes," he mumbled.

"You do that. One day, I just might say yes," I reassured him, and I meant it. At that moment, I couldn't imagine that there was anyone else in the world that I could want more than him. Even though we still hadn't even kissed on the lips, I knew that losing him would feel like I'd lost myself.

I opened the door and found a big glass of water, aspirin, and towels waiting for me.

I handed him the water, and he gave me a drunk, gorgeous half-smile as his way of saying thank you. "Take a sip of the water."

He took a big drink and handed it back to me just in time for him to start losing his bourbon. I sat down on the edge of the bathtub. I rubbed his back, played with his wavy hair, and whispered soothing words to him.

I could tell how frustrated he was with himself. Every time another episode of the retching started, he would cuss. A couple of times he begged me to leave him alone. I ignored him and maintained my contact with him.

When he thought that he was finished, he leaned back against the bathroom wall. We were sitting across from each other, staring into each other's eyes.

"I feel like hammered shit," he finally said, sounding much more alert.

I flushed the toilet and grabbed him a towel, wetting it for his face. "You look like hammered shit. You need to drink some more water. Once you can prove to me that you can keep it down, I'll let you go to sleep," I ordered.

"I'm sorry that I overwhelmed you last night," he said.

"I don't want to talk about it right now. I want to get you better, and then we'll discuss this like adults," I reassured him.

Unfortunately, the water didn't stay down, but that round of sickness left him dry-heaving with nothing coming up.

He was so weak that when he stood, he reminded me again of the Colin that I met that looked like Bambi on ice. I followed him into the bedroom and watched him sit down on the bed.

I removed his very stinky T-shirt and made the joke while I was stripping off his shorts that this was not the way I thought my first time seeing him naked would be. I did allow myself one quick peek at the bulge in his underwear. *Hmm ... That will be very fun in the near future.*

He fell back snuggling into the spot that I had slept.

I pulled the covers over him and gave him a kiss on his forehead.

"I'll come check on you every hour. Sleep tight."

"Hey Charlie," he mumbled.

"What?"

"Marry me."

"No Colin. Not today," I replied sweetly.

***

About six hours later, Colin emerged from our bedroom looking like a spring chicken. He was freshly showered and smelled like my body wash. He walked straight to me and gave me our first kiss on the lips. I couldn't help but notice both Jennifer and Rachael raise their eyebrows at us.

He apologized to Quinn and Jennifer and promised to replace the Jack. I seriously didn't think that they cared.

We took the pontoon boat out, and turned a day that started off like a nightmare into a lot of fun. We all grabbed inner tube floats and jumped in the cool water of Lake Travis. The water was refreshing compared to the hot sun that beat down on us. As soon as Colin could get me alone, he whispered to me, "I'm a mission statement, huh?"

I laughed and shrugged. "You're apparently my mission statement."

I made him blush, and I loved it. He pulled my inner tube next to his and said, "I'm sorry that you had to see me like that. I will not drink again."

"You're a twenty-one-year-old guy; that's what they do. It's okay. I promise," I reassured him, not wanting him to feel ashamed. "Can I ask a question without you getting angry?"

"Um … sure, I guess," he replied, anxiety etched around his eyes. I have no clue what he thought that I was going to ask, but I had obviously made him uncomfortable. He began to fidget with the string of his board shorts. I'd never seen him this unsure of himself. The confident and usually cocky Colin that I knew had faded away, and a six-foot, five-inch anxious little boy floated next to me in the water.

I grabbed the hand that was rolling the board short string in its fingers and brought it into my lap. I grasped it to stop the nervous tic. "Why has it taken so long for you to tell me how you feel about me?"

I turned my inner tube so that I could see him better. We were facing each other, but still side by side, so that I didn't have to break contact. I got the impression that he needed my touch for this conversation.

"Well, Charlie," he began, "I guess I've never had a real girlfriend before."

The look of surprise must have registered loud and clear on my face because Colin laughed. "I've been with girls before, just not any that I actually got to know and really cared about before we … you know … had sex." He sheepishly looked at me and blushed pink with embarrassment. It was really cute.

At least a thousand emotions raced through my mind, but the most surprising one was jealousy. I was jealous of the unnamed girls who'd had his attention before me. I silently implored him to continue. Discussing his past conquests was not high on my list of interesting topics.

"At first, I just wanted to get to know you. Then I started to really look forward to our Tuesday drives to Houston. But, let's face the truth, Charlie, I dropped a lot of flirtatious comments and you didn't once flirt back."

I knew that he was right. I had been so scared to flirt because I didn't want him to think that I was just a stupid fangirl. Then there was that nagging promise that I had made to myself to not get involved with guys until after medical school.

I smiled at him while I continued to rub his hand. "I've been accused of being aloof by more than one person."

I could tell that he was trying out that word in his head for a moment. Apparently, he decided to not respond to my comment about my possible personality flaw, and he continued. "By the time that I ran into you at Hurricane Harry's you had me so fucked up that I didn't know my head from my ass. I wanted my celebration dinner to be our first date. You looked smokin' hot in that lavender dress, by the way. But, you gave me no signal that you were interested in me.

"I called Jennifer and Quinn when I got back to my dorm that night. They both agreed that you were obviously not into me like I was into you. Jennifer even pointed out that maybe I liked you so much because you were the first girl that didn't just roll onto her back for me."

Quinn interrupted by yelling at us, to see if we wanted beers from the cooler. Colin accepted water, and I gratefully took a beer. I was getting more information from this conversation than I had expected when I'd asked the question. I'd thought that Colin wasn't a good communicator of his feelings. I was beginning to think that I was the one who had the problem with communication.

Jennifer, Quinn, Rachael, and Aiden got back on the pontoon boat to make sandwiches. Colin continued once we were sure that no one was paying any attention to us. "I spent the rest of that week being a real asshole to everyone. I didn't know if I would ever see you again. I was scared to call you and ask you out because I didn't want you to say no. Finally, on Sunday, Aiden and Quinn had an intervention of sorts," Colin said laughing.

"They kidnapped me and insisted that I go dancing with them. They wanted me to go to Harry's and pick up a hot piece of ass. I was supposed to get laid and forget that I'd ever met you," he said, smiling at the memory.

In my sassiest voice, I interjected, "And boy did you find one hot piece of ass."

He leaned over and tickled my tummy. "Except that hot piece of ass had already deleted my number, confirming for me that you wanted nothing to do with me."

"Colin, you were such a jerk when you saw me. I couldn't believe it when you grabbed my phone without permission and started scrolling through my contacts."

He widens his eyes. "Well, Caroline, I was pissed. I didn't want you at some bar picking up guys when you had a perfectly good one—me —who you wouldn't give the time of day. One flirty comment back would have been all I needed. I decided in that moment, when my number had been deleted from your phone, that I was going to take you on that dance floor and embarrass you. You'd never told me that you could dance." Colin paused momentarily, no doubt thinking about that night. He started to chuckle. "You made me want you more than anything I have ever wanted in my life when you could dance as well as me. While we were jitterbugging, I decided that I would just have to convince you how fucking perfect we were together."

I laughed at the memory and remembered it well. Now, he'd confessed that he'd wanted to show me up with his dance skills and I was just as good, if not better than him. I silently added a point to my side of the scoreboard.

"Instead of being angry and confused by you, you became my goal. I decided that it didn't matter how long that it took: I was going to make you realize that you wanted me." Colin paused taking a sip of his drink.

"I texted you the next day after Hurricane Harry's, and you didn't respond until six days later when you asked me if I was going dancing again that night." I paused for a split second "What gives, McKinney?" That had been gnawing at me for a while.

Colin looked away from me and his mood shifted to one of darkness. The light left his eyes, and he ran his hand through his hair. It was another facet of his personality that I didn't know, and I wasn't sure how to respond. I decided to just wait it out and let him talk when he was ready.

He gripped my hand tighter, "You terrify me, Charlie. You aren't easy to read. Even though we spent so much time getting to know one another in the car, I still didn't know you then, and I don't think that I truly know you now.

"Football is a game of predictions. I can watch my receiver run a route that we have practiced hundreds of time. I know exactly when to release the ball and at what speed for him to catch it. I can watch the defense and predict what play they're going to run." He trails his hand through the water. "I can't predict a fucking thing about you. I can't read you. I'm never sure where I stand with you. For someone who has always been the best at reading plays and predicting outcomes, you scare the shit out of me." His words were almost a whisper, and I had to lean closer to him to hear the last part.

What he confessed made me choke on the sip of beer that I was attempting to swallow. I mean, Rachael had told me before that I have an unattainable air about me, but I always thought she was full of it. Now, essentially, Colin had just said the same thing. I made a mental note to reflect on his words later while I ran.

"I spent that week making myself crazy. I wanted to call you so bad. It hurt even more that Aiden couldn't quit talking about Rachael. I wanted to duct tape his mouth so I didn't have to hear how fucking perfect she was. I knew she wasn't perfect because she wasn't you. After I lost my temper in spectacular fashion at practice with one of the assistant coaches, I knew that I couldn't continue like this. I decided to invite you to Harry's. If you went dancing with me again, it was because the universe wanted us together. If you said no, I had to let you go and move on." He paused for a split second and then flashed me his Colin McKinney half-smile. "You know, with another hot piece of ass."

I knew that he was teasing because he gives me the cutest little smirk. He was ready to end this conversation. I took the bait and launched myself into his inner tube flipping us both into the water. We came up spurting water and laughing hysterically. Apparently we caused a scene, because when we turned around, everyone was standing on the boat watching us.

Colin yelled, "Nothing to see here, people. Move along. Move along."

We swam to the boat and made ourselves sandwiches. Rachael whispered in my ear, "We apparently have a lot to discuss when we get home." She smiled and nodded her head toward Colin.

***

Because of Colin's disturbed sleep schedule, he wasn't ready for bed when everyone else was. I was sleepy, but I wanted to spend some time alone with him, so I grabbed a Diet Coke out of the refrigerator and snuggled up to him on the couch.

"Would you like to have a do-over of last night?" Colin asked while tucking me under his arm.

"I would love that." I giggled.

While he grabbed his iPod, I located the blanket that we had cuddled under the previous night. He had the two sun loungers pushed together and old country music playing when I stepped outside.

I could have sworn that the stars were even brighter than they had been the previous night, or maybe I just noticed because I wasn't nervous to be alone with Colin.

He pulled me to him and I laid my head on his muscled chest. He started pointing out some of the brighter constellations. I recognized them, but I let him show me.

"I love your hair. It's so soft," he said while running his fingers through it.

"Thank you," I purred. "That feels good."

"Your hair and your eyes are the first things that I noticed about you when you walked into your dad's office," he confessed while continuing to play with my hair.

I looked up into his beautiful face. "I thought you were even hotter in person than on TV. When you touched me, I got butterflies in my stomach." I sat up and looked at him. "Colin McKinney, you are the only boy who has ever given me butterflies."

He flashed me his half-smile and said, "I'm glad to be the first."

I leaned toward his mouth and kissed his lips. It felt so natural … so right. Our tongues began a slow dance exploring each other's mouths. We weren't hurried. We were getting to know each other in a way that we hadn't yet.

He pulled away first, and looked at me with such longing that it made me feel weak. "Will you dance with me?"

"Of course." I smiled and took his offered hand.

He chose one of my favorite songs, "What Might Have Been" by Little Texas. We danced under the bright Texas stars, holding each other tightly. It was three minutes of bliss until he started laughing.

"Charlie, what a horrible song for us to dance to," he said through his belly laughs. "I've always loved this song, but the lyrics are about a guy telling himself that he can't change the past and that there's no way to know if their relationship could be anything more than friends. I'm so sorry." His laugh was infectious and before the song was over, we were both chucking. It was just what we needed.

Thankfully, he redeemed his taste in music by playing some more appropriate songs for us. After the fourth dance, I was beyond tired. I asked him to come to bed.

"Caroline Collins, I thought you would never ask," he said making me blush.

I glanced at the clock and saw that it read 3:32 when I felt the bed dip. Colin wrapped his big arm around me and pulled me to him. We lay in bed, holding each other. His front pressed against my back. We felt so right.

I fell asleep, optimistically dreaming of our future together.

We got up the next morning and took the boat out for one last hurrah. Everyone was in a great mood and agreed that we should make this a yearly trip. By the time the house was cleaned and put back together it was four p.m. I decided to ride back to College Station with Colin, even though it had to be in Big Bertha.

Colin motioned for me to scoot over next him. I now understood the draw of bench-seating in a truck. His hand only left my thigh to shift gears. My hand lazily rested on his knee, and my head was tucked under his arm. I couldn't get enough of his touch.

I had craved this level of contact since I met him, and I had been scared that my feelings were not mutual. Now that I had his touch, I didn't want to give it up.

When we reached my apartment and turned off Big Bertha, I did the boldest thing that I had ever done in my life. I invited him to stay with me. I wasn't ready to give up the contact just yet, and I, frankly, wanted him.

He smiled a cocky smile and took out his phone sending a quick text.

I frowned, "Who are you texting?"

Colin gave me his half-smile and said, "Aiden. I want to make sure that Rachael stays at his place."

"Oh." I bit my bottom lip.

The sexual tension between us could be cut with a knife. I don't know how we actually made it to my apartment, but we did. When the front door shut, he was on me so quick that I could barely keep my balance. The stress of admitting how we felt about each other, plus six months of not touching was just too much for either of us to hold back.

He kissed my lips, forcing them open with his tongue. I ran my tongue over his perfectly straight white teeth. He then began to consume me. His six-foot, five-inch body pressed against my five-foot, seven-inch slender athletic frame.

I could feel his erection poking into my stomach through his jeans. His hands were in my hair. My hands ran up and down his back. We stayed like this, passionately kissing and exploring each other's bodies over our clothing for a long time. It was every bit as good as I had imagined. A fire was burning in my lower stomach, and I ached for his touch.

He hugged me and held me close to him. "Are you ready to do this?"

I smiled, biting my bottom lip and nodded yes. I took his hand and led him to the red chair in my bedroom.

"I've fantasized about you in this red chair since I met you. Colin McKinney, I want to make love to you for the first time in this chair," I said. It's the boldest statement that I had ever made.

I gently pushed him down on the chair and stepped back. I slipped off my yellow sundress, doing a simple striptease for him and allowed my dress to pool at the floor around my feet. I stood in front of him in nothing but my white lace bra and thong panties.

He took a deep breath and his pants strained to contain his very large bulge.

"Caroline, just when I think that I have you figured out, you do something like strip in front of me," he said with lust and appreciation in his eyes.

Instead of moving close enough so he could touch me, I decided to stay at arm's length and touch myself.

I started by kneading my breasts through my bra. I tweaked my nipples until they were so hard that they looked like pencil erasers. I crossed one arm over my body and continued to massage my breast while I slipped the other hand in my panties and began to rub my clit.

Colin's eyes got that lazy look of a man filled with lust. "God, Charlie. That's the hottest thing that I've ever seen." He reached for me. I stopped massaging my clit to shake my finger at him. Once he leaned back in the chair and settled down, I continued.

I massaged my breast and vagina, running my finger inside and back out without ever taking off my panties. I was nearing orgasm. Watching him get so turned on by watching me pleasure myself was beyond erotic. I loved it. I loved that I could make him moan for me without touching him.

In a choked up voice, Colin whispered, "I can't just sit here any longer. Please let me touch you."

I put my hands down at my sides and walked very slowly towards him. I started unbuttoning his shirt. He tried to touch me, and I slapped his hands away. I pulled his red polo over his head, tossing it on my bed. I then reached down and started teasing and playing with the button on his jeans. He gasped each time he thought that I was unbuttoning his pants.

"Please, you're killing me, Charlie," he begged with his words and pleading eyes.

I finally let him pick his hips up so I could slip his jeans off. There was a small, wet circle on his underwear and his bulge was throbbing.

He sat back down in the chair. All he had on were his long boxer-briefs, jeans pulled to his ankles and loafer shoes. I bent down and slipped each shoe slowly off his foot, then I made quick work of his jeans.

His hands reaching for my waist. "If you touch me, I'll stop," I said. "This's my turn. You can have a turn later. Nod your head if you understand."

He nodded.

I slipped his underwear off, freeing his erection. "Oh, my!" I said, licking my lips in approval. It jerked and twitched for me, and it was so long that it lay against his stomach. There was nothing I wanted more than to shove his erection inside me and ride it until I came, but I wanted this to be his pleasure. I wanted to make him feel special. I wanted to remind him that I was not one of the groupie girls.

I reached around my back and undid my bra. I let it fall lazily to the floor. I then sat on his lap, straddling him. My breasts were mere inches from his mouth.

"Oh God, I want to suck your tits. Please let me," he begged.

"Not yet."

Then, through my white lace thong, I started gyrating on his penis. I rubbed my clit against it, dancing to my own music, swaying to my own rhythm.

"Oh, God," he moaned. "Please let me make love to you."

"Not yet, Colin." It was all I said.

I was so turned on that I was about to make myself come. I stood up and grabbed his jeans. I pulled out his wallet and looked inside. Sure enough, my boy scout had a condom.

I walked back over and stood in front of him while I tore the condom packaging open with my teeth. I knelt in front and took his penis in my hand, and held the tip of the condom while I rolled it down his considerable length. I then climbed back on top of him with my knees on either side of his thighs.

His hands were suddenly on my hips, "Charlie, I want you. I want to be inside of you right now. I've taken many a cold shower because of you. I've waited six long months for this moment. If I can't touch you while I make love to you, I'll feel like you're a stripper. Please let me touch you."

I nodded my head yes.

He was on his feet so fast that I couldn't register what he was doing. He picked me up and tossed me on my bed. He was on top with his hands going crazy all over my body. He reached down and ripped my lace panties off, then his hands were all over me again, first touching my breasts and then massaging my clit. He slipped one finger and then two inside. I moaned in appreciation. He knew exactly what he was doing, and it felt like heaven.

Suddenly, he stopped and stared at me. "Oh God, you're the most beautiful thing that I've ever seen. You told me that I was your mission statement. You know what, baby? You're mine. You are so fucking perfect. I can't get enough of you."

With love and lust and admiration in his eyes, he entered me. His hot breath was in my ear. His hands were supporting his upper body. His moaning matched mine. I was able to take all of him. He fit perfectly.

I reached up and grabbed his hair and pulled him to me. I whispered in his ear, "I want you to make love to me so hard that I can still feel where you've been tomorrow."

He groaned in appreciation of my words.

That set him in a steady, pounding pace. I was just on the verge of orgasm when he reached up and tugged hard on my erect nipple.

I came loudly with each tug.

Suddenly, he grabbed my hips and thrust into me, moving my hips in a circular motion. He yelled "Charlie" as he came.

Colin fell on top of me. I let him lie there for a moment, stroking his back in a soothing motion. Finally, I felt like I was being smothered so I gently rolled him off me.

The word *complete* is the only way that I know how to describe it. We made love like we danced together, like he tackled football and me my studies. Our lovemaking was athletic, passionate, driven for perfection, and challenging. We'd spent six months getting to know each other before we took that step, and with hindsight being 20/20, it was worth waiting for.

He put his arm under my head and whispered, "You're the most amazing woman, Caroline Collins. I'm not sure what I did to deserve you, but I'm sure glad that I did it. Will you marry me?"

I leaned over, kissed his cheek, and cuddled into his side. "Not today," I said.

We lay there for another two hours, exploring each other's naked bodies. I eventually got up, fixed myself a glass of wine, and brought him a bottle of water.

He'd started a bath while I was gone. When I followed the sounds of running water to the bathroom, he looked up at me with an apologetic grin. "I want to bathe you."

I slithered into the hot bath and drank my cold wine.

"Where did you develop a taste for red wine?" he asked as he took the glass from me to take a sip.

"My mom always drinks red wine. It was served to us starting at around the age of ten as something that you have with nice dinners. Mom wanted to take the mystique out of drinking," I explained.

"I like that it's cold. I bet it feels good going down while you lay in the hot bath," he said.

It did.

He meticulously bathed me. He washed and conditioned my hair and shaved my legs. It was the most intimate experience of my life.

February, Senior Year

"CHARLIE, I need a date." Colin, of course, decided to ask me when he was lying nude on my bed after giving me a record number of orgasms.

I sat up and looked at him, and then rolled my eyes as dramatically as possible. "Details." I absolutely hated doing public appearances with him. Colin could work the crowd and be so charming. I felt like a fish out of water. The fans were there to see him and not me.

I hated when the girls gave me dirty looks and assumed that they were more right for Colin than I was. I warred between being very possessive of him in public and disappearing. So far, we had made numerous public appearances together, but I had yet to find my comfort zone.

"You know how Subway asked me to be an athletic spokesperson ..."

"Yes, Colin. I vaguely remember that. I think that's how I got the ridiculous car," I said, while he completely disregarded my comments about his spending.

"Well, they're having some sort of meet-and-greet in Los Angeles. It's during your spring break. I thought it might be fun to go and then fly down to Cabo for the rest of the week," he made a puppy dog face that he knows that I can't say no to.

"Fine. I guess I can be persuaded to be your date if I get Cabo in return."

"I knew that I could bribe you with the beach and sun."

He knew me too well ...

The more time that I spent with Colin, the more I was reminded just how crazy I was about him. The two nights he spent back in Dallas were a nice break, but I was always ready for him to come back to me. That was what I'd learned about our relationship. When he was with me, I couldn't get enough of him, but when he was gone I tended to be okay. I made a mental note to think more about that on my next run.

Tomorrow, we were going to visit the kids' wing of the hospital, like we'd done every Thursday when he was still a student. Then, he was taking me to our gas station barbeque joint. My Statement knows how to show a lady a good time.

He arrived the next day at quarter to three to pick me up. He had a bag of signed Aggie footballs and Dallas merchandise to hand out.

We took off to brighten some kids' days. On the way, he reminded me about how he was supposed to be born with a genetic abnormality that should have taken his life within hours of being born. His parents had tried for years to have a child. They were not willing to terminate the pregnancy. Then, when he was born, the doctors were shocked. He was perfectly healthy. His mom said that it was divine intervention. His doctors said that they'd screwed up. Colin believed that visiting kids in hospital was his way of thanking God that he was okay.

He grabbed his bag of goodies and stepped around to my side to help me out of the truck. He held my hand as we walked into the hospital.

Nurses, doctors, and patients greeted him, congratulated him and fist-bumped or high-fived him. It was awesome to witness. He kept introducing me as his girlfriend to these people he had obviously built a relationship with over the years. I knew some of them from past visits, but some were new. "Hey, Doctor Jones, meet Caroline Collins. She's my girlfriend." It made me smile, and my heart sing.

We took the elevator up to the pediatric wing. We were met by a social worker, who indicated which rooms that we should visit. Colin shook hands with the kids, talked to them about football and posed for pictures. One little guy really busted Colin's chops about a bad decision that he felt Colin made during a game. Colin was so cute. He thanked the boy for the advice. The last patient's room that we entered was a little boy's. He obviously had spent a lot of time in the hospital because he and his parents had a relationship with Colin. I wondered how I'd never met him. Colin talked to the parents first, and got an update on the boy's condition. He was on the heart transplant list. They were anxiously waiting, and praying that one would become available. Colin took my hand and led me to the hospital bed.

"Hi, Colton. I would like for you to meet a special friend of mine. Her name is Caroline," he said.

"Hi, Colton. It's a pleasure to meet you," I said politely staring at the little boy with bright red hair and huge green eyes.

Colton looked at Colin and said, "Way to go. She's a hottie."

I laughed out loud. Colton's poor parents were mortified and sighed in defeat.

He continued, "If you don't kiss her, I will."

"Colton, that's some great advice. Thanks," Colin said flashing me his half-smile.

Colton was precious. We stayed about thirty minutes in his room. He gave Colin lots of advice about football, what ladies liked, and good movies to take me to.

It was so hard to say goodbye to him and his family. Colin leaned over and whispered in Colton's dad's ear, "Call me if anything changes. I'm praying for you." The older man teared up, and shook his hand.

We walked back to the elevator. I reached up and gave him a kiss. "Thank you for bringing me. This is one of my most favorite things about my Statement."

My heart was so full of love for this man. There was no press to take pictures and splash Colin's good deeds on the front of a newspaper. He did this for the kids and himself.

After we left the hospital, we headed to the gas station barbeque. It was literally a gas station about five miles outside of Bryan that sold the best ribs and brisket in Texas. I'm not even sure that the restaurant had a name.

Colin discovered it one afternoon his freshman year, and it became his secret hole in the wall that he just shared with a few important people. He loved going because the food was amazing, cheap, and everyone left him alone. If he wanted an honest assessment of how he was playing, gas station barbeque was the place to go. The old timers who hung out there were more than willing to tell Colin exactly what they thought of his game, if he asked. Their advice was rarely unsolicited.

"Hey, baby," he asked me. "Would you like your usual?"

"Sure," I replied. "See if they have banana pudding." I needed to eat more calories, and quick, before Colin started getting suspicious about my weight loss.

I chose a bright orange booth and took a seat while Colin placed our order. I studied him while he waited at the counter. He carried himself with such confidence. His size made him stand out in a crowd, but not in a scary way. Colin had charisma. Even if he were an average-sized guy with average looks, people would still have been drawn to him. I knew why he had become such a popular football player so quickly in the NFL: every guy wanted to be his best friend, and every girl wanted to sleep with him. He was special.

He turned and looked over his shoulder, as if he could feel me studying him, and flashed me a heartwarming smile. It made my whole body tingle. This beautiful man was smiling just at me. I smiled big and waved at him. He winked and turned back to the counter to place our order.

He grabbed our drinks and walked to our table. "Hey there, pretty lady. Were you checking me out?"

I giggled and said, "I think I was."

He reached out and took my hands across the table. "I've missed bringing you to gas station barbeque. I'll always think of this restaurant as our place."

"I brought you to-go orders a couple of times when I came up for games because I know how much you love it," I reminded him wanting to hear his gratitude.

"You did, and I appreciated it. It's not the same, though, as sitting here across from you, knowing that this is our place to just be Colin and Charlie. No one cares who we are, or what we do for a living. We're just us."

I rubbed his hands and said, "I love you. Just you. I forget to tell you sometimes, but even if you didn't throw a football I would love you."

"I know that you do. It's one of the things that I love most about you," he said while he caressed my hands in response.

When our food arrived, I asked Colin to tell me about the upcoming football season.

***

"Wake up, sleepy-head. Today's the day that you marry me," Colin breathed into my ear at six-fifteen in the morning.

I rolled over to try to escape him. "Not today, Mr. Sunshine," I replied in a hoarse voice.

Before I knew it he was on his feet, the covers were on the floor, and I was being dragged out of bed by my ankles. He yanked my naked body to his and grumbled in my ear, "One day, you will say yes."

I rolled my eyes and was rewarded with a swat on my bare behind.

Oh! I thought while I tied my running shoes, *He will pay today.*

Colin and I stretched near what we had come to call the Statement Bench. Apparently, Colin liked being my Mission Statement.

At mile eight of our run, I asked him very nicely if he would buy himself a new truck or car. I assured him Bertha could stay, but I would feel more comfortable if he were in something equally safe ... You know, like my car.

He flatly refused without so much as a discussion. So, I increased our pace by fifteen seconds.

At mile ten, I once again politely asked him to purchase a more reliable vehicle. Once again, he politely refused.

I increased our pace by thirty seconds this time. I could run like this all day. We'd see how long Colin could take it before he gave in.

At mile twelve, as I heard him huffing and puffing, I asked again very nicely if he could trouble himself to spend some of his ridiculous money on a new car.

He huffed and puffed and said, "I can do this all day, baby."

"Awesome, because we are increasing our pace," I said, barely breathing hard.

At mile fifteen, still able to talk while I ran, I said, "Colin, you are the love of my life. I adore you. That's why I want to keep you safe. Please allow me to buy you a suitable car for you to drive while you crisscross Texas. Big Bertha will always be a part of our lives. Hell! She can be the best man at our wedding, if I ever say yes. Please let me do this."

He stopped running, bent over, and sucked in huge gulps of air. "Fine, buy whatever you want with the credit card. Oh! And you will marry me."

I did a quick victory dance and allowed him to walk back to the apartment.

The rest of my day was spent fantasizing about what I was going to purchase for him. Part of me was tempted to buy him a tiny car like a Fiat, but the practical side couldn't waste money. Then, about halfway through one of my study groups, I had a stroke of pure genius. I knew exactly what he needed.

I was relieved that he wasn't at my apartment when I got home. I took his credit card out of my wallet and Googled car dealerships, giggling to myself as I made my phone calls.

There was only one located in the state of Texas. I gave the very stunned salesperson my credit card number over the phone, and then provided him with my delivery address. I asked the very nice gentleman if he could take care of personalized plates for me. Of course, he obliged.

If I had not had Harvard hanging over my head, I would have felt a whole lot more lighthearted. So far Colin hadn't noticed, but he was going to pick up on it soon enough.

My deadline for a decision was the first week of April. I hadn't shared my acceptance with anyone, and it might be time that I unloaded my burden on someone else.

I grabbed my phone and texted my advisor to ask for an appointment. He quickly responded with a time that worked with my schedule tomorrow. I knew what he was going to say: Choose Harvard. However, I was hoping that he would give Dallas a few more pluses in the yes column.

I felt overwhelmingly lonely and my secret was resting on my shoulders like a one hundred pound weight. It had been a long while since I had been alone in my own apartment. The quiet was deafening. I sent a text to Colin.

Me: Hey, big boy! How's it hanging?

Colin: A little to the left ☺ How are you?

Me: I miss you. Come home to me.

Colin: You know if you marry me, we'll have our own home …

Me: Home is where the heart is ☺

Colin: Touché, Caroline, touché. How about if I pick up my best girl and take her to dinner tonight?

Me: How long will you be?

Colin: Probably at least one more hour. I'm stuck at a 12ᵗʰ Man function.

Me: Have fun. Guess I'll have to pull out B.O.B.

Colin: You wouldn't?!?

Me: I would!

Colin: If I find him, he's getting smashed.

Me: Guess I'll hide him super well …

Colin: I hate that bastard. Be home in ten.

I smiled and hugged myself. Usually just the threat of my battery-operated boyfriend got me Colin on my terms.

I slipped off my jeans and long-sleeved shirt, and slid on the lavender wrap dress and silver ballet flats, the outfit he'd bought me on our first date.

True to his word, by the time I finished changing he was parking Bertha and headed toward me like a man on fire.

I stepped out of the apartment and met him on the front porch.

"I'm ready for said promised dinner," I said as I planted a chaste kiss on his cheek.

"What about B.O.B?" he asked. His eyebrows drew together in confusion and the obvious bulge in his pants told me that he was anticipating skipping dinner.

"It was a movie from the 1990s. I was forced to watch it as part of family night. I'm famished," I said as I looped my arm through his.

"You think you're funny, don't you?" He smirked.

"I know I'm funny." I gave him a girly wink.

"Fine, Funny Girl, I'll take you to dinner, but you have to ride in Bertha for the little stunt you pulled this morning."

As we were walking towards the ugly hunk of metal, "Does that mean that you will help me in the truck?"

"Always, Caroline, always. By the way, I know the game that you're playing. The dress and shoes are a nice touch," he said as he grabbed my behind.

***

After the 417th time our dinner was interrupted by one of his biggest fans, I wished that I hadn't played sassy, and we had just stayed home.

He could sense my unhappiness because he flashed his pleading eyes for me to be patient. This was part of the Colin McKinney Mission Statement, but it had never gotten easier. I really wanted to ask these people, "Do you not see that he's having a private dinner?"

Finally, when our food arrived his fans got a clue and left us to eat in peace. By that point, I was in such a foul mood that I was no longer hungry, but I didn't dare push my plate back. I didn't want the masses to sense weakness and swarm us again.

"Colin, you know how Rachael and I are getting our Aggie rings on Friday?" I started as I pushed my food around my plate.

"Yes. Of course. How could I forget?" he said.

"Well, we want to dunk them on Saturday at the Dixie Chicken with everyone else," I stated.

Aggie rings are a huge deal at Texas A&M. Every Aggie gets a ring their senior year and most Aggies wear their ring the rest of their lives. The tradition is that when you get your ring, you must place it in a pitcher of beer. You have to finish the pitcher in the number of seconds that is your graduating class. For example, if you are class of 2006, you have to drink your pitcher of beer in 106 seconds. Then, you have to catch the ring between your teeth. Most Aggies dunk their ring at a bar called the Dixie Chicken. It's a local legend. Colin didn't dunk his ring because he doesn't drink.

He got a look of horror on his face and put his fork down. "Charlie, you can't do that. You'll be all over the Internet if you dunk your ring at the Chicken. What about if I fly you and Rachael to Cabo? Y'all can dunk your rings down there where no one will see you."

How did my super fun day turn into this nightmare? I tossed my fork on my plate with a loud clank. "Colin, I don't want to dunk my ring in Cabo. I want to dunk it at the Dixie Chicken with all of my friends. I want to be a normal senior for once and do something that everyone else who isn't dating Colin. Fucking. McKinney gets to do." I know that I sounded like a brat, but I didn't care. I longed to be anonymous again.

I hurt him … badly. He dropped his head and ran his fingers through his hair. I hated the look that was on his face. "Fair enough, Charlie," he whispered. "What about if I see if I can get us a section reserved?"

"No!" I raised my voice. "I just want to go up there on Saturday and throw my ring in a pitcher of Miller Lite like my friends. I don't want special treatment."

"Fine," he said with lines etched around his eyes. "I won't go then. I'll get Aiden to video it for me."

I began to cry into my paper napkin. "I want you to come, but I don't want to be on the Internet, and I want everyone to leave us alone."

"Baby, it's not this bad in Dallas. I promise," he said while he rubbed my hand from across the table. "In fact, half the people still hate me for taking the other quarterback's job."

As if on cue, a college kid approached our table with paper and pen in hand. Colin waved him off with a dismissal nod never taking his eyes off of me.

I contemplated what I wanted to say next and took a deep breath before I continued. "Colin, this is very hard for me. Not only do I have to be jealous of the damn supermodels and actresses that throw themselves at you, but we're constantly swarmed in public. It freaks me out. What if we had a baby? Would you like these people crowding around your child?"

He removed his napkin from his lap tossing it on the table in defeat. "What do you want me to do? The only girl that I want is the one looking at me like this is somehow my fault. I do understand that it's my problem. To answer your question, no Charlie, I wouldn't like it if people were crowding around our child. I'd be fucking psychotic if strangers approached our children. I hate that because I can throw a football far and accurately that we can't have dinner in public, and I can't watch you dunk your ring. Once again, what do I do? Do we start acting like celebrities and only go places that can give us private rooms? You tell me the solution because I'm all ears."

I dropped my head as the tears flowed down my cheeks. I knew that he was right. There was no solution. We would never have privacy when we were in public. Everyone knew who he was, especially in College Station. Maybe he was right. Maybe Dallas would be easier.

He got up and walked around the table crouching down to comfort me. I looked up into his beautiful green eyes and saw the pain in them that I'd caused. "I'm sorry. I never feel like I have peace when we are in public."

He rubbed my leg trying to soothe me. "I don't either, baby. It's just part of me being the Statement, right?" His smile was forced and didn't meet his eyes.

We were making a serious scene. Restaurant guests had their phones out videotaping my melt down. Colin motioned for the waitress and handed her his credit card. She brought him his receipt to sign and to-go boxes. I boxed up our food while Colin took care of the bill.

It was dark out. He steered Bertha back to our safe haven in College Station … my bedroom. It was where we could just be Colin and Charlie, two young twenty-somethings who were in love.

"Is there any way to salvage this evening, beautiful girl?" he asked.

All I felt like doing was putting on a T-shirt, closing the blinds and making sweet love to my Colin, not the world's Colin. "I don't want to share you with anyone. Let's lie in bed and watch a movie in my room and make out."

"Like we're in high school?" he asked with a twinkle in his eyes.

"Yup! Like high school. I might even let you touch my boobs, but only through my shirt," I said, getting into the spirit of this game.

"Oh, Charlie. This is going to be one fun movie. I might even leave a hickey on your neck, just like high school," he teased.

I punched his arm. "You better not or my dad will see it and get really mad at you."

Before he could respond, my phone began blowing up with text messages. I opened the first one from my oldest sister Chelsea.

Chelsea: Did you and Colin break up? Why are you crying? What's Libby Maxwell doing with her arm around him? She's a whore. Let me know if I need to drive up.

"What?" I shrieked as I shoved my phone at Colin to read.

"Motherfucker! What's going on?" he said in utter confusion.

We quickly got inside my apartment and pulled up the hottest gossip website. Sure enough there was a video of me crying in the restaurant with Colin attempting the console me. The headline read *Is CharCol over?*

Beside the video was a picture of Libby Maxwell, an actress from some dumb reality show, with her arm around Colin's neck. Apparently, undisclosed sources had confirmed that Colin and I had broken up because he has been dating Libby for the past two months. Colin was reading this nonsense over my shoulder. When I looked up at him, he was as white as a ghost.

"It's just a stupid story, Colin. We know it isn't true. No need to let this garbage ruin our evening," I tried to placate him. "We have a movie to make out to."

Then I saw why he was so upset. I read the first comment under the story: "Finally, her hot ass can be mine. I'm going to show her how a real man fucks. I'm going to tie her up and shoot my cum in her long hair."

He reached for his phone and dialed his agent because Mark is always the first phone call when there's a problem. His hand was on my back, and he was rubbing my shoulder more to reassure him than to calm me down. He did this every time that he got upset.

"Mark. It's Colin." There was a pause in the conversation.

"Fucking fix this nonsense before I do. Have them remove the comment immediately," he screamed into the phone.

There was another long pause. I knew Colin did not like what he heard because his grip on my shoulder tightened to the point that it was painful.

"Mark, I pay you a shitload of money. Get your people out there fixing this story."

There was another pause where I guess Mark was talking. Then Colin replied. "No. I met her at some event that was held in Dallas. Her dad is a big fan, and she wanted a picture. I AM NOT FUCKING HER! I don't care about the fabricated story. I care that someone wants to rape Caroline," he screamed into the phone.

Whatever words Mark was saying were working because Colin loosened his grip on my shoulder.

"I know, Mark. But, this is my girl. I can't take much more of the bullshit," he said in a much calmer voice.

He nodded his head as if Mark could see him. "Okay. I'll talk to the university tomorrow."

He ended the call and looked at me with pleading eyes. "I know that you're upset, but you have to hear me out. Mark said that he would have the comment removed from the website and contact the College Station and campus police. We need to leave here for Rachael's sake and go back to our apartment in Dallas until we are sure that this asshole isn't a threat, and the paparazzi are no longer digging for a story. Mark said that reporters are on their way to your apartment right now. We need to go."

I balled my fists and stomped my foot like a petulant child. I yelled much louder than I intended to. I was just so damn frustrated. "Colin, in case you've forgotten, I will not get into medical school if I don't complete college. I want to pick up my ring on Friday. I can't run to Dallas because some lunatic thinks I'm hot, or reporters with nothing better to do sit outside of my apartment. There are some things in my life that do not revolve around you," I added with acid in my voice.

His volume level matched mine. "I know that you're upset. I'm upset too, but there's no need to be angry at me. This is just part of being Colin. Fucking. McKinney the motherfucking statement, Charlie," he said sarcastically.

I ran into my closet and shut the door sobbing. How could this evening have gone so badly? I had so much fun getting to buy him a car and playing sexting games with him. I just wanted to have dinner in a restaurant like everybody else. Yet, here I found myself crying in my closet with the media going crazy over break-up reports and assholes threatening to rape me. All I wanted in that moment was to just be a normal college girl again.

He opened the door and joined me on the floor under my neatly hung pants. "I'm just a girl who loves a boy," I sobbed. "Why can't they leave us alone?"

He tried his best to soothe me, but I was beyond calm at that point. I knew in my heart that Colin was completely devoted to me. He'd made it clear time and time again. I was his future. I just hated that I knew that THIS was our future. We'd have to run off and pay a fortune to get married because CharCol's wedding would bring in big paparazzi dollars. God forbid if we brought a little one into this madness. There would be a bump watch to see how fat I got, and high-dollar shots to see the baby. What if someone tried to kidnap our child because they knew that Colin could pay the ransom? I sobbed harder because I didn't know if I could deal with this future.

In my heart, I knew that I had an out. There was a golden ticket to Harvard that would take all of this stress out of my life, but it would also remove Colin.

"Let's get our bags packed. We'll go to our apartment in Dallas. The security is top notch. We'll eat delivery and watch shitty movies. I'll even watch *What About Bob?* We'll play high school make out. That sounded like fun," he said, winking at me. "We'll give Aiden and Rachael a break. The media isn't going to stay long once they know that we've gone into hiding. We'll let the police do their thing." He wiped a tear from my cheek. "I'll put a personal phone call in to the President of Texas A&M. God only knows the amount of revenue that I've personally generated for this university. They owe me this favor. I will guarantee that you will graduate in May if I have to hire bodyguards for you, and we'll get you your Aggie ring."

His plan and assurances made me feel better. I stood up and started packing my duffle bag. Colin grabbed a bag for himself and threw in a few essentials.

"You get changed, baby. I'm going to text Rachael and Aiden and let them know to stay away from the apartment for a few days," he reassured me.

I changed out of my beautiful lavender dress and shoes and put on yoga pants and a lightweight sweatshirt. *So much for seducing my boyfriend,* I thought while I put on my comfies. Dallas was about three hours from College Station. We had a drive ahead of us.

I gathered my school essentials and threw them in the duffle. Colin quickly grabbed our stuff and headed to the Porsche. I followed behind him with my absurdly expensive purse and newest cell phone. The car was ready and waiting to whisk me off to the fortress that is Colin's apartment.

"I need to make some phone calls. Do you mind if I do it through your car's Bluetooth?" He asked once we were on the road.

"It's your car. Do whatever you want." I knew that he was really upset, and I wished that I had just said okay.

Even in the dark car on a stretch of road with no lights, I could see him glaring at me. I pulled out my phone and started working on my text to all those who loved me, letting them know that I was fine and headed to Dallas.

I tried to ignore Colin's conversations. His first phone call was to his parents. He reassured them that we were not breaking up and there was no other woman. Then, I heard the stress in his voice when he told them about the threat and about the reporters headed to my apartment.

I rolled my eyes. Should he really have to have these sorts of conversations with his parents?

His mom went on and on about how much she loved me, and how Colin needed to reassure and protect me. Now, it was his turn to roll his eyes. I needed to remember to call her tomorrow.

His next call was to leave a voicemail canceling his public appearances for the next three days.

Finally, he grabbed his phone and took it off Bluetooth. I was now suspicious.

"Why can't I hear this conversation?" I asked.

"Because I am calling Mark. He has the media people working on what stories the trash tabloids are running with. I also want an update on whether or not they've tracked down who this asshole is. There's no need for you to hear this shit, Charlie," he said with utter disgust in his voice.

My heart dropped into my stomach. We'd had to deal with this right after Colin got the starting quarterback job. I was about to go for a run in Dallas in my sports bra and shorts. Someone snapped a very unflattering picture of me while I was stretching with my behind in the air and bent over a bench. A website had a *caption this picture* contest. When Colin found out about it, he just about lost his mind. He had his attorney write a nasty letter to the magazine, he called and apologized to my parents, and lost himself in a bottle of bourbon. Unfortunately, we had another repeat of the lake-house weekend.

I reached over and rubbed his leg. "Look, I know that you love me. You know that I love you. What the media reports doesn't mean anything to me. The people that we care about know the truth. You can't threaten to sue every time there is a story about us. To be perfectly honest, I would have the media run stories about us every day if it meant that we could eat out or go shopping without being mobbed." I knew that this was much more about the threat. I'd learned some time ago that loving Colin meant I was media fair game.

I moved my hand from his leg to his hair. I could feel the tension leaving his body as I rubbed his scalp and played with his waves.

"That feels good, baby," he purred.

"If that feels good, how good would this feel?" I said as I moved my hand from his hair to the rock-hard bulge in his jeans. I played with him through his pants for a little while. When I went to undo the top button, he let out a loud moan.

"Charlie, what are you doing?" he asked.

"Watching TV," I said playfully as I pulled down his zipper. "Now, we need to do something about these pants."

He rose up just a fraction of an inch and allowed me to work his pants to his knees, freeing his huge, throbbing erection. I reached over and started stoking and massaging it.

He put the seat back on the driver's chair and set the cruise control.

"Do you think that this is a good idea?" he whisper-moaned.

I undid my seatbelt and wrapped my mouth around the head of his penis. I took it in all the way, wrapping my lips around my teeth and gently biting while I sucked.

I lifted my head up and said with syrupy sweetness in my voice, "I could stop if you wish."

"God, no. Please finish. This is a great idea," he reassured me.

I leaned back down and ran my tongue up and down the shaft, making sure that I licked the top when the pre-cum started dripping. His sounds of pleasure made me aware that I would do anything to hear him like this. I loved making him crazy with want and need for me and only me.

I wrapped my mouth around his penis again, working hard to break my own personal record for the best blowjob given.

His breathing became more erratic, and his movements frenzied. I took his huge balls in my hand and gently pulled and squeezed.

"Fuck, baby. I'm going to come," He panted.

I continued my ministrations, and he shot his come down the back of my throat while he pumped his hips into my mouth. When he was spent, I licked every bit of him clean.

I leaned up and kissed him gently on the mouth and scurried back to my seat and put my seat belt on.

"I think I deserve a Diet Coke for that," I said very confidently.

He laughed out loud, and it made my heart sing to hear him happy. He reached over and ran his hand over my hair petting me. "You deserve much more than a Diet Coke for that."

Once his pants had been restored to normal, he called the twenty-four-hour concierge at his apartment building and informed them that we would be arriving in a couple of hours. He asked that the refrigerator be filled with the basics and added a six-pack of Diet Coke for me, and three good bottles of Malbec wine. He also advised them of the threat.

I smiled and thanked him.

We stopped at the first convenience store that we came to. He got his customary water while I grabbed a fountain Cherry, Vanilla Diet Coke, a bag of Doritos, and gummy bears.

"What are you, five years old?" he teased.

"I just performed my personal best blowjob. This is my prize," I whispered back.

"No, your prize is that I am not letting you out of bed tomorrow. I'm going to worship your body all day long." He tossed at me while we were standing at the counter to pay.

I sucked in a deep breath and mummered, "Oh, my."

September, Junior Year

"CHARLIE, YOU plan on sitting with my parents, right?" he asked while shoveling a fork full of roast in his mouth. I'd made a pot roast in the crock-pot, and it was damn good.

"Umm ... I had just planned on pulling a ticket to the game with Aiden and Rachael. Why?" I asked while I marveled at how much food he consumed. Now that two-a-day practices were over, I'd thought he would start eating like a normal human again. That wasn't the case. It was gross to me how much food he put away. The Aggies first game of the season was Saturday. I was looking forward to it, which was new for me because I hated football.

"But then you will be on third deck, and I won't be able to see you," he reasoned after swallowing green beans.

"Why do you need to see me? Just throw the damn ball to whoever is supposed to catch it. I don't think you need to know where I am to do that," I replied flippantly. *Was this conversation even necessary?*

He threw his fork down, slamming it against his plate. It startled me and I jumped. "Because you are my girlfriend, at least the last time I checked, and I want you there because I love you and I need your support."

"Well, if you had just said that instead of assuming that I'm a mind-reader, then I guess that I will sit wherever you want me to. I don't know your parents all that well, but sure. It won't be the least bit awkward," I said, while rolling my eyes.

He picked up his fork and started the inhaling of food again. Apparently, getting mad at me didn't squelch his appetite. "Good. I'll get tickets for you, Rachael, and Aiden. That way you won't have my parents forced on just you," he said with venom in his voice.

"Colin, that's not what I meant and you know it," I huffed. I had met his parents that one time in Dad's office, but we were not introduced.

He shoved back from the table and grabbed his plate and put it in the sink. I heard him banging around and slamming drawers. I sat at my kitchen table and watched him throw his snit fit.

Finally, I said, "Your reaction does not match this conversation. What's going on?"

He walked back over to the table and directed his green-eyed glare straight at me. "I have sat here and watched movies while you've studied for the MCAT. I have purposely stayed longer at practice to give you your study time, and you can't even sit where I ask you to at the first game of the season? Do you understand, Charlie, that this is my future?" Now he was yelling. "If I fuck up this season, instead of playing in the NFL I'm sitting behind a desk, banging away on a keyboard all day. This is my medical school. The next four months define my life.

"I love you, but sometimes you are the most selfish person I've ever met. Do you think that your medical school is any more important than my NFL career? You just need to keep in mind that I have dreams too." He stormed. His eyes were dark green with anger and his fists were balled at his side.

I felt awful. I hadn't realized all of this. He was right. I'd take my MCAT in three weeks. All I had done that summer was take practice tests and study. "So, if I asked you to come watch me take the MCAT, you would?" I asked in my sweetest way. *Why can't I just say that I'm sorry?*

"I would wear a fucking cheerleader outfit and carry pompoms, if you asked me to," he said, still furious.

I had no idea what came over me, but I reached up and grabbed his penis through his athletic shorts and started massaging. It was flaccid, but it didn't stay that way for long. "What if I asked you to give up football, run my medical practice, and be my house husband?"

Before he could answer, I pulled his shorts down and took his now erect penis into my mouth, and started sucking it with everything that I had.

"Oh … Charlie … Shit …" he moaned while tugging on my hair.

I began sucking so hard that my cheeks hollowed in. I knew that he was close to coming when he started pumping his hips. I stopped what I was doing and looked at him.

"What are you doing?" he gasped.

"I'm showing you how it makes me feel when you just assume that I know what you are thinking and feeling. If you want me to do something, just ask me. Don't assume that I can read your mind." I prayed that he got the message as I stood there terrified of his reaction.

He picked me up and carried me into my room, slamming the door behind him. Before I knew it, I was up against a wall with my panties off, naked and my legs wrapped around his waist. He pounded his huge penis inside me, making me gasp as he stretched me completely. It surprised me more than it hurt. He paused for just a split second and then continued his assault. I leaned into his mouth and kissed him hard, passionately matching his intense pounding. His eyes were crazed and his breathing was erratic. Sweat covered his chest and forehead.

"Colin," I said into his mouth. "You don't have a condom on."

He growled back at me and kept up his relentless assault on my body. I threw my head back and screamed his name as I came.

He finished inside me for the first time ever. His hot liquid filling me up. It felt so sensual to have him naked inside me.

He carried me back to my bed and tossed me on it.

"That is how you make me feel when you use sex as a weapon," he spat at me.

He turned and walked into my bathroom and slammed the door. I could hear the water running. I lay on the bed terrified to see what was coming next.

He emerged from the bathroom about ten minutes later wrapped in a pink, fluffy towel monogrammed with my initials. He looked so ridiculous that it might have been funny, if he didn't look murderous. He walked into the kitchen and grabbed his shorts. He came back into my bathroom and shut the door again. He emerged a few minutes later fully dressed.

"Where are you going?" I asked with dread in my voice. I was thinking about the Jack Daniels at the lake-house and didn't want a repeat.

"I'm going to my place. You want communication? Well, here is some communication for you. I am pissed at you," he said, running his fingers through his wavy, wet hair. "I need you, Caroline. I think about you constantly. I wonder what you're doing. I go to sleep dreaming about our future together. I don't think you give a fuck about me as more than a convenient pastime and fuck-buddy when you need a study break. I shouldn't have to ask you to sit with the families at my football games. You should want to. You should demand that you sit with my parents. You should put down your MCAT study shit and ask me to spend time with you. Let me leave you with this thought," he said, yelling down at me while I lay naked on my bed feeling so exposed. "Have you ever been to my dorm room? No! I chase you. It would be nice to be chased back."

His semen was running down the inside of my thighs and on to my sheets. I was completely paralyzed. I didn't know that he had these kind of feelings for me: feelings that made him behave this way. He'd said that he loved me.

Colin wasn't done. He was usually so laid back. I'd never seen him this angry at anyone especially me. "To answer your question, I need you and football. I hope that you would never make me choose. However, after my football career is over, I'd love nothing more than to devote my life to supporting you and our kids. I don't think that you can say the same for me."

I went into ugly-cry mode because I knew that he was right. He'd just hit a spot inside of my heart that was very, very tender. My parents' divorce had scarred me far deeper than I'd admitted to him or really anyone else.

"I'm leaving. Call me when you can't breathe without thinking about me, because that's what I deserve." He turned on his heels and walked out my room, slamming the front door behind him.

My body shook as I sobbed into my pillow. The only man that I had ever truly loved had just walked out of my life.

I grabbed my phone and quickly texted Aiden.

Me: Colin is really angry at me and just stormed out. Please keep him from drinking.

After a couple of minutes, he replied.

Aiden: Shit, Charlie. I'm sorry. Rach is headed to you. I'll find him.

Me: He's so mad. Please tell him that I love him and let me know that he's okay.

Aiden: Sure thing. Hang in there.

I lay there for an eternity, convinced that I would die of a broken heart and not being able to control my tears. I had never felt pain like this, and I just wanted it to stop.

My best friend and angel soon had me wrapped in her arms. She rocked me like a baby. I was grateful for the compassion. At some point, I realized that I was still naked.

Later, I became conscious of Rachael helping me into my pajamas. I kept trying to breathe without shuddering, but I couldn't seem to take a breath.

I heard the trill from my phone telling me that I had a text. I mumbled for Rachael to check it.

It was from Aiden. "I'm with Colin. He is not drinking."

I think that I asked her to reply, but I don't remember.

At some point, I knew that there was sun coming in my windows. I tried to sit up, but my head immediately screamed at me. I fell back down. Rachael stirred next to me.

"Hi, honey. How are you feeling?" she said while she stroked my head.

"I have a migraine. Please close the curtains," I groaned.

"You haven't had one in a really long time. What can I get you?" she asked, with a raised voice. "Please call my dad and ask him to call in my medicine. Don't tell him why," I instructed her.

Just her rising from the bed made me nauseous. She came back a few minutes later and said that the prescription would be ready in thirty minutes. She handed me a cold cloth that I put on my head.

"Your dad said that this will help until I can get your prescription. He also said that he loves you and to call him when you're feeling better," she reported.

I grunted a thanks.

"Aiden called last night and said that Colin is very upset. I'm not sure what happened, but Charlie, he's crazy about you," she continued.

"He is. He doesn't think that I'm in love with him," I responded with no more than a whisper.

"You need to talk to him. You need to make him understand that you guys have very different perspectives on relationships. I know that his perfect family dynamic can be intimidating."

I knew that she was right, but I couldn't think about anything right then except keeping my stomach contents down.

She left me to grab my medicine and Gatorade. This was not the first migraine that my best friend had nursed me through. Like the angel that she was, she helped me sit up enough to take the pills and wash them down with the sports drink. The question was, would they stay down. The last time that I'd had one of these, we wound up in the E.R. with me getting a shot because of the nausea.

Fortunately, she had the garbage can ready because I vomited everything in my stomach. My wonderful friend stood there holding the garbage can until I was done. God bless her, because I couldn't have gotten out of bed. At least I was able to keep the medicine down the second time around.

"I'm going to close your door and keep the apartment as quiet as possible. Call me if you need me," she said as she kissed my cheek. "I love you. You and Colin are made for each other. You guys will figure this out."

I wished I could be as sure.

February, Senior Year

"HEY, CHARLIE. I need to call Mark now since I was bit distracted earlier," he said, giving me his half-smile that makes me weak in the knees.

"Oh, my! Whatever happened to distract you?" I asked, doing my best Scarlett O'Hara impression.

He threw his head back and laughed as he massaged my knee. "You are my funny, beautiful girl."

We were back on the road and heading Dallas.

"Fine. Go ahead if you must." I pouted. I knew that as soon as he talked to Mark, my lighthearted fun Colin would disappear. I was too tired to perform any more fellatio so I was going to have to deal with his bad mood.

When I heard him say hello to Mark, I pulled out my phone and checked my calendar. Shit! I was supposed to meet with my advisor tomorrow about Harvard. My plan to ignore my life-altering decision was not really working out for me all that well.

Colin had been too preoccupied to notice, but I had been exercising a lot more. I was trying to offset my potential weight loss by drinking smoothies in between meals, and eating Doritos and Gummy Bears. Exercising was the only time when I could have my head absolutely silent so I could concentrate on a problem and work through it until I had a solution. Running was either a mental break or problem-solving time.

I had considered calling my dad and asking for some sort of antianxiety drug, but that made me feel weak. Plus, he would want to know what was going on. If he found out that I might choose Colin over Harvard, his dream school that rejected him, he would be so disappointed in me and he'd probably never forgive Colin. I couldn't let that happen so I was all alone with this decision.

Sometimes I thought that I should tell Colin. I might be surprised, and he might demand that I go to Harvard and marry him after I graduated. However, I knew things like that only happened in fairytales. I knew my man well enough to know that just us being separated for the past year had killed him. I had classes to occupy my mind. He had football during the day, but at night, he would get lonely and anxious for me. On more than one occasion he'd wanted to see me so badly that he drove to my apartment in College Station to spend a couple of hours with me before turning around and going back to Dallas. I teased him that that was the most ridiculous booty call ever. Fortunately, he could laugh at his addiction to me.

There was a part of me that thought his level of dependence on me was not healthy. Then, I thought that maybe the divorce rate wouldn't be so high if couples that didn't feel this way didn't get married. What would happen if I died? Could Colin cope without me? Was it okay that I knew I could live without him? Don't get me wrong. I wouldn't want to, and I wouldn't be happy, but I knew in my heart that his need for me was stronger than my need for him. If it weren't, I would not even be considering Harvard.

My heart raced, and I felt nauseous. This was why I went for a run, swim, or bike ride. When I was exercising, these thoughts would stay out of my head if I wanted them to, and I felt free.

"What's wrong, Charlie?" Colin's conversation with Mark must have ended a while ago. "You're white-knuckling your phone."

I quickly tried to pull myself together. "I'm fine, baby. I just got lost in my own head."

"Is everything okay? You seem to be really distracted lately," he asked with clear concern in his voice.

Shit! He's noticed. I should have known by now that I couldn't hide anything from him.

I fidgeted with my phone. "Only four more months and I graduate. I guess I'm getting a little nervous." *Not true, but it's the best excuse that I've got.*

He chuckled. "Baby, your future is so bright. You're going to agree to marry me. I'm going to buy you your dream home. You're going to go to medical school, and take lots of study breaks with me. I'm going to lead Dallas to lots of championships. You're going to set up your practice and treat all the players that my O line takes out. When my career is over, I'm going to devote my life to you, your practice, and our family. See? What's there to be nervous about?"

He made it sound so easy. Before my brain could even stop the words from exiting my mouth, "What if I don't go to medical school in Dallas?"

The hand that was gently stroking my leg paused. "Why would you not want to do that?" he asked, sounding confused.

"I don't know," I lied. "You just have this wonderful little life planned out for us. I guess the pessimist in me just wonders what happens to us if one of those variables doesn't come to fruition."

He began stoking my leg again. "Well, all you have to do is say you'll marry me. That's not hard. Money isn't an issue for a home. You've already been accepted to medical school in Dallas. Sex has never seemed to be a problem for us. Our team is young and only getting better. We already made it to the playoffs. Championships don't seem to be out of the picture. My offensive line smells blood. My life is already devoted to you. Looks like kids are the only variable, as you put it, in this equation. How many should we have?"

"God, you make it sound so easy." It was my only reply.

I reclined my seat and pretended to be asleep while I processed what he'd said. What's wrong with me that I couldn't be as sure about this plan as he was? He was adamant about making me his wife. Why didn't I feel the same way about making him my husband? Maybe because my parents' divorce had shown me how ugly marriage could be. He'd never had to witness a family being ripped apart. Then I started to wonder if I could ever marry anyone. Would I consider giving up Harvard if Colin and I could live together without getting married?

I pondered the idea of suggesting to Colin that we live together and worry about marriage after medical school. The thought brought me enough comfort that I was able to fall into a dreamless sleep, something that hadn't happened in a long time.

September, Junior Year

IT HAD been five days since I had seen or heard from Colin. I knew from a very reliable source—Aiden —that Colin had thrown himself into football like a mad man. I was relieved that it wasn't Jack Daniels. I'd thought about calling him hundreds of times, but I didn't know what to say. I knew that Colin was right. I had been very selfish.

I'd been in a constant debate with myself if I should go to the game. I knew in my heart that if I didn't go, he would never speak to me again. I also knew that there was a part of me that thought that it was okay. I had never intended to fall in love until after medical school. God knows that I'm living proof of what happens to medical-school marriages. Maybe we were too young to feel this way about each other.

I also knew that the last five days had been crushing. I was a zombie. I moved through life, but wasn't present. I was so distracted that I couldn't study.

All I had done since I got over the migraine was exercise. I wasn't stupid. I knew that if I didn't get that under control, my dad was going to have the eating disorder talk with me again. It's easy to slip into old patterns.

I hadn't told Colin about my past struggles with an eating disorder, and I knew that if we had a future he needed to hear some pretty shitty stuff about me. Sometimes I thought it was easier to just run or swim or bike.

"Charlie, it's time to get ready for the game," Rachael pointed out. "Go in your room. Put on your short blue jean skirt, a cute Aggie T-shirt, and your cowgirl boots."

I nodded. I guess the decision was being made for me.

I emerged forty-five minutes later looking like a homeless person. Everything hung on me. My hair was dull, but it looked awesome compared to my eyes.

Rachael took one look at me and gasped. "When is the last time that you ate?"

"You mean that I didn't throw up?" It wasn't the answer that she wanted.

She walked me into the kitchen where she watched me manage to choke down a slice of cheese and a banana.

Next, she braided my hair, smeared makeup on my face and found me a shirt that was made to fit loosely.

"Caroline Jane Collins, so help me God, if you don't start eating and quit this exercise schedule I will call your parents," she admonished me.

I knew that she would. I promised to get my act together.

Rachael and I took the bus to campus and met Aiden at the will-call ticket window. We arrived early enough that the players were still warming up on the field. I was so nervous that I thought that I might lose what little was in my stomach.

Rachael must have sensed my panic because she reached over and squeezed my hand. "Honey, if he didn't want you here he wouldn't have left a ticket."

I let out the breath that I had been holding, hoping that she was right.

As we walked to our seats I saw him. He was warming up with a trainer. It didn't take more than a second for our eyes to lock together, his green to my lavender. He motioned to the trainer that he was heading my way. I walked to the cement railing unable to stay seated even if I had tried. I was so drawn to him – an inexplicable force – that made me need his touch.

I'd really thought that I had my act together, but as soon as he flashed me his half-smile, I burst into tears. I reached down and hugged his neck.

He was sweaty, and I just didn't care. I craved his touch, and his forgiveness.

"Baby," he soothed, patting my back. "Will you marry me?"

"Not today," I said while I laughed through my tears.

I whispered in his ear, "I'm sorry. You were right. I will start making you more important in my life. Every time I take a breath, I think about you. I love you. Good luck."

He stepped back and waved to Aiden and Rachael. "Thanks for coming. I've missed you like crazy."

I nodded my head. "I've missed you too."

"Quit crying, baby," he said as he wiped away my tears with his thumb. "I have a game to win." He brushed a kiss over my lips and turned and ran back on the field to finish warming up.

I headed back to Rachael and Aiden with a big smile on my face while I wiped my tears. I was so thankful that Rachael had made me come. There was nowhere else that I'd rather be.

She looked at me and said, "I think we have recruit tickets. These are amazing."

I noticed that we weren't sitting with Colin's parents. I wondered if he had done that on purpose just in case I didn't show up.

The Yell Leaders were warming up the crowd. We did all the Aggie yells and then the starting players ran out on the field. Everyone cheered and clapped. The band played. Even I had to admit that it was a little fun.

Then I saw him in his full uniform. Even though he had his helmet on, I could tell by his body and the way that he moved that it was him. He was number eight; I noted that for future conversations. He ran to the sideline and pointed to me in the stands. I flashed him my biggest smile and gave him a little wave.

Finally, the game got underway. The Aggies won the coin toss and opted to be on defense. I watched him on the sidelines. He was talking to the guys, his coaches, so in charge and serious. The defense didn't allow the other team to get a first down so it was Colin's turn to take the field.

The stands went crazy when he stepped on the grass. I wasn't sure if he heard the screaming fans because he didn't acknowledge them. *Maybe he was concentrating too hard?*

He took command of his team. He quickly passed the ball to a receiver and the Aggies picked up a first down. This pleased the crowd, and they cheered their approval. The next play he faked a pass and handed the ball off. The player made it one yard past the line of scrimmage. On second down and nine, he handed the ball off again. We picked up eight yards. It was third and one. Colin dove over all of the other players trying to get the first down.

My heart stopped beating, and I held my breath. The other team was on top of him. Colin was somewhere underneath all of the guys, who were much bigger than him, attempting to knock him back. Finally, the whistle blew and the other team let him up.

When I saw number eight, my heart started again.

They brought out the chains … First down. The crowd went crazy.

Colin got up and quickly had his team in a huddle. They formed up on the line of scrimmage. Colin got the ball. He spotted his receiver. He let the ball go in a high spiral pass. The receiver caught it. He turned and ran it forty yards for a touchdown.

The stadium went crazy. The band started playing. Everyone was kissing. When the Aggies score, everyone scores. The team congratulated Colin, the receiver, and each other. Even I had to admit that this was really fun.

Aiden and Rachael kissed like mad next to me, and I felt like the third wheel until Colin found my eyes and held up one finger. The next time the Aggies scored, he looked at me again and held up two fingers. I quickly understood. That was the number of kisses I owed him after the game. Deep in the third quarter, I got the distinct impression that he was purposely running up the score just so he could "score" more with me.

The game was over. I owed him nine kisses. Somehow I thought those nine kisses would get turned in for one amazing night of make-up sex.

The Aggies won by a lot, and the players lined up and did the Aggie War Hymn along with the fans. His eyes never left mine the whole song.

Rachael leaned over and said with a chuckle, "I think you guys could just throw down right here."

I smiled knowingly at her.

After the fight song and the school song were over, the players headed into the locker room. Rachael, Aiden, and I did quick check to make sure that we didn't leave anything and made our way along with the throngs of people out of the stadium.

My phone vibrated while we were waiting for our bus. I dug it out of my purse and saw that it was a text from Colin.

> Colin: You owe me nine kisses ☺ I'll see you at your place when I am done here.

I quickly texted back.

> Me: I'm looking forward to it.

The game could not have gone any better. We had issues to work out, but at least we both seemed willing to try.

My lifted spirits had improved my appetite. I had a fruit and cheese plate when we arrived home. Rachael gave me a hug and squealed with delight when she saw that I was eating.

I put my dishes away and took a shower to wash off the sweaty, sticky Texas humidity. I changed into a pair of shorts and a tank top, but when I saw my appearance, I knew that I needed to put on something baggier. Colin wasn't blind, and he would freak out if he saw the amount of weight that I had lost. I opted for sweat pants and a big T-shirt. Certainly not a make-up sex outfit, but it did a nice of job of camouflaging my appearance.

I picked up my abandoned MCAT study guides and dove in. I would take the test in mid-September. Most people take it three or four times, so I was looking at this round as practice. However, that didn't mean that I didn't want to kick its ass all over the place.

Later, I heard a knock on the front door. Rachael was waiting for Aiden to pick her up so I assumed that it was him. To my surprise, I heard Colin's voice in the living room, greeting Rachael. I leaned back against my pillow and closed my eyes drinking in the sound. I loved his voice. It was masculine and deep, but it was also good-humored. I really think that he could tell someone off and that they would thank him for bringing their faults to their attention. Charisma oozed from every pore in man's body.

A few seconds later, he opened my door. He looked ravishing. His wavy hair was still damp from his shower and falling in clumps around his chiseled face. His full mouth drew into his half-smile. I wanted to consume him.

I pushed my MCAT study paraphernalia to the floor and ran to him. I jumped up to reach his mouth, and he caught me while I planted kisses all over his face. He walked us over to my bed and laid me down very gently, as if I might break.

I put my hands on either side of his face and kissed his mouth with all the passion and desperation of the past week.

"Did you miss me, baby?" he asked while kissing me.

I broke our kiss and took his dear face in my hands. "Please don't ever leave me again," I begged. "I love you. I'm sorry. I'll do whatever you want me to do so you don't walk away." I smothered his forehead and cheeks with kisses.

He took my chin and held it steady while he looked into my eyes. "I love you, baby, and we need to talk, but right now I want to be inside you. Is that okay?"

I nodded my head, but my heart started racing and my palms became clammy. The bedside lamp was on. I needed it to be dark so he wouldn't see me.

I scooted towards the headboard and flicked off the light. The room was washed in moonlight that spilled in through the half-opened blinds. In his lust filled daze, he didn't question why I had turned off the light and for that I was grateful.

He knelt on either side of my hips towering over me. I ached for his touch and tried to grab his waist – craving the feel of his smooth skin. Colin met my wrists and placed them over my head. Shaking his head, "Let me look at you, Charlie. I've missed your gorgeous face." He secured them with one hand and caressed my cheek with the other.

I nuzzled into his touch. His callused fingers brushed over my cheeks and outlined my chin. I closed my eyes as he stroked my eyelashes. It was so sensual that I moaned in carnal appreciation.

"Colin, I need to touch you," I begged.

He released my hands, and my eyes flew open taking in the sight of my Statement. His erection tented his maroon athletic shorts and I licked my lips in appreciation. At some point he must have removed his shirt. The grey light of my bedroom perfectly highlighted his defined chest and abs. My God, he was gorgeous. I reached for his pants and slid them down freeing his penis. He removed his shorts the rest of the way and tossed them on the ground by my study material.

I grasped him in my hands and worked him back and forth enjoying his moans of pleasure.

He made quick work of my shirt and sweat pants adding them to the pile of things on my floor that were standing between us. When he tried to touch my breasts, I grabbed his hands and moved them so that he could feel how wet I was for him. He groaned in appreciation and started massaging my clit in the same rhythm that I was pumping him.

"I can't take it anymore," he gasped. He pulled out of my hands and placed the head of his erection at my opening. I reached around, grabbed his incredibly tight ass, and shoved him inside.

He found my lips and kissed me tenderly while he slowly moved inside me. It felt like heaven, and being home. I finally was whole again. I didn't realize how much I'd craved him until he was gone.

I ran my hands up and down his back until I couldn't take it any longer. This slow pace was killing me. I needed my release. I needed for him to feel me pulse around him. Colin needed to feel how much I loved him. I put my hands back on his behind and directed his hips to push harder. He gladly obliged.

"Baby, you going to make me come," he breathed into my hair.

"I need you, Colin. Please, baby, I am so close," I whispered back grabbing his ass with more strength.

With that, he pounded into me with four hard thrusts. We came together. Then, we clung to each other basking in our lovemaking both of us were silent. It felt glorious and perfect, but mostly it felt right.

His warm wetness ran out of me, and I loved it. I loved having proof that he needed me like I needed him.

After a few minutes, I began to feel smothered and I had to use the restroom. I tapped his back, not wanting to speak, and he rolled off of me. I got up and walked into the bathroom and flipped on the light.

"Charlie, what the fuck is wrong with you?" he said, with obvious shock and worry in his voice.

Shit! Shit! Shit! I had forgotten. I quickly flipped off the lights and sat down on the toilet.

"Nothing, Colin. Why?" I asked, trying to keep my voice neutral.

I should have known that this wasn't going to fly. In an instant, the bathroom light was flipped back on. He was gloriously naked with a semi-erection, looking at me with horror on his face.

"Privacy," I yelled while I tried to hide my body with my hands.

He yanked my hands away and stared at me with panic-filled eyes. Here I was in the most vulnerable position ever, sitting naked on a toilet while he examined me from head to toe. Thankfully, I finished and stood up, not bothering to wash my hands, and pushed past him to find my clothes.

From behind me, "I asked you a question. What. The. Fuck. Is. Wrong. With. You?" he said, pronouncing each word very clearly. "If you tell me nothing again I'm going to assume that you're a liar and walk out of this room."

Everything had been so perfect just minutes ago. I put my clothes on and collapsed in my red chair. He walked over and pulled up the matching ottoman, staring into my face. His huge arms were resting on his knees so he could better lean into the personal space that I was trying to maintain.

A little more calmly, "What's wrong Charlie? Talk to me."

I very quietly replied, "When I was in high school, I had an eating disorder." I pulled my knees to my chest and buried my face in my hands not wanting to see his reaction.

"Had?" he said with anger, sadness, and worry in his voice. "You look like a Goddamn cancer victim."

I picked my head up and opened my eyes. My poor Statement looked panicked. His eyes were dilated and his body was rigid. I had to make him understand. I hated that I'd made him this worried.

"When I feel like that I don't have control in my life, I sometimes slip back to my old ways. I've already started eating again, and I promised Rachael that I will cut back a ton on my exercising. Just give me a few weeks, and I'll be okay again," I pleaded.

"All those hours in the car together and you didn't think to mention this?" he said with obvious hurt in his voice.

"I'm sorry. It's not something that I like to talk about. It's in my past," I tried to explain as I leaned forward and rubbed his leg reassuringly.

He let out a rueful laugh. "Yeah. It's obviously in your past. You did this because I left?" he asked in horror.

"Colin, it's not something that I plan to do. I don't sit down and say, 'Today, I am going to run twenty miles, bike forty, and swim for two hours. Then, I am going to eat a hamburger in front of Rachael. Ha! Except, I know when she goes to bed, I will force it all back up.' It's a disease. I just do it until I feel in control," I explained.

"I'm sorry," he said, while he ran his hands through his hair in obvious angst. "That came out wrong. I know that you didn't do this to hurt me. I'm just trying to understand. I'm worried about you. Do you need help again?" he asked, as concern creased his forehead.

"No, I don't need help. I've done a great job managing my disease for almost five years. When I got out of treatment, they told me that there would be setbacks. I'm like a recovering alcoholic. I'll always have the tendency to over-exercise. I'm not going to lie and tell you that when I eat a big meal, I don't think about how good it would feel to shove a spoon down my throat and empty my stomach. However, I don't act on it because I know it's not healthy."

He pulled me to him cradling my body against his. His heart was wildly beating in his chest. "I love you, Caroline. I never want to see you look like this again. Promise me that before you do this to yourself that you'll talk to me. I'm in this relationship for forever. I want us one day to be Mr. and Doctor Colin McKinney. If you come to me, I will get you the best doctors that money can buy."

I nodded my head against his chest. He held me tight and kissed my hair over and over. I could feel his love, and it was all consuming.

After what seemed like hours, he got up and carried me carefully to the bed as if I was breakable fine china. He laid me down on my side and crawled over wrapping his huge body around me. I was cocooned in Colin. This felt like it should, and I made a promise to myself that I would never do anything that would make Colin leave me again. I wanted to be wrapped in his arms forever.

As we were falling asleep, I told him how sorry I was that I hadn't shown more interest in football. I vowed that every day I would ask him about practice and learn more about what it meant to play professional ball. He had been so supportive of my studying, and I wanted to show him that I was just as supportive of his passion.

February, Senior Year

"WAKE UP, pretty girl," he whispered in my ear.

I turned over grumbling and scooted away from him.

"I know that you're sleepy, but we need to call your professors to see what can be done about you missing class," he said.

"Shit … I forgot," I said as I flopped onto my back. God only knows what time we'd arrived in Dallas last night/this morning. I'd walked straight into his apartment and crawled in bed. I was still wearing my yoga pants and sweatshirt from last night.

"I'm hoping that I can Skype into lectures. Isn't the Internet great?" I gave him a sleepy smile.

He brought me my computer, cell phone, and book bag, and placed them around me. I looked at my watch. It was almost ten o'clock. "I guess I'll have to go for a run later," I mumbled to myself as I began to unpack my laptop.

"Speaking of that, I've noticed you exercising more. Anything that you want to talk about?" he asked with such genuine concern in his voice that it made me cringe.

I found myself turning away from him when I responded and fiddled with the power cord. "Like I said last night, or this morning, or whenever it was, I'm just a little nervous about graduating. I'm fine. I'm eating. I am not making myself sick. I've just been exercising a little more. I promised you that if I were slipping back into old patterns I would ask for help. I'm okay," I reassured him. What he didn't know was that I might wreck his world in a few months. I might choose the path less taken and run off to Harvard. And changing the subject … "Anything about the guy that posted the comment?"

"Yeah. It's some dickhead in California. He seems like an Internet fan of yours, but no one that would actually act on his threats. However, everyone still thinks that it's a good idea if we hang here for a couple of days and just let the dust settle. There are three media outlets camped outside the College Station apartment," he explained.

"And who is everyone?" I inquired, knowing full well what the answer was going to be.

He turned my face so that I was looking into his very serious eyes. "You know, Charlie … your parents, my parents, Mark, the attorneys, the police …"

"Colin, what happens if I'm in medical school and some freak threatens me? Are you going to keep me home from class?" I asked, trying to keep the hostility that I felt out of my voice, but I did throw my arms up in despair.

"We'll cross that bridge when we come to it. We'll both make more of a conscious effort to stay out of the public eye." He made it sound so easy.

I worried about future patients snapping a photo of me and selling it to the tabloids. Ever since my introduction to the media, I had been extra careful. The stupid photo of me stretching was just an accident that made it online.

Colin was setting in the middle of the bed cross-legged. His hair was a mess, and he had stubble on his cheeks. He would have looked good enough to eat if his worry line wasn't creasing his forehead. I hated making him anxious over me. He had enough on his plate with his career without me being an added burden.

"Fine. I will be your prisoner for a couple of days. However, I will be in class on Monday, even if you have to hire me the promised bodyguards." My shoulders slumped in defeat.

"Awesome! Tomorrow is Valentine's Day, and I don't have to worry about Aiden or Rachael crashing my party. I'm going to make dinner reservations while you take care of your professors," he said smugly. I had made him very happy. He bounded off the bed with one leap.

"Dude! You can't make reservations for Valentine's the day before. That's a gigantic pile of fail. And what happened to my day of not getting out bed? I was promised mind-blowing sex," I yelled as he walked out of his massive bedroom.

He paused at the door and turned around giving me his beautiful half-smile. "Charlie, I'm Colin. Fucking. McKinney, your Statement. Do you really think that I can't score a reservation? Take care of your professors, and you're mine the rest of the day."

I fell back in bed with a thud. It was soft and very large. I had to admit that it was nicer than the two of us sharing my queen-sized mattress.

Other than his bed, I hated his apartment. It felt like a modern furniture showroom. It was cold and harsh.

Colin hadn't decorated it. He'd rented it fully furnished. That had been a huge argument. When Dallas drafted him, his starting position was not a guarantee. He wanted me to choose a McMansion in some Dallas suburb. I put my foot down. He could railroad me into a lot of things, but picking out his house when I was a junior in college was not one of them. Hell! I couldn't legally buy alcohol, and he wanted me to pick out real estate?

It took his dad, Mark, and me flat-out refusing to look at homes to convince him that renting an apartment was the best idea. He chose a nice three-bedroom furnished apartment in a building with great amenities. The only thing that he insisted on buying was his bed.

It had been such a fight over where he lived that I didn't care if he chose the most expensive bed in the world. He could have it, if it would end that chapter of our lives.

I'd been dragged to every mattress store in Dallas to test them. I was finally put out of my misery when I asked Colin in front of the salesperson if we could try it out (wink, wink) before we bought it. Colin said that we would take it and handed the guy his credit card.

I grabbed my phone and sat up in his fabulous bed, fluffing the pillows behind me. I knew it was time to begin making my phone calls.

I hated this. What was I supposed to say? "Hi, this is Caroline Collins. I happen to be fucking Colin McKinney, and there is some guy who's ready to take his place in the bedroom department because the media thinks that we broke up. Therefore, I have been whisked away in the middle of the night to Colin's apartment because his parents think that it is a good idea. Yes! I know that this is the last semester of my senior year, and I need your class to graduate. Care to make an exception for me, excuse my absences and let me Skype into your lectures?"

This was so ridiculous. I flopped back down on the bed. I decided to start with my advisor. He was the easiest to reschedule.

As I was ending my call, Colin walked back into his bedroom. "All taken care of?"

"Not even close. Every time that I try to formulate what I'm going to say to my professors, I sound like a spoiled brat. If I were my professors, I would ask me if I was going to pull this sort of stunt in medical school," I explained. "Can't I just say that I'm sick?" I groaned.

"You say whatever you want. However, you have to remember that if you lie and we get photographed out together, you're busted," he reasoned.

I knew that he was right. I just hated how uncomfortable this portion of our life made me. If I went to Harvard, I could be anonymous again. The freedom to go for a run and not worry about someone snapping a picture, the ability to eat in public without being swarmed—right now, it sounded pretty damn good.

"Let me think while I take a shower," I said as I brushed past him to make my way into his palatial bathroom. I started the water and brushed my teeth while it warmed up.

He followed me in and watched me with caution. He knew that I was upset, but I think that he was clueless as to why or what to do about it.

I decided to head him off at the pass. "There is nothing that you can say or do to fix this. This is the part of your life that I have always had a difficult time accepting. I don't want to rehash old arguments; let it go, and just let me feel angry for a little while." I stepped into the hot, glass-enclosed shower and the delicious warm water ran down my body. His shower could do all sorts of fancy stuff like give me a massage. I just wanted a plain shower.

He stood outside the glass, staring at me like I was fish in an aquarium. I was very thankful that the steam had fogged the glass so I felt less exposed. Silently, I begged him to leave me alone. I was feeling desperate, raw, and out of control.

I lathered my hair with shampoo and massaged it in. He was still standing there watching me through the fog with a haunted look in his green eyes. I turned my back to him and rinsed the shampoo out.

"Please don't turn away from me. It makes me feel like you're rejecting me," he quietly pleaded.

Instead of his words making me want to embrace him, they made me want to run away. I felt like a caged animal. Without turning back towards him, I said, "Colin, please give me some space."

I felt him silently stalk away leaving me to finish my shower with the peace that I craved. I even took an extra few minutes and shaved my legs. I had to admit to myself that for a few seconds there, I thought about how good it would feel to make myself sick. My stomach would be empty, and I would be in control of how I felt for once. Colin and his life didn't have a say in my emotions. I just wanted to be in control of something, and I knew that these feelings were wrong.

I got out of the shower and wrapped my hair in a towel, and slipped another towel around my body. I prayed that Colin wasn't in the bedroom. I needed to get my head on straight. I put on my running shorts, T-shirt, and shoes. Colin had a gym in his building. I could go for a run. That would help me to feel more stable.

Busted! He was sitting on the ultra-modern white leather couch in the living room. "Where are you going?"

"I'm going to run on the treadmill in your secure building's twenty-four-hour gym," I said flatly. "No one can touch me. Isn't that why you rented the fortress-in-the-sky?"

"No, you aren't," he said, standing up and walking over to me. He put his arms around me and pulled me to him very tightly. I didn't hug him back.

I knew in that instant that my decision had been made a while ago. He was frantic for me to hug him back, and I couldn't. The tension was rolling off of him in waves as he grasped me against his chest tighter. And I couldn't bring myself to pick my arms up. I just wanted to go for a run and be left alone.

He picked me up and carried me to the couch, snuggling me to him, but I remained rigid. He kissed my hair over and over again. "Baby, we need to talk. I'm very worried about you."

I moved away from him so that I could look in his eyes and have my own space. His eyes said how anxious he was. "Let me begin. I just want you to listen to me and not interrupt. Then I'll give you the same courtesy."

My head was reeling as his words made me feel like a child, but I nodded in agreement anyway.

"This past year has been hard on us: I had to leave you in College Station, the uncertainty of the draft, having Dallas draft me, spending long hours away from you, fighting hard for the quarterback job, playing at a higher level and all that entails … I didn't see you near as much as I'd hoped. Then we've been thrown back together for the last six weeks, trying to make up for lost time." He pauses and takes a deep breath. "I can see the toll that it has taken on you. You've lost weight. You're distracted. You keep pushing me away. I'm too selfish to let you run from me. I need to know what's going on in that pretty head of yours, because the thoughts that I'm having are very scary."

I let out a sigh. Everything Colin had said was true. Part of me was really relieved that he'd called me on it. The other part of me hated having these sorts of conversations, and had hoped that I could dodge it as long as possible.

My heart was beating out of my chest. My palms were sweaty. I knew that I was on the verge of a panic attack. I took a couple of deep breaths. *Breathe in. Breathe out.*

His face turned from one of concern to one of terror. I think he knew what was coming next, and it wasn't what he had expected when he started this conversation with me.

I started, "Colin, I ..." I stopped. I couldn't seem to make the words come out of my mouth.

I tried again. "Colin, I ..."

"For God's sake, Caroline! You are scaring me. Just fucking say whatever it is." His pupils were dilated and his fist were clenched so tightly that his knuckles were white. He was the most terrified that I had ever seen him.

I took a deep breath. "Colin, I was accepted to Harvard Medical School."

February, Senior Year

COLIN LOOKED at me, very confused, and finally said, "Congratulations on getting into Harvard. Why are you upset? You did it, baby." He was scooting toward me with a huge smile on his face.

Oh goodness! My poor Colin doesn't get it. I took a deep breath and put my hand up to stop him. "Harvard has the best medical school in the country. No one turns down Harvard. It's every medical student's first choice. My dad would've killed to have gone there."

"I know, Charlie, and to think that they accepted you. I'm so proud of you," he said, beaming his half smile at me.

We sat there in silence for a couple of minutes. I let the realization hit him before I took a deep breath and said, "I'm going."

Those words changed the course of two lives forever. He looked like I'd kicked him in the gut. He became pale and his shoulders slumped forward. I reached out to grab his hand, but he moved away from me. That broke my heart. He never denied me himself except one time, and it had nearly killed me.

I started crying. "I'm so sorry, Colin. I can't pass up this opportunity. I've struggled with the decision. I've beaten myself up over it. What I know in my heart of hearts is that I will end up resenting you if I don't get to follow my dream. You deserve the best of me! I can't give you that if I know that I turned down a shot at my dream school because of you. Can you understand that?"

He dropped his elbows to his knees and hung his head. He looked the same way that I found him that morning at the lake-house after his bender. This was killing me. I felt as if my heart were being ripped out of my body.

"I think it might be best to cool our relationship off while you focus on football, and I tackle medical school," I whispered through my tears while I fidgeted with the hem of my running shorts.

Then, I noticed that my six-foot, five-inch hulking Statement of a man had a tear rolling down his cheek. I watched the tear as it hit the ground with a tiny splash.

All I wanted in the world was to crawl in his lap. I wanted to kiss the tears away. I wanted to tell him that I could be happy marrying him and going to medical school in Dallas, but I knew that I couldn't. In all honesty, this was the most gut-wrenching moment of my life, but there was a huge part of me that felt relieved. I hated that part of me. I would love to have gone to a surgeon, had it taken out and replaced it with contentment for the life that he wanted.

I had to make him understand. "Colin, I've tried to be the person that you want me to be. I love you with everything that I have. This is not about my feelings for you. This is about me. I'm a crazy, fucked-up person from a divorced family. I make myself puke to feel better. How absurd is that? I love you enough to not give you second best, which would be me right now. I'm not saying that I never want to see you again, or that I don't want you in my life. I just want to move to Boston, complete medical school, and then pursue a future with you," I pleaded.

He didn't say anything. I watched more tears fall from his cheeks and on to the floor. My chest was so tight that I couldn't take a breath. I scooted next to him, afraid that he was going to push me away again. He thankfully didn't. He pulled me to him, and we sat next to each other, held hands, and cried.

Finally he spoke in a broken voice. "How long have you known?"

I had to make him understand. "I found out about Harvard in early January and have struggled with the decision. I made up my mind just moments ago. I started thinking about how I could eat with you and then sneak off to vomit. I thought that I might not go into the restroom because that would too obvious. I developed a plan to vomit in Ziploc bags. That way I could do it in any room, and you wouldn't be suspicious. Then I could hide them in the garbage. When I stepped back and realized that I was doing it again, I knew what my decision had to be." I hated sharing all of that with him, but he needed me to be honest. I owed him complete honesty.

He wiped his tears away with the back of his hand. He picked his head up and looked at me with the saddest eyes I had ever seen. "I'm sorry that I made you feel that way. I've only wanted to make your life better. Not worse."

I kissed his tear-streaked cheek. "You've made the last two years of my life wonderful. I think that we're soul mates who met at the wrong time in our lives. I can't stand to lose you."

He didn't respond.

"Colin, please don't tell me that you are cutting me out of your life. We don't have to break up. We will just have to work harder to see each other. I'll even let you buy me a place in Boston so when you visit you don't have to stay in a dorm room. I may not get to see you every weekend, but I bet we can make it work once a month," I pleaded.

He leapt to his feet, towering over me. "I spent six months only getting to see you every other week, or a stolen day or weekend every now and then. I can't do that for four years." He began pacing the room, running his fingers through his hair. "Don't you understand?" he yelled. "I can't be without you." He was a man torn apart.

I wanted to take it all back. I wanted to offer him a compromise. I would go to medical school in Dallas if he would not ask me to marry him again. Even in my desperation to make it better, I knew that this wasn't rational. I loved him, but he was stifling me. I was losing myself in this relationship. I was going to fall back into my eating disorder if I stayed with him. I needed space. I needed to find me again. I needed to not be CharCol any longer.

I curled up into a ball on his couch, sobbing. I thought that my heart was shattering into pieces.

He stopped his pacing and walked over to me. I looked into his blazing green eyes, and he screamed, "You are fucking breaking my heart!"

I reached for him but he turned and walked into the bedroom, slamming the door behind him. I was distraught. I didn't know what to do.

I decided to follow. I knew if he'd just let me touch him that he would feel better. I was his soothing balm. He had told me that on more than one occasion. I opened the bedroom door cautiously, and looked for him. I didn't see him so I walked in. The door to the bathroom was shut. I softly knocked.

In a broken voice, he screamed, "Go the fuck away Caroline!"

I ignored him, because I knew that he really didn't want me to leave. I opened the bathroom door to find him sitting on the floor, leaning against the egg-shaped bathtub. One leg was crossed over the other, and he was resting his head in his hands.

I walked over to him and sat down, making sure that my body was gently touching his. I was so relieved when he didn't move away.

We sat like that until he was ready to talk. "Is there anything that I can do to change your mind?"

I knew that there wasn't. This wasn't about him. It was all about me. "What I had hoped would happen was that you would be happy for me to go to Harvard, and we would find a way to make it work for four years. Then, I'd marry you."

When he didn't say anything, I finished, "However, we both know that with the demands of your job and my schooling that we would spend four years frustrated as hell because we can't be together."

He nodded his head in agreement. "Charlie, when you walked into your dad's office on the first day we met, I knew that you were something special. These last two years haven't always been easy, but I never once regretted meeting you until this moment. You're the only person that I've ever given my whole self to and you're destroying me before you've even given me a chance to make our lives complete."

His words should have sent me over the edge in ugly tears, but they didn't. He was right, and I knew it. The truth was a bitter pill to swallow.

"If it makes you feel any better, I hate myself. I wanted to want the life that you planned for us, but I would not be me, the girl you fell in love with, if I turned down Harvard. It's my NFL," I explained.

He threw his head back and laughed. "How fucking lucky am I? I have to go and fall in love with the only girl in the world who's more competitive than me. No. You're right, Charlie. One of the qualities that I love the most about you is the one that is shredding me right now."

I put my hand on his gorgeous thigh, pausing for just a second, making sure he wasn't going to slap it away. When he let me touch him, I pushed my luck even further and rested my head against his shoulder. I knew that I would miss touching him the most.

With a little calmer voice he said, "Promise me that you'll see a therapist. I can't let you walk out of my life worrying that I'm going to get a phone call from someone telling me that you dropped dead in the middle of a run. You need to work through your issues over your parents' divorce. Not every man walks out on his woman."

"I promise that I'll find someone to talk to," I reassured him.

"I've got two more days before I have to take you back to College Station. Can we pretend that this isn't the end?" he asked with a hint of desperation in his voice.

Tears rolled down my cheeks as I said, "There's nothing that I would like more."

September, Junior Year

I WALKED out into the warm September Saturday sunlight after five of the most grueling hours of my life. It was over! Now I just had to wait to see how I did.

I could hear the fans at Kyle Field cheering. Unfortunately, the MCAT exam had coincided with a conference home game. Colin understood why I would be missing one of his games, but I hated not watching him play. Things had been so great since our breakup and makeup. I'd actually spent some time at his private dorm. He'd quizzed me on some stuff for the MCAT. I'd made an effort to ask more questions about football and did some research on the draft. I had gained back some of the weight that I had lost, and Colin made a point of running with me every morning. I think that he did it to make sure that I wasn't overdoing it. I knew that I had dodged a bullet this time. My eating disorder was something that was never going to go away, but at least I had beaten it back. Things were really, really good right now.

I sent my family, Colin, and Rachael a quick text, knowing that at least Colin and Rach wouldn't receive it until after the game.

Me: It's over! I'm mentally spent. I feel good about it. I can't wait for October to see if I will be taking it again.

Then, I sent a text just to Colin.

Me: I'm sorry that I am missing you running up the score. I love you. See you tonight, whatever time that might be.

When I got home, I took off all my clothes and crawled in my bed for an afternoon nap. My clean, cool sheets felt awesome against my naked body. My fan was turned on high and my curtains were pulled, making my room feel like a cave. I hadn't felt this stress-free in years.

I fell asleep thinking about my quarterback.

"Hey, baby, wake up."

A huge, warm hand brushed my hair out of my face. I barely opened an eye and saw that it was six thirty. I had been asleep a long time.

I rolled over and looked at him. In a very raspy voice, I asked, "Did you win?"

"Don't I always?"

There was no denying that the boy had swagger.

"How many kisses do I owe you?" I asked, stretching.

"Four, but I'll let you off the hook if you get up, throw some clothes on and join me and my parents for dinner."

"Ugh! Colin, please, for the love of God, don't make me," I grumbled pulling the covers over my head. "Anyway, what's the deal with asking me to put clothes on? Usually you are begging me to take them off." I tried to roll on my stomach, but a huge hand reached out and stopped me.

"Please. My parents are dying to meet the girl who will not marry me," he stated.

I pulled the blanket from my face. "That's just great, Colin. Did you tell them about our game?"

"No, but I will if you don't come eat with us," he said, knowing that he had me.

"Fine, but I want it noted that I am doing this under duress, and I'm naked. You're asking a naked girl in bed to put clothes on," I grumbled.

I had met Colin's parents twice before. Once in my dad's office, where we were not properly introduced, and the other time before the lake-house weekend. They had come for a visit, and Colin had invited them to go to Harry's on Sunday night and watch us dance. They were very nice and bought everyone's drinks for the evening. However, I'm sure that they were just as confused as I was about our relationship status. They were very nice people, but I wanted to celebrate the Aggie's win and taking the MCAT. I didn't want to sit under a microscope for his parents to examine.

I sashayed to my closet, taking my time. I wanted to make sure that Colin saw what he was asking to cover up.

"I know what you're doing. That body of yours is gorgeous, but my parents are waiting," he scolded.

I ignored him. I bent over, exposing my behind to him as I pulled up the tiniest pair of thong panties that I owned.

"God, you have a gorgeous ass," he complimented me.

This game was obviously not working out how I'd planned. Damn him!

I marched into my closet and pulled out a pair of jeans.

"I don't mean to be difficult, but can you wear a dress? And maybe take those nothing panties off and put on some panties that are big and baggy?" he asked with a smirk.

I threw my jeans on the ground and huffed back in my closet. I spotted the lavender wrap dress and silver ballet flats. I silently congratulated myself. Two can play at his game.

I slipped the dress on in my closet and walked out for him to admire.

"Thank you. That dress looks smoking hot on you. It must be because I bought it," he said, smiling at me.

I brushed out my long hair and put makeup on. I made sure that my eye shadow really accentuated my lavender eyes.

"I'm ready, lover boy. Let's go meet the fam," I said as I flashed him my bare behind.

***

I held his hand as he led me into the restaurant. I saw a man about Colin's size wave in our general direction. We walked to the table.

His parents had a table in the corner of the restaurant. I was pleased, because I had noticed the stares that we were getting as we made our way through the maze of tables. Also, I was very thankful that Colin had insisted that I go back into the closet and put panties on. I felt like an exhibit at the zoo for everyone's prying eyes. *Maybe the Aggie fans will just let us enjoy our meal*, I silently prayed.

His father stood and introduced himself. "Hello Caroline, I'm Colin's father, John. I know that we've seen each other before, but I don't think that we have been properly introduced." He was a tall man, maybe the same height as Colin. He had the same wavy hair, except his was greying around his temples. He was trim and fit. He obviously took good care of himself.

His mother was one of the tiniest people that I had ever seen, and I lived with Rachael. She was maybe five-foot one-inch in her flat sandals, and if she weighed more than a hundred pounds I would have been shocked. Her hair was Texas-blond and perfectly hair sprayed in place. She had on a maroon blouse, tucked into trouser jeans. I stuck out my hand and we shook as I introduced myself. "I'm Caroline. It's a pleasure to see you again." Even her hand was dainty.

"I'm Susan, Colin's mother."

It was clear that Colin had gotten his father's size and wavy hair, but he looked just like his mother. He shook his father's hand and gave his mother a kiss on the cheek. They both clearly adored their son. There was no denying that.

His dad began discussing the game. They were throwing around statistics like percent completion, and quarterback rating. I just listened politely and drank my water.

The waiter mercifully came and took our drink orders. No one else ordered alcohol, so I opted for a Diet Coke.

After the waiter left, it was apparently my turn to be quizzed.

"Caroline, I hear that you are one of six girls. Your mother must be so busy," Susan said.

"Two of my sisters are from my father's second marriage, but yes, we've kept my mom busy," I politely replied.

"Oh, your parents are divorced? Colin didn't mention that," she said.

Whose parents aren't divorced? Is that a big deal?

"You know Colin's an only child. I'm not sure I'd know what to do with girls." Susan laughed.

Colin grabbed my hand and said with pride in his eyes, "Caroline took her MCAT today."

That thankfully turned the conversation to a topic that I was much more comfortable with.

While dinner was on the table, they told me some funny stories about the small town outside of Austin that they still lived in and where Colin had played football.

Colin's dad worked for Dell Computers headquartered in Austin, but he'd preferred to raise his only son in a small community. His mom was the principal at a preschool in the town.

She said that the students make Colin good luck cards before each game. I thought that was so cute.

I glanced at Colin's face while his mother was talking. He looked so relaxed and happy; I guess he was pleased at how well dinner was going. My heart warmed for the man next to me. I loved seeing him this laid back.

After we'd finished our meal, John steered the conversation back to football. "Mom and I are still trying to find cheap airfare for the game next weekend."

I hadn't realized the game wasn't in College Station. *Guess I'm going to need to get a copy of the schedule.*

Colin said, "I understand if you can't make it. Even though it is a conference game, we have a better record than the other team."

Susan quickly added as she stroked his arm, "Colin, you know that we don't like to miss a game. We'll be there even if Daddy has to open his wallet a little wider than he wants."

Susan and John then looked at me. "Are you traveling to the game?"

Nothing like being put on the spot. Considering that I didn't even know that the game was out of town, the answer would be no.

Colin spoke up for me. "We haven't discussed it yet."

I gave his knee a thank-you squeeze under the table. He winced.

"Colin, are you okay?" his dad asked.

"I'm just a little sore."

As our dinner was drawing to a close, the waiter came over and said that someone had picked up our tab.

Colin quickly told him, "I can't let someone pay for my meal."

His dad took out a $20 bill and handed it to the waiter. "Please make sure that this covers my son's food."

They seemed so unsurprised that I guessed this happened frequently when they went out to dinner.

We looked around and saw a table full of Aggies dressed in maroon waving at us. Colin stood up and walked over to their table shaking their hands and thanking them for picking up our tab. He had to take at least three pictures with everyone at the table.

His mom gave me a very pointed look. "Caroline, it's all part of dating my son."

I nodded. *But it doesn't make it any easier.*

Colin joined us back at the table and pulled my chair and his mother's chair out from the table. We all made to the front door except for Colin. He stopped numerous times to sign an autograph or receive congratulations. His parents and I stood outside talking about nothing in particular while we waited on him.

When Colin finally made it out of the restaurant, his mother reached up and stood on her tiptoes and gave her son a hug around his neck. Colin kissed her on the cheek.

He said, "Mom and Dad, thanks for coming to the game."

"I love you Colin. Please take care of yourself," Susan said.

John shook his hand and reminded him to take his supplements.

They both graciously told me goodbye, then his mother gave me a hug and said in my ear, "Don't hurt my baby."

She didn't see the look on my face, because she was already walking toward their car, but Colin did, though.

"What did my mother say?" he demanded when we were a safe distance away.

"She said to not hurt her baby," I answered.

He apologized and I made a joke. That seemed to be our pattern for uncomfortable situations.

He helped me into Bertha, and I noticed him climb a little more gingerly than usual into the driver's seat.

"Colin, are you okay?" I asked.

"I'm just sore. Even though I wasn't sacked today, I still get sore every time I play. Your body never fully gets used to the abuse," he explained. "What shall we do tonight, Ms. Collins?"

"You're the one who played a football game today. You tell me," I replied as I buckled myself in.

"You're the one who kicked the MCAT's ass today. You tell me," he countered.

I looked pretty in my dress and wasn't the least bit tired after my marathon nap, so I suggested going out.

"What are Quinn and Jennifer doing tonight?" I really liked them and had missed hanging out this past month while I'd done nothing but study.

"Well, actually, they're having a party. Rachael and Aiden are going. We're invited," he said.

"That sounds like fun. Why didn't you tell me that to begin with?" I was really curious. An invite to their house seemed like a good idea.

"It's going to be a lot of the football team. I didn't know if you were ready to walk into the lions' den yet," he explained with a hint of apprehension.

"What's wrong with the other players?" Okay. Now, I was really, really curious.

"You know. We're guys. We give each other a hard time. They might not be as respectful to you as I would like." Now he really sounded apprehensive.

"Oh, Colin. How bad could it be?"

***

Quinn and Jennifer had a cute, little two-bedroom bungalow in Bryan, the town next to College Station. It's the kind of neighborhood where kids still played in the streets and climbed trees.

I was sure that the neighbors were horrified of Quinn and Jennifer. They liked to throw parties, and the guest-list often included most of the Aggie football team. Those boys could drink.

We had to park about a half a mile up the road and walk to their house. Before I could spot their driveway, I heard, "Do my eyes deceive me? Is that Colin McKinney at a party?"

"Fuck off, Ethan," Colin said, laughing as we watched the guy approach us. He grabbed my hand giving it a reassuring squeeze.

"Who is the lovely lady? Could this be the mythical girlfriend?" he teased.

I stuck out my hand and smiled sweetly. "My name is Unicorn. It's a pleasure to meet you."

He laughed and grabbed me in a huge bear hug tearing me away from Colin's side. "I knew that anyone that would make Colin McKinney settle down had to be awesome."

After the fourth or fifth time that one of the guys made a comment about me taming Colin, I knew that Mr. McKinney had some explaining to do.

I whispered in his ear, "What kind of male slut were you?"

He laughed and smiled back, whispering, "The kind that always wore condoms."

That was not quite the answer that I wanted my potential children's father to give me, but it could have been worse. I knew his reputation around campus before I agreed to date him, but I guess I had hoped that it was all just rumors. It also explained why he just assumed that we were dating. In his mind, it was black and white. He didn't have random sex with chicks because he liked me, therefore, we must be dating. Guy logic!

We finally made our way to the house. Jennifer enveloped me in a hug. "I'm so glad that you finally agreed to come to a team party. "

I shot Colin a questioning look. This was my first invitation.

"Jennifer, don't overwhelm her. We want her to come back," Colin admonished her, tucking me into his side.

Jennifer was having none of Colin's passiveness and took my hand leading me around. She introduced me to more people than I could count. They all seemed to know who I was. Most said that they'd heard a lot about me. I didn't know these people from Adam.

After what felt like hours, I spied Colin surrounded by a group of people. I was shocked. He had a red Solo cup in his hand. I had only seen him drink water, except for at the lake-house. I walked up beside him and touched his back. He was in the middle of telling a story and pulled me to him while he finished. He was so animated. I didn't know this version of Colin.

"Everyone, I'd like for you to meet Caroline Collins," he said to the group surrounding him.

"Hi. I go by Charlie," I said giving the group a little wave. "I would love to say that I've heard all about you, but I haven't. Colin seems to not share much," I flashed him an evil look.

One of the guys chimed in and said, "It's probably better that way." The group gave a collective chuckle.

I still hadn't spied Rachael and Aiden. I was tired of feeling like an exhibit at the museum and needed my best friend.

Colin must have noticed my distress because he leaned down and asked me, "Is everything okay?"

"Why does everyone at this party seem to know me, but I haven't heard you mention any of their names even one time? I also have had confirmed for me that you have a reputation as a guy who sleeps around. So no, Colin, I'm not okay," I said all of this quietly with a smile on my face to make sure that no one heard what I had said. I didn't want the spectators to know that I was upset.

Colin excused us from the group and walked me into the backyard where we had a little more privacy. Before he could say anything, I added, "Also, the only time that I've seen you drink, you got so drunk that I was worried you had alcohol poisoning and now I see you drinking a beer."

He stopped walking and turned to me. His hands were clenched in tight fists, and Colin's whole body was so tight that he looked brittle. "First of all, I warned you that the guys give me a hard time. That's how I know that they like me." He reached up and ran his hands through his hair, staring up at the stars before he began speaking again. "God forbid that I've shared stories about you with them. I love you. That's what people in love do: they talk about each other. Second of all, I was not a male slut, as you called me. I bet if you took a poll of how many different girls that these guys have slept with, I would be near the bottom. I always wore a condom. You're the only person that I've ever slept with when I didn't. I haven't asked you to explain who you've fucked, and I frankly don't think that I could stand to hear the answer because I know that you weren't a virgin when we slept together for the first time." He paused and held his glass up to emphasize his next point. "Finally, I'm sipping on one beer. That doesn't make me an alcoholic. I'm really fucking sorry that you had to see me like that at the lake-house. I haven't done it very often, but sometimes I have to do something to shut my head up. You, of everyone, should understand that. Now, do we need to go home, or can you go in there and act like an adult instead of a petulant child?'

Once again, I was dumbfounded by his reaction. Sure, I made a few snippy remarks, but I didn't realize that I was going to be lectured like an errant pre-teen. I was still trying to figure this man out that I had only really been dating for a couple of months.

I was not going to let him have the last say again when he was angry. I grew a backbone and placed my hands on my hips. "Wow! That's some kind of soliloquy. Are you finished? Because I've got one for you, Colin," I said matching his tone. "First of all, I could care less about the guys teasing you. I think that it's funny. What I don't like is that you haven't shared any of these people with me before. Jennifer said that there were other invitations that you neglected to mention. These people are obviously important to you; I give a shit about anything and anyone that's important to you.

"Second of all, I don't think either one of us cares about whom we slept with before each other. I would have just liked a clue so I didn't feel blindsided when people were joking about it. I think that's only fair.

"Finally, how dare you throw my eating disorder up in my face? You have no idea what it is like to have grown up in a divorced family. I watched my mom struggle with four little girls while my dad, his new wife, and two daughters lived like royalty. I had to be perfect so she wouldn't have any more stress on her than she already did. Without any help from my father, she got four little girls dressed for school every day. She made our lunches, ironed our uniforms, polished our shoes, and helped us with our homework. She then worked forty-plus hours a week so we had food on our table. Don't even get me started on her running us to after-school activities. Her life was exceptionally difficult because my dad broke his promise to her." I paused making that I knew exactly what I wanted to tell him while I wonder how this conversation took this turn. "You asking me to marry you every day scares me to death. I want a life with you, Colin, but I don't want to end up like my mom. My dad broke her and me when he left. I can't put my heart out there and have you break it also. I have to have medical school so I can at least have a stable career if you decide that you want someone else instead of me. So you see, you putting yourself in a bottle of Jack Daniels a couple of times is not even in the same league as my eating disorder. If you ever bring it up like that again, I will be hard pressed to ever share anything that personal with you again. Now, do we need to go home, or can you go in there and act like an adult instead of petulant child?"

He stood there, staring down at me. I was not backing down. We were two incredibly stubborn people, refusing to give in to each other. I was prepared to stay all night. I didn't make it in a family with five sisters and not learn to fight.

Finally, he said as he took my chin in his large hand forcing me to stare into his eyes, "I love you, Charlie. Get that through your head. I'm not your dad. I'm not going to walk out on you and leave you broken. You are my fucking life!" In a much calmer tone, he added, while brushing a stray piece of hair out of my face. "I'm sorry about bringing up your eating disorder. You have no idea how proud I am of you. I love you, and I'll never bring it up in an argument again. I haven't mentioned the other invites because you were studying for the MCAT. Can we call this a draw and go enjoy the party?"

I tucked piece of hair behind my ear while I thought about it for a moment. This was our first party together, and I didn't want to fight with him.

"It's a draw," I said, taking his arm and walking back to join the action. However, this argument was not forgotten.

Thankfully, I spotted Rachael and ran to her side. It was nice to have an ally. We helped ourselves to the keg of beer and found the porch swing empty. Rachael was my oasis in the middle of this sea of unknown. For the most part we were ignored and it felt nice to not be the center of attention. I hadn't seen Colin, or Aiden, for that matter, in quite a long time. We chitchatted about girly stuff and laughed over old memories. It was such a relief to have the MCAT over with for the time being and feel free again.

Somehow our drinks seemed to be bottomless. Suddenly, I had the urge to go to the restroom. I knew from stolen bits of conversation that Jennifer and Quinn only had one toilet and the line was a mile long.

I leaned over to Rachael, "Honey, I have pee, and there's nowhere to go." That was obviously the funniest that thing I had ever said because that launched a laughing fit. I guess the beer was getting to me.

"I think we should pee out back behind that tree." She pointed into the darkness at the shadow of a tree that had hidden Colin and my little spat. That set off another fit of giggles.

"Let's do it," I said. That might be the craziest thing that I had ever done. The only time that I had ever used the restroom outside was when my mom took all four girls camping.

We locked arms and headed off toward the tree. As we got closer, I saw the shadow of a girl and a boy in an obviously heated discussion. Then, to my horror, I realized it was Colin and another woman.

Even in the moonlight, it was obvious that she was gorgeous. She looked like Eva Longoria, complete with rocking curves.

Rachael tried to hold on to me, but she really didn't have a prayer. I walked up, wrapped both arms around Colin's waist and said in my nicest voice, "Who's this, baby?"

The tension was palpable. Whatever I'd just stumbled into was not a place that I was meant to be. Colin reached down and rubbed his hand on my back, and then he squeezed my shoulder.

"Caroline, this is an old friend: Jenna," he said without further explanation.

I just stood there like a big dummy. Surely, one of them was going to clue me in. I looked around for Rachael, but she was gone. I thought, *Thanks for abandoning me.*

I stuck my hand out, toward Jenna. "It's nice to meet any friend of Colin's."

She did not shake my hand. She looked at me like I was garbage and said, "I had him first. Before you, there was me."

Colin screamed at her, "We've been over for a long, long time, Jenna. Leave me alone." I had never heard Colin scream before. Even when he was angry with me he didn't sound like this.

About that time, Rachael came running up with Aiden. Colin and Jenna were locked in a glaring match. There was obviously a lot of tension and history between them. My guy apparently had some more explaining to do, considering he'd told me that he'd never had a girlfriend before.

Ignoring Jenna, I looked up at Colin. "Baby, I am so tired, and I have to use the restroom. Can we go home?"

That seemed to get his attention. "Let's go, Charlie," he said, turning toward me while still glaring at her.

Jenna yelled. "This is not over, Colin McKinney. Either you tell her or I will."

This night was an epic disaster. I grabbed Colin's hand and made sure that she saw me holding it as we walked away. I didn't know what was going on, but I trusted Colin enough that I was not going to let Jenna see an ounce of weakness between us.

"How much have you had to drink?" I asked.

"One cup of beer," he replied.

"Awesome. I've had many more than that. Drive me home."

"Like you could drive Bertha anyway," he attempted to tease but it came out as very flat.

"Not in the mood, Colin," I spat. "I'm assuming that was more than one of your condom fucks."

"Well, she was a little more than that. She was my high school something," he admitted.

Fortunately, we were at Bertha. I had never been so happy to be inside of his horrible truck.

When he started the engine and had maneuvered the warship on to the road, he continued, "We dated all through high school. We were dumb kids. We would date a couple of weeks and break up. It was never serious for me. I didn't love her and 'girlfriend' is a word that does not describe how I felt about her."

"And ..." I said. I'm a girl. I knew that whatever was going on behind that tree was more than high school drama.

"And she got pregnant," he said in a soft voice.

"And ..." I repeated, a touch more sympathetic.

"She told me the baby was mine, but I'd never had sex with her without using a condom. The condom didn't break. I knew that they weren't one hundred percent, but I knew that I used them correctly," he said, running his hand through his hair. He was obviously upset at reliving this memory.

We were stopped at a red light. I unbuckled my seatbelt and turned so I could read his face in the light of the streetlamps. "Oh, Colin. Do you have a child?" I gasped. It had never occurred to me to ask that question.

"No, Charlie!" he declared loudly. "Please put your belt back on and keep listening."

I settled against the seat back and buckled up, feeling like I couldn't breathe. She must have had an abortion. *Fuck! What do I even think of that?*

He sighed and then continued, "She kept pressuring me to accept responsibility. I freaked out one night and broke down and told my parents. They put me in the car and drove me to her house. She hadn't told her parents yet. It was a huge, ugly scene. I was eighteen, and she was sixteen. Her father threatened to file charges against me."

I gasped. I could understand her parents being upset, but accusing Colin of statutory rape? That was over the top.

He continued, "She was planning on having an abortion and not ever telling them. They demanded that she have the baby and put it up for adoption. When the baby was born, my parents demanded a paternity test, and I was not the father. I was beyond relieved. However, it ruined her life."

"Colin, I'm so sorry. That's an awful story," I said as I reached across the cab and took his hand.

"It is," he said very quietly. "She blames me. Being from a small town, no one ever looked at her the same. Her grades were messed up from missing so much school due to her pregnancy. She wound up dropping out and getting her G.E.D."

"Why is it your fault, Colin?" I was genuinely confused. He squeezed my hand and then brought our joined knuckles up to his lips for a kiss.

"Well, if I hadn't told her parents, she could have had an abortion. The rest wouldn't have happened," he clarified.

"Oh!" It was all that I could say. What a horrible story. Colin would also have been left thinking that he had fathered a child.

We sat in silence for a couple of stoplights. Finally, I said, "Colin, this isn't your fault. You did what an eighteen-year-old should do. You told your parents. That's what they're there for. You didn't ruin her life. When she decided to have unprotected sex with someone else, she incurred the risk." I pause to collect my thoughts, "I don't understand why she was at the party."

He let out a huge sigh. "She heard that I had met someone. I haven't dated anyone since her in high school. I think she wanted to make one last attempt to see if I would get back together with her. I, of course, told her about you.

"She thought if I told you what I did, you would run away." He sighed again. "She thinks that I owe her for ruining her life."

That made me bristle. "Well, she's wrong. Let me say this again: You did nothing wrong. I love you. This doesn't change how I feel or think about you. I hope that if we have a son he will be that open with us," I reassured him.

What a day and night! I wanted to crawl in my bed and see if tomorrow could be better.

Colin apparently had other plans. I walked into my apartment and went straight to my bathroom. I still had to use the restroom. With the door shut, I washed my face, put on moisturizer, and brushed my teeth. When I walked out of my bathroom, I went in to my closet to take off my pretty lavender wrap dress and silver ballet flats. I put on my sleep shorts and tank top, and I walked over to my side of the bed and crawled under the covers.

Colin curled up behind me and started kissing behind my ear. "I love you baby." He whispered, "Let me love you."

"No, Colin. I've had a heap-load of shit dumped on me tonight. I want to go to sleep," I replied.

Colin did not get to be starting quarterback for Texas A&M by taking no for an answer. So he used his patented wraparound move into my panties and gently nibbled on my ear.

"I said no, Colin. You aren't changing my mind. I love you. I'm not mad at you, but I'm telling you that tonight, if you want to spend the night with me, we're only going to sleep."

"I would rather lie here with the hardest dick in College Station than be anywhere else," he replied while kissing my temple.

"Good night, love," I mumbled.

October, Junior Year

RACHAEL AND I were lying on my bed, solving the world's problems. Colin was either at practice, making a public appearance, or meeting with a coach. I couldn't keep track of his schedule any longer. I saw him when I saw him, which was as often as he could make time for me.

The Aggies were ranked fifth in the country. They were doing better than had been predicted, and Colin was playing like a man on fire. There was already buzz on where he would go in the draft. I tried not to listen to the speculation or really think about him leaving in January. I was trying to take it one day at time. We had gotten so close, though, that I'd really started feeling anxious at the idea of him not being around.

"Aggies are out of town this weekend. We should go home," Rachael proposed.

"That's not a half-bad idea. I haven't seen my family in a couple of months. Want to leave Friday after class?" My oldest sister, Chelsea, had graduated college and lived in a cute little apartment in mid-town Houston, which was the place to go and be seen.

"Sounds like a plan. I'll drive. I don't trust the Honda," Rachael said, poking me. The Honda was in really bad shape. The old girl just had to last three more semesters.

"When do you get your MCAT score, or scores, or whatever it is?" Rachael asked.

"Any day now. I keep checking the website. I have to admit that I am a bit anxious. I haven't done much studying since I took them. If I have to retake them I'm going to be in a boat-load of trouble," I answered hoping for the best. I'd spent all my free time with Colin. He was bad for my grades.

"Oh, Charlie, you'll be fine. You always think the worst about yourself." I knew that she was right, as much as I hated to admit it.

"What's Aiden doing this weekend?" The two of them had been attached at the hip since March.

"He's actually thinking about flying to the game. His dad offered him miles, and a bunch of his frat brothers are going," she explained.

"Lucky him! I'd like to go. Colin said that this is a season-defining game. We're playing a team ranked higher than us and not expected to win. If we can pull it out, we might play for the national championship."

"Your parents wouldn't loan you miles for a ticket?" Rachael knew better than to even ask that sort of question.

"If it wasn't in the divorce settlement, I don't get it," I replied. Sometimes being a poor college student with divorced parents sucked.

***

"I'm thinking of going home this weekend with Rachael," I said to Colin while we were on an early-morning run.

"Will you watch the game?" he asked, slightly out of breath.

"Of course! I just haven't seen my family in a long time, and it's a good time to go because you'll not be back until early Sunday morning. I promise to leave before noon on Sunday so we can spend the day together." I was not at all out of breath at all. I loved being able to school him in something.

"Is Rach driving?" He'd shortened her name so he could talk less. *Ha!*

"Yeah. I'm not sure the Honda has the drive in her anymore," I replied, feeling great.

"I don't understand why your dad doesn't get you something reliable. It's not like he doesn't have the money." Apparently he'd found his second wind, because that statement had some venom behind it.

"It's not in the divorce agreement." In my mind, that explained everything.

Oh shit! Now, he was really mad. He stopped running and grabbed my arm. He was huffing and puffing, but his words were clear. "That's why we aren't going to get divorced. If it's not an option, then you're forced to work through your issues." He drug his fingers through his hair and gave the ground a disgusted look. "I'm turning back around. I'm too pissed to finish this run."

We were seven miles in and still had at least two miles back to my apartment. *Now might be a good time to talk about medical school marriages,* I thought.

"Wimp!" I couldn't help myself, but I quickly added as we began our jog home, "Medical school is hard on marriages. They make you sign an agreement that you will not have an outside job, because school occupies so much of your time."

"So does football, but we'll make it work." He gasped in a deep breath. "That's my point, Charlie. Me playing professional football and you finishing up school and then medical school will not be easy, but if we're both equally committed to making it work it will," he said, as if this were the God's honest truth.

"If I hadn't lived through it, I could be as sure as you are," I said.

We didn't say anything else to each other until we got to the park for our cool-down stretches.

As I was sitting in a straddle position, he launched himself pinning me to the ground with his hips. I giggled while relishing the attention. "I fucking love you. I will not let your parents' mistakes ruin us. They already have taken enough away from you." He glanced at my still nonexistent boobs. "We aren't them. There's no one else that I want to be with more than you. I know you think that I'm teasing about marrying you, but if you said yes, we'd be on a plane to Vegas tomorrow. That's how serious I am about our future," he said while he gave me his serious don't-fuck-with-me look.

I licked my lips. What could I say to that, except "Dear God, Colin. That's the hottest speech that I've ever heard. Take me back to my apartment and make love to me."

***

I hadn't even been in my mom's house for five minutes, and everyone was already driving me crazy. Amy and Julie had bombarded me with questions about Colin. I promised that before the season was over I would invite them to a game.

My mom was fussing over how skinny I was. I wasn't anymore, though. I had just about regained all the weight that I had lost, but my boobs were still pretty flat. I needed to get Chelsea to take me bra shopping for something that would give me cleavage.

While my mother insisted on us making chocolate-chip cookies, a ploy to fatten me up, I pulled out my phone and sent Colin a text.

Me: I hope you had an uneventful flight. Tell Quinn that I said to be nice to my Statement. I'm in hell. I'm being forced to bake. Hope you know that you shouldn't marry me for my baking skills.

Colin: We are safely on the ground. Quinn talked to me the whole flight, and you think you're in hell. Baby, I'm not marrying you for your baking skills ...

I was sitting in our small kitchen surrounded by my nosy family, but I just couldn't help myself.

Me: What skills do you approve of???

Colin: You exceed expectations in the classroom, the gym, and most exceptionally, the bedroom.

"What're you smiling about, Charlie?" Julie said as she reached for my phone, but I snatched it back in time.

"None of your business," I yelled. Being with my family made me twelve again.

"Girls, leave Charlie alone. She's entitled to her privacy." My mom slid naturally back into referee mode.

Me: I love your answer ☺*My sisters are being nosy brats. I have to go. Call me before you go to bed.*

Colin: They can't be any nosier than Quinn. He is trying like hell to see my phone right now. Love you. I'll call you later.

"So, what are your plans this weekend?" Mom asked.

"I'm going to hang out with you guys tonight. Tomorrow, I'm going over to Chelsea's to watch the game, and then we're going dancing. I'll probably crash at her place and then leave early Sunday," I stated.

"Sounds like a good plan. Now, what do you girls want for dinner?"

Going home for me was always bittersweet. I loved my family deeply, however it was very hard to see my half-sisters' lives compared with how we'd struggled at that same age. God bless my mom. She'd carted us all over Houston to make sure that we didn't miss out on any activities, but she had not been on one date since my dad left.

Her life was so different than what she had signed up for. She'd put my dad through medical school and gave him four daughters. He gave her no help, just child support checks and grief when he didn't like her parenting.

Let's just say, that when I was in therapy for my eating disorder, the divorce came up a lot.

***

"Oh my God! We won! Oh my God! We won!" I kept whispering to myself. I grabbed my phone and sent Colin a text.

Me: I am so proud of you. I love you. I love you. I love you. Congratulations! My Statement did it!

The watching party was going crazy. Everyone kept congratulating me. I just wanted to keep my eyes on the TV. I wanted to see him. I wanted to hear his sexy voice. I wanted to touch him. He was right; this being apart business sucked.

The camera found him after the game, sitting on a bench staring at the field. He had a slight smile on his face. He looked more relieved than happy. I wanted to hold him and touch him. I was so angry with myself for not finding some way to get a ticket to the game.

They interviewed him when he was in the locker room. He gave them all the standard media-training answers. I couldn't help but stare at him. He was gorgeous. He was freshly showered and his wet wavy hair was pulled back from his face. I knew why websites had popped up dedicated to his movie-star good looks.

Finally, Rachael convinced me to get ready to go out. She was right. They were just going to keep replaying his interview again and again. I secretly would have watched it every time that it aired, but I knew that was a little crazy.

My phone rang while I was slipping on a navy blue, very-short party dress. I dove for it.

"You did it, baby!" I said instead of a standard greeting.

"I did it, Charlie," he said. He sounded exhausted, deflated. I had read his body language correctly.

"I watched every second of the game. By the way, your ass looks so hot in those pants. Can we have a pair for the bedroom?"

"I adore you. I'm so fuckin' wiped out. The adrenaline has worn off. I'm ready to be in bed, lying naked with my girl." He was so forlorn.

"I know, baby. I'll see you in about twelve hours. I'll call as soon as I'm back in College Station. There's a big group of us about to go dancing, and they're waiting on me so I need to run."

"Be careful. I love you." He sounded so pathetic that I wanted to crawl through the phone and hold him.

"I will. Love you too," I replied, not wanting to hang up.

"Are you going to hang up, baby?" he asked very softly.

"I can't hang up when you sound like this. I want to be with you."

"I want you to be with me too. Touching you makes me feel better," he said just as softly.

I heard Quinn yelling and screaming in the background.

"Go celebrate with your friends. You deserve it. You played a fantastic game. You made the Aggies, your parents, and me very proud. Go enjoy your success. We'll celebrate tomorrow," I said, trying to give him a pep talk.

"You're right, baby. I love you. I'll see you tomorrow," he said as he hung up.

He had really just rained on my parade. Part of me wanted to see if Rachael would go back tonight, but I felt bad about ruining her fun.

As I put on my makeup, I gave myself a mental pep talk. I couldn't let him dictate my moods. By the time I was dressed and ready to go my spirits were back up.

***

We were dancing like lunatics at some fun club that Chelsea frequented. The music was insanely good. The drinks were flowing like water. I hadn't felt this carefree since Colin entered my life. Guys kept asking Rachael and me to dance, but we politely declined. Even though Colin and Aiden would never know, it still felt wrong.

In the middle of one of the songs, a bar employee tapped Rachael and I on the shoulder and asked us if we wanted to dance in one of the go-go dancer cages. Did we? We were born for that moment.

We nodded happily and headed toward the center of the dance floor with him. He lifted us up on the platform and we entered the cage together. Apparently this was a big deal, because the crowd went crazy and started cheering us on.

I briefly wondered if this was how Colin felt when he was on the field.

Rachael and I danced. The more the crowd yelled, the freakier Rach and I got. I was dripping with sweat and crazy thirsty, but I just didn't care. I was in the moment.

We cage-danced for six songs and then the bar employee helped us off the platform and helped two new girls up. He gave us free drink passes for the rest of the night.

By closing time, we were drunk, sweaty, drowned rats. Chelsea, Rachael and I stumbled back to her apartment. I hoped to God that Chelsea had food in her refrigerator, because I was starving. To my relief, my sister had a frozen pizza. Just what the doctor—I mean, me—ordered!

We were sitting around her kitchen table, shoveling pizza and water in our mouths when my phone rang.

It was Colin. *He must be calling to tell me that he's home.*

"Hi, baby," I said, hoping that he was in a better mood.

"Charlie, what the fuck have you been doing?" he growled at me.

I immediately got defensive. "You know what I've been doing. I went dancing with Rachael, Chelsea, and some of her friends. What's the problem?" Had he forgotten the whole conversation that we'd had earlier?

"The fucking problem is that your ass is all over the Internet, and it looks like Rachael is going down on you," he screamed at me.

Oh shit! I never thought about that.

"I don't understand. Tell me where to go and see the pictures," I said. He gave me more than one web address. *Double shit!*

I asked Chelsea for her laptop. She grabbed it and pulled up the websites. It was way worse than I had imagined.

At the top of the page was a picture of Rachael and me dancing together in the cage. It very clearly looked like we were about to have crazy sex. The headline read, *While the boyfriend is away, the bunnies will play.* The rest of the article identified my unknown dance partner and me as engaging in lesbian acts in a cage after Colin had just won the most important game of his college career. He looked like a saint. I looked like an unsupportive whore.

"Are you still there?" I asked.

"I'm here," he whispered.

I started to cry. I was beyond embarrassed. *My family will see this. His family will see this. Hopefully medical schools don't Google applicants, or they'll see thi*s. He let me cry for a long time before he said, "Come back early tomorrow. We have a lot of damage control to do."

Then he hung up.

He was furious. He hadn't been this mad at me since the night that he'd accused me of using sex as a weapon. Even then, I don't think he was this mad.

I overheard Rachael in another room pleading with Aiden. Oh no! She was in trouble also. This was so bad.

She walked back into the kitchen and joined me at the kitchen table. "We need to drive back to College Station tonight. Colin just stormed out of his private dorm and is headed to Jennifer and Quinn's house. Aiden is with Colin. He said that he has never seen him this upset before."

I grabbed my phone and dialed his number. He immediately ended my call. I called back ten more times, then I sent him a text.

Me: Please don't do anything stupid. Rach and I are getting in the car. I'll be there in two hours. Where are you?

I sat there and stared at my phone, willing him to respond to me. He had never done this to me. He'd never ignored me before. I was desperate. I was losing my mind. I wanted to be with him. I knew that if I could see him and touch him, I could make him better.

My phone rang. I grabbed it and didn't even bother to look at the screen.

"I'm so sorry," I cried.

"Caroline, you should be," my dad said, to my surprise. "You should know that Colin called me. I have woken up my attorney. This is going to cost a pretty penny. He is working on a sternly worded letter to all the media outlets that ran this story. I am not sure what good it's going to do, but we have to do something."

I tried to plead my case, but he cut me off.

"I have no idea what you were thinking but this is very bad, Caroline. You better pray that my attorney can stop this wildfire."

The phone went dead.

Chelsea gave me a knowing look. Our father was our father.

Rachael had us packed and were ready to go in ten minutes. Not surprisingly, we were both dead sober now. Off to College Station we went to try to fix this nightmare.

***

Rachael called Aiden when we were about ten miles outside of College Station. I could hear from her tone that the call was not going well.

She hung the phone up and looked at me. "Aiden has asked us not to come over. They are at Quinn's house playing poker, they finally have Colin calmed down, and he's drinking water."

I grabbed my phone and tried to call Colin again. This time, he had turned his phone off.

"Rachael, I don't care what Aiden says. I want to see Colin. He can't pull this business that we're getting married one minute and divorce isn't an option, and then he ignores me when I screw up. Granted, this is monumental, but I'm suffering too. The article makes him look like the second coming of Jesus Christ and me a groupie whore."

"That's exactly what I hoped you would say, Charlie. Let's go to Quinn's."

***

In hindsight, we should have listened to Aiden. When we arrived at Quinn and Jennifer's we were met by Quinn. He all but begged me to go home. I ignored him and pushed my way inside.

When Colin saw us, he said, "If it isn't the lesbians. Come to put on a private show on for us? I bet we could all chip in $20."

No one had ever spoken to me like that before. I chose to ignore him and recognized that it was his hurt heart talking. "Colin, I'm fucking exhausted. I know that I fucked up, and you're furious. Come home with me. It's not like I did anything that millions of college students don't do on a regular basis. I went dancing. I had a good time. Someone snapped a picture from just the right angle. Aiden isn't condemning Rachael," I offered.

Colin stood up and flipped the kitchen table over causing me to jump. He came barreling towards me, standing over me and yelling in my face. I could hear the rustling behind me as Quinn and Aiden moved toward him, but I did not take my eyes off him or back down.

Right now, we were six-foot, five-inches staring down five-foot, seven inches. We were green eyes pitted against lavender. We were the two most determined and stubborn people in the world.

"Aiden isn't furious with Rachael because she's the 'unidentified friend.' You are Colin. Fucking. McKinney, Quarterback for Texas A&M's fucking girlfriend. Your pretty little face is captured on TV every time that you're in the stands. They're waiting to see if you flinch when I get hit, or how your now nonexistent boobs jiggle when you're happy that I scored. For God's sake, Caroline, the media has already nicknamed us CharCol. How fucking cute is that?" he bellowed at me.

I was not backing down. I'd done nothing wrong, but somehow this was my fault.

My voice was deadly calm as I continued our staring contest. "Colin, I'm giving you one more chance to come home with me. A few days ago, you gave me the speech about how divorce wasn't an option. You said that if I agreed to marry you right now that we would fly to Vegas and be husband and wife the next day. Here's the first rough patch that we hit since that speech, and you're ready to write me off. If I had been cage dancing with a guy instead of Rach, how would you feel? Would you have already broken up with me? It's time to put your money where your mouth is. Pick up the table, tell your friends goodbye, and come home with me."

This was it. It was time for Colin to put up or shut up. I needed reassurance that he truly believed what he had been preaching.

He spun away. For a quick moment, I thought that he was walking away from me and my heart seized in my chest, but he stooped down and righted the table. He pushed all the chairs neatly around it. He grabbed my hand, and we walked out of the house and to Big Bertha.

"Are you okay to drive?" I asked as I ran to keep up with him.

"You can't drive the truck, and I'm not riding home with Rachael. So yes. I'm okay to drive," he answered coldly

He opened my door and helped me inside the cab. Before he shut the passenger door, he said, "If it had been a guy instead of Rachael, I'd have fucking killed him for touching my future wife."

We didn't say a word to each other as we drove to my apartment. I kept wondering what we were going to do when we were in my room. Were we going to fight? Did he want to rehash this? Were we just going to go to sleep?

My questions were soon answered when he slammed my bedroom door behind us and locked it. "What song was playing when the picture was taken?"

"I … I am not sure," I stammered. He had completely caught me off-guard. "We danced for five or six songs in the cage, I think."

"Well, then name of one of the songs that you danced to," he spat at me, treating me like I was a child.

"I don't know … Maybe Britney Spears' 'Toxic'?" I answered, very confused.

He grabbed his iPod and started searching. I was standing on the other side of the bed from him, completely clueless as to what to do. After a few minutes, I heard the first notes of the song begin to play.

"Dance for me, Charlie. Show me the moves that you were doing in the cage with Rachael," he commanded.

Okay! How awkward is this? I'm bone tired. My eyes are puffy from crying. He's staring at me like I'm an alien. I can't dance for him.

"This is ridiculous. Let's just go to bed," I pleaded.

"Caroline, move your fucking body to the music. Do I sound like someone that you care to fuck with tonight?" he barked.

From somewhere deep in my soul, I found the strength to start dancing. The more that I swayed my body and moved to the music, the more turned on he became. This was actually kind of fun. His erection strained against his jeans making me move my hips more.

"Do the move that you were photographed doing," his raspy voice commanded.

As I moved my body to the ground and back up, he pounced on me. My dress was pushed up over my hips, and my panties were shredded as he shoved his erection inside me. It took me by surprise, and it hurt for just a second.

He paused until he felt me get wet, then he started his punishment of my body. I was bent over my bed. He was holding my hips and slamming into me repeatedly. It was grueling. It felt like the night that he'd fucked me against my bedroom door when he left me.

I wasn't sure if I should stop him or let him use me like this. My body was begging me not to say no; my mind was telling me that I was in a heap of trouble. Before I could make up my mind, he reached one hand around my hips and started massaging my clit. My body won. I screamed out as I came, and he finished a few seconds later.

We were so spent that I didn't get up to clean myself. In the early dawn hours of Sunday morning, we somehow managed to crawl to the top of the bed, holding on to each other for dear life.

"Colin, I got an almost perfect score on the MCAT," I whispered.

"That's wonderful, beautiful girl," he said as we drifted off to sleep.

February, Senior Year

I WATCHED him walk out of my apartment. The last two days had been hell. We had done nothing but spend the last forty-eight hours grieving the loss of this relationship together. We'd hugged, cried, screamed at each other and made desperate, passionate love.

The drive back to College Station was awful. Every time that I thought I had it together, I would remember that this was it. He was walking out of my life. During our last conversation, Colin admitted that he needed all or nothing from me. He couldn't take being my friend. I was desperately sad that he'd made that decision, but I respected it and understood. We were ripping the Band-Aid away from the wound instead of gently coaxing it off.

I'd texted Rachael to let her know what was going on and asked her not to be home. She graciously obliged.

We were like ghosts packing up his things. We didn't talk much. I handed him his clothes from my closet. He folded them neatly and put them in his duffle. I bagged up his toiletries. He silently carried his things to Big Bertha.

He insisted that I keep the Porsche SUV. He said that he at least had to know that I was safe on the roads in Boston. I didn't want the car, but I knew not to try to argue with him. I just smiled and thanked him.

When everything was in his truck and he was ready to go, we stood there like two stupid fools in my living room. Neither wanting to say the word *goodbye*.

He slowly slid my key off his key-ring and handed it to me. I begged the tears to stay away, but they wouldn't.

I looked up at him and said, "I never want you to doubt that our relationship was real, strong, and filled with all the love that I have to give you. I'm not going to Harvard because you're inadequate. I am going to be Harvard because I'm inadequate."

He kissed me tenderly on the lips, reassuring me that he knew. "You'll always be important to me, Charlie. If you ever need anything, I want you to call me. I can't be your friend, but I can be your guardian angel. Do you understand me?"

I nodded.

With that, he turned and walked to Big Bertha. I watched him climb inside that awful truck and drive away. I knew that my heart was in that ugly pickup truck.

***

Three days later, I got a call from the car dealership confirming a delivery time for Colin's new car. I had completely forgotten. I told the salesperson that there was a change in the delivery address and gave them Colin's apartment information and cell phone number. I asked the salesperson to start dealing with him directly.

I sent Colin a quick text to let him know what was going on. We hadn't spoken to each other since he'd driven away from my apartment. It was brutal, but I knew in my heart of hearts that Colin was right. This was the best way for us to try to move on with our lives.

> *Me: The car dealership was supposed to deliver your new SAFE car today. I gave them your address in Dallas and phone number, and asked them to coordinate with you. I know that you are very upset with me, but please don't return the car. I want you to be safe on the roads in Dallas, like you want me to be safe on the roads in Boston.*

He didn't reply. I didn't expect him to. Blissfully, Aiden and Rachael were not mentioning his name to me. There were no sides to take in our breakup. We were two people who desperately loved each other, but we knew that we couldn't make a four-year long-distance relationship work.

***

Five days later, I was getting out of the shower when I heard my phone trill, telling me that I had a text.

It was him: it was from Colin. My heart fell in my stomach. I hadn't realized how much I missed seeing his name on my phone.

I grabbed it and opened the text.

Colin: The maroon hybrid Cadillac Escalade was delivered today. I am assuming hybrid is so I can try to make amends with the environment after driving Big Bertha for so long. Thank you. It's a great car. I'll keep it. However, I can't keep the license plate STATMNT. It's just too painful. I hope you understand.

And that was the last time that I heard from Colin McKinney for eight years …

The Present

Chapter One

I STEERED my red Mercedes CLK convertible into my reserved parking spot and turned the engine off. I always take a few minutes to get my head straight before I head into the chaos that is my day. Today's a patient day. I like surgery days better because I can just do what I've been trained to do and not have to play good-bedside-manner doctor.

I grab my purse, phone and head into my office in Smith Tower.

I'm greeted by Carmen, "Good morning, Caroline. I love the dress. It looks stunning on you." I have on a black, knee-length dress. It's nothing special. She must be trying to butter me up for something.

"Thanks, Carmen. When do I see my first patient?" I ask. This is our morning routine. I have an assistant, but I don't see him until I get to my office, which is in the back of the practice.

"Ten o'clock, and you are booked solid today," she replies.

"Great news," I say, tying not to sound sarcastic.

I know that my dad is already here. He beats me every morning. I swear the man doesn't sleep. I stop by the break room and try to fix a cup of coffee without being spied upon. Coffee is a fun addiction that I picked up in medical school. I'm not particularly happy with it, but every time that I try to give it up, my coworkers insist that I have a mug.

"Made it! Yes!" My dad hasn't seen me yet. I mentally high-five myself. My wonderful assistant, Brad, is waiting for me at my office. He knows the drill. We do everything that we can to avoid my father until I've had coffee. Brad is my savior.

He holds my office door open for me and scoots in behind me. He closes my door, and we both collapse in my office, letting out a sigh of relief. My office is large and comfortable. I have a big desk with lots of drawers. They are mostly empty. I have a large credenza behind my desk that's also empty. My dad insisted that I have this desk and credenza because he said that it makes patients feel like we have lots of knowledge and importance behind us. In reality, all of our patient records are kept digitally. With a few clicks on my keyboard, I can access any file that I need.

I have two club chairs in front of my desk and a couch along the wall. Sometimes I need to accommodate families. I sit down behind my desk and Brad takes his spot on my couch. He looks more like he's watching TV than having a meeting with his boss.

"So, Brad, tell me about my patient load today," I instruct. He's obviously gay. He has copper-colored hair, brown eyes, and smattering of freckles across his nose. He is a yoga and Pilates enthusiast. He has become a dear friend and personal shopper for me. There are times that I wonder how I lived so long without him. He's an R.N. by schooling, but he needed a break from the hospital world. He doesn't like whiney patients, vomit, infections, or anything dealing with vaginas. That's what he told me as his opening line when I interviewed him. He's also meticulously organized, has a great bedside manner and everyone loves him. Working for me, he's still able to dabble in medicine while he gets to run my life. This is something that he takes great pride in.

"Doctor Collins, just let me tell you, you are slammed today. I don't know who's doing the scheduling, but they must think that you wear running shoes instead of those fabulous high-heeled Christian Louboutins," he gushes.

"I have some sort of stupid fundraiser tonight. I'll slip on more practical shoes. I don't want our patients to think that I get paid too much." I wink at him.

"Well, whatever the reason, you're a busy little beaver today," he reaffirms for me.

We make it about halfway through my patient list when there's the inevitable knock on the door. "Come in, Dad," I call. Brad rolls his eyes.

My dad steps into my office and barely acknowledges Brad. It's nothing personal. My dad doesn't have time for niceties.

"Good morning, Caroline. I need to talk to you," he says.

Brad takes the cue and leaves, flashing me an exaggerated grin as he walks out my door.

"What's up?" I ask. This is our morning routine. Thankfully, he let me have some coffee first before he decided that we "needed to talk." Dad is an expert at helping professional athletes extend their careers. He exclusively deals with the world's best athletes, and they all fighting to see him.

When I graduated from Harvard, we went into practice together. I see the everyday athletes. Mostly my patients are weekend-warrior types who play beyond their age. His side of the practice is cash only. He doesn't accept insurance, and he doesn't take too many athletes on at one time. There's a waiting list a mile long to get in to see him. It's the who's who of professional athletes. We've been known to have some seriously great offers of persuasion show up at our office. My dad hasn't missed a World Series or Super Bowl in years.

"Have you had your coffee?" he replies. Maybe he isn't as clueless to my coffee addiction as I'd thought.

"Yup. Just finished my second cup. Am I going to need a third?" I ask.

"Brad," he yells. "Bring Doctor Collins another cup of coffee."

"Absolutely," Brad yells back.

Great! What is this about? It has to be either really bad or really good. Dad doesn't behave this way when it's nothing.

He dives right in. "I've been invited to attend a formal dinner honoring the long and successful career of Clay South. Mainly because Clay passionately believes I extended his professional career by three, very important, years. He has asked that I sit at his personal table with him and his family."

Clay South retired at the end of the football season after playing seventeen years as quarterback. He led his team to five championships. He's a god and legend in the football world.

Clay came to Dad five years ago. He was suffering from a neck ailment that was preventing him from throwing the football with the maximum velocity he needed to stay at the top of his game. He had seen numerous other doctors and they'd all suggested surgery, but it could have been career-ending. My dad was able to rehab Clay's neck during the off-season and fix the issue without him going under the knife. I seriously think Clay is crazier about my dad than he is about his own kids.

"That's fabulous, Dad. What an honor," I reply. It's very cool, but I am not sure what this has to do with me.

Just then, Brad knocks on my door and comes in without waiting to be acknowledged. He hands me the cup and says, "Let me know if you need some Baileys."

My father admonishes him, "Inappropriate, Brad."

I give Brad a wink as he shuts my door.

"Caroline, I think that it would be good for the practice if you joined me as my date. The top athletes in the football world will be there to honor Clay. It will be wonderful networking for you," he concludes.

I agree that it does sound like a good opportunity for me. I would ultimately like to do what Dad does, and just work with professional athletes exclusively. "When is it?"

"Saturday," he replies. "It's in Los Angeles. I'll have Brad book your ticket."

"Saturday, as in, four days from now?" I ask, incredulously.

"That would be the one," he says without a hint of humor in his voice.

"Dad, I have nothing to wear. Ugh! Why are you just now telling me about it?" I ask, suddenly suspicious.

"Take Brad shopping with you. Buy whatever you need and expense it to the practice," he says, obviously bored with the details.

"You didn't answer the question. Why am I just now hearing about this?" I ask again.

He crosses and uncrosses his legs. Shifting in his seat, "I suspect that Colin McKinney is on the guest list. I don't know if he is attending," he says it as if that explains everything. "You can't avoid him forever, Caroline."

"I'm not avoiding him. I just haven't had the opportunity to attend a function that he's also attending," I explain. He doesn't have to know that I have Brad call before I R.S.V.P. to any event that Colin might be at to check and see if he is on the guest list. If he is, I politely decline.

It's been eight years since I last saw him. Don't get me wrong; I've seen him in magazines, websites and on TV. I have followed his career because you would have to be blind or deaf to miss him.

I had a panic attack the first time that I saw his underwear campaign. The man that I had been crazy in love with was blown up ten-stories high on the side of a building in nothing but his tighty whities, which I knew for a fact that he didn't wear. I'd gasped, felt sick to my stomach, and avoided that part of town until I was sure that the ad had been replaced.

"I love you, Caroline. Don't overthink this. You're a very accomplished young lady and doctor. You need to hold your head high. You are the new face of our practice, and this is your time." He stands up and walks out of my office. As soon as my door shuts, I start doing some serious breathing exercises. I finish the rest of my coffee and try to compose myself for my first patient of the day. I vow not to think about Colin again.

First, though, I pull out my phone and message Rachael.

Me: Colin. Fucking. McKinney

There's no need to say more. Rachael will get the meaning.

Rachael: I need details. I'll call you on my way home.

Fortunately, the rest of my morning goes much more smoothly. Patients are on time. They don't try to make idle chitchat with me. By one, I'm on such a roll that I hate to break for lunch.

Brad is waiting for me. "Where shall we eat today, My Lady?"

"Well, kind Sir, I was thinking about just going down to the building deli."

Brad makes a face. "I was hoping for somewhere amazing."

"Sorry, Brad. You keep my schedule. If you want to go somewhere amazing, keep appointments from slamming me," I admonish.

"That's a deal, Caroline." He smirks.

My after-lunch appointments have been just as awesome as the before-lunch patients. Ask any doctor, and they'll tell you that this is generally how their day will go. In medicine, you either have a kick-ass day or a day that kicks your ass. Today, we're kick-ass. I even had one patient who was very nice looking ask if I was single. I have a rule against dating patients, but it's always nice to have a gorgeous guy show some interest.

Brad hands me the last chart of the day. He starts messing with my hair, flipping it over one shoulder, and pinches my cheeks. He smiles at me and says, "Go get 'em, Tiger."

I have completed my marathon day. I walk out of the exam room and hand Brad my notes sheet and collapse in my office. Brad follows in behind me.

"I've taken the liberty to schedule you dress fittings at three luxury department stores. Our first appointment is in an hour," he informs me.

"What?" I ask.

"Your dad said that you need a formal gown for the dinner on Saturday. He left me with such short notice that we're going to have to buy off the rack," he says making a face. "Come, Doctor Collins. Let's see what Neiman Marcus has to show us."

I roll my eyes. "Brad, you know my size. Can't you just grab me something? Plus, I have the fundraiser tonight."

"No. I need to see you in them, and I already put a generous check in the mail to the charity with your apology note," he states firmly.

"Brad, how much do you love me?" I ask.

"I love you enough to make sure you look so hot that every man there goes home and takes a cold shower," he gushes.

"Fine. I'll go tonight. That's it. You're picking something. Then, you are taking me to eat sushi and drink sake. Got it?"

"Got it, Doctor Collins. This is going to be so much fun," he exclaims, clapping his hands.

***

I've tried on every bloody beaded gown in the store. Brad is fussing over me. He can't make up his mind. The sales associate, sensing a big commission, is passing out white wine like it's water.

Brad has it narrowed down to a full-length ivory halter-neck beaded gown with a slit that is so high I'm sure my panties will show. The other dress is also full length. It's a shade of light aqua, strapless, also with a slit, but it shows a little less leg.

Brad is wailing about how he likes the cut of the ivory, but the aqua is a better color for me. Another sales associate scurries off to pull accessories for both looks.

I go back into the dressing room and change into my work clothes. I check my phone. No missed calls. I note that I really need to make more friends than just Brad. I'm tired and hungry. I can't take this nonsense any longer. It's just one stupid dinner; I'm not being buried in this dress.

When I walk out, Brad is discussing my dress options with the sales associate. "She has such great shoulders, and both dresses really show them off."

"We'll take the aqua," I say.

"Really, Caroline? It's a little conservative," he suggests.

"We'll take the ivory, then."

"I don't know. I'm worried about that slit," he counters.

"Brad, if you value our friendship and your job, pick one," I almost scream at him.

"She'll take the aqua," he says to the sales associate.

My little red convertible is loaded with the dress, shoes, bag and jewelry. "How am I going to get all of this to Los Angeles?" I ask Brad.

"I'm shipping it tomorrow," he says.

I should have known that he would have the perfect solution. He really is amazing.

After Brad and I are halfway through our first bottle of sake, I tell him that Colin might be at the dinner.

Brad raises eyebrow. "And you're going?"

Brad doesn't know the whole Colin saga. He knows that I dated him in college, and then we broke up. He knows that Rachael and I now refer to him only as Colin. Fucking. McKinney. He also knows that I'm avoiding him.

"My dad didn't give me a choice. Plus, if I want to play with the big boys in the professional athlete arena, I'm going to have to see him," I explain.

"Look, Caroline, I don't know what went on between you two, but it's been eight years. People grow up. They change. Maybe it would be good to see him and realize that you've both moved on," he reasons as takes another sip of sake.

That's just it, though. Have I moved on? I haven't had a serious relationship with a man since Colin. It's not that I don't get asked on dates, but no one has intrigued me enough to make it past two or three dinners and attain the boyfriend title. There was one guy during medical school and residency, but he liked me significantly more than I liked him. In hindsight, he probably thought we were dating. I was just passing the time.

Sure, I graduated from Harvard and my career has shot through the roof. Personally, though, I don't have many friends, and no guys that I want to date. Rachael told me once that there was no settling for second best when I've had the Statement. I'm secretly worried that she's right.

"You're right, Brad. I know you are. If he's there, he's there," I concede, wishing that I felt as confident inside. *What will I do if he has a date?*

Soon our table is filled with sushi rolls. Before we start, Brad reminds me that I have to rock the dress on Saturday so I shouldn't eat too much. He doesn't know about my past struggles with my eating disorder. If he did, he would no doubt be horrified that he'd just said that.

By the time dinner is over, I'm completely sated. I drop Brad off at his home and head to my townhome in the museum district. Even though it's brand new, it has fabulous old world charm. The wall the fireplace is located on is antique brick. I chose either antique or antique replica lighting. My furniture is neutral colored with pops of primary colors.

Instead of traditional granite, I chose Carrera marble. My cabinets are antiqued black.

The first floor is my garage and guest room. My second story is open concept. There are no interior walls. I love how spacious it is. My third floor is my master bedroom and bathroom.

I love my townhome. I decorated it, and it looks just like me. This is my refuge.

I carry myself upstairs and crawl into bed. As I fall asleep, I reflect on my life. I have everything that I wanted for myself, but I have no one to share it with. I'm so busy that I can't even get a dog.

My sisters have encouraged me to join a singles' group. I might look into it when I get back from Los Angeles. I'm lonely, and it sucks.

I get up and take a sleeping pill. I've gotten myself worked up, and six-fifteen comes very early at my house.

Chapter Two

BRAD DROPPED my dad and me at the airport Friday afternoon. He reassured me that my dress and accessories would be waiting for me at the hotel when we checked in. He'd come over last night to pack my suitcase while we watched reruns of *Sex and the City,* and ate Chinese food. I was really thankful that he'd offered. If left to my own devices I would have packed a pair of jeans, two shirts, pajamas, and running clothes. Instead, I've got a suitcase filled with Los Angeles appropriate attire.

My hair instantly rebels when I step off the plane at LAX. Thankfully, Brad made an appointment for me at a salon that one of his friends recommended. When I protested, he reminded me that Colin might be at the dinner. Then he told me that I wanted to look as fabulous as I could. I knew he was right, but I hated being fussed over.

Dad and I are staying in the same hotel that's hosting the dinner. Sure enough, when we check in I'm informed that a package will be brought to my room shortly. I quickly send Brad a text thanking him.

However, we're also informed upon check-in that there's a reception this evening for out-of-town guests. I quickly ask what the dress code is. I'm told that it's casual.

As soon as I walk into my hotel room, I call Brad. "Help me out here. What do I wear for a casual reception?"

"Thank goodness I packed for you. If I hadn't, you'd have been in running shorts and a tank top." Brad likes nothing more than reminding me how much I need him.

"You're a rock star, Brad. Now, tell me what to wear." I can stroke his ego if it gets me what I want.

"I packed you a sleeveless lavender dress. Pair it with your silver, high-heeled sandals. Blow-dry your hair with soft waves. Put on makeup, but not too much. You want to look effortlessly fabulous," he instructs.

"Thanks! You're a lifesaver." I hang up with him and start the process to look effortlessly beautiful.

At six o'clock on the dot, my dad knocks on my door. I grab my phone and room key and slip them into a small purse that Brad packed for me. I really need to get him a great thank-you gift while I'm here.

Dad looks stunning. For a man who's almost sixty, he's really dashing. I inherited my light olive complexion and lavender eyes from him. He's about six-feet tall with a full head of salt-and-pepper hair, and his build is slender, like mine. He has on a white, very expensive-looking golf shirt and pressed khaki pants. The Rolex he's wearing really helps sell the doctor image.

We don't say much to each other. I have butterflies in my stomach. I'm comfortable with networking, so it must be the prospect of Colin being there that's screwing with my digestive system. I almost hope that he's at the reception so I can get seeing him over with.

What if he's with a date? Then, he just is. I'll be polite and wish them well.

Ideally, I hope that I can make it one more event without running in to him. I'm not even sure what I would say. Then an ugly thought enters my brain. *What if he doesn't remember me?* It's been eight years. I'm sure that our relationship has been chalked up to nothing more than puppy-love in his mind.

The doors of the elevator open, and just as I step off I remember that I left my business cards in my other purse. "Dad, I need to run back up to the room. I'll be back in a second."

My dad nods his head and exits the elevator. I hit my floor button as I silently reproach myself. Here I am coming along to network for our practice, and I leave my business cards in the room. *Not smart, Caroline. You're too distracted by the thought of Colin. Fucking. McKinney.*

Fortunately, they're right where I left them. I stick them in the small purse and do one last appearance check in the full-length mirror in my hotel room. I primp my hair and lick my lips. This just has to be good enough.

I walk to the bank of elevators and wait impatiently for mine to arrive. I know that Dad is waiting on me, and he hates to be kept waiting.

I hear the *ding* of the elevator behind me and turn around to get on.

My heart falls into my stomach. My eyes grow wide with shock. The last time I saw him in person was when he was walking out of my life for good. He's standing there – in the elevator. Colin. Fucking. McKinney. I gasp. He looks just as surprised as I feel.

"Hello, Charlie. It's been a very long time," he says. His voice is just as smooth as I remembered it. *Well, I guess he remembers me.* He's just as gorgeous as he was at twenty-two. He's more muscular, and his wavy, dirty-blond hair is now shorter and darker. His clear green eyes are still just as hypnotizing. He doesn't necessarily have wrinkles around his eyes; they just look more knowing. He's still a beautiful, perfect Mission Statement.

I'm stunned to see him. I just stand there, as if I'm glued to the floor looking like a damn fool. I had thought of this happening over the years, but it was always in a more open place and not an elevator. Our eyes would lock across a room filled with people. We would say a few polite things to each other. I'd introduce him to my wonderful husband, who'd cured cancer. Colin would give me a kiss on the cheek and tell me how nice it was to see me again, and my gorgeous husband would then take me home, and we would make passionate love, reaffirming that my life had turned out like it should have.

Instead, I'm very successful professionally, but haven't had sex with anyone beside myself in more than two years.

"Are you going to get on the elevator?" he asks, flashing me his half-smile.

"S … s … sure," I stammer.

I step on the elevator and the doors shut.

"It's Caroline. I don't go by Charlie any longer," I find myself saying. I'm amazed that I can speak.

"That's a shame. I always thought Charlie was a great nickname for you. By the way, I love your lavender dress," he says as if we're sharing an inside joke.

I'm facing forward. I can feel him behind me. My body recognizes him instantly. I'm drawn to him. My body wants to touch him. It wants to hold his hand, or touch his thigh that only seems to have gotten more muscular. I feel the tingling rush of electricity go through my body. My mind tries to reason with my body that we no longer know him, and remind myself that nothing has changed: he's still a professional quarterback and has even more baggage than before. I plead with the elevator to go faster.

"I assume you're here for the Clay South event," he says.

I love how deep and masculine his voice is with its hint of lightheartedness. *God, I just thought that*, I tell myself. *Get it together, Caroline.*

"Yes," I respond without turning around.

The doors of the elevator open, and I race off. Thankfully, my dad's waiting. I see him smiling. My heart floods with love for that man. Then, I realize that he's not smiling at me. He's smiling at Colin, who is walking behind me.

"Hello, Colin. How nice to see you again." Dad beams at my ex-boyfriend, shaking his hand.

"Doctor Collins. It's been a long time. I guess that's good in my line of work." Colin laughs, but it's strained. *Maybe time doesn't forgive and forget.*

"Yes. I guess it is. I have enjoyed following your career. You're one hell of a quarterback." My dad slaps Colin gently on the arm. "You know, Caroline's practicing with me."

I realize that Colin is still standing behind me. I turn and orient myself more appropriately into the conversation circle. This is so awkward.

"Is that so, Charlie? I mean, Caroline," he says.

"Yes." I'm completely detached from my body. "I've been working with my dad since I graduated from Harvard Medical School and completed my residency."

Fortunately, the waiter walks by offering trays of red and white wine. I quickly snag a glass of white. My dad and Colin refuse.

"Well, it's nice that you made your dreams come true," he says with just a trace of bitterness in his voice. I pick up on it only because I know/knew him so well. Wow! He's still a little hurt. That snaps me out of my zombie-like state.

"You know me, Colin. I was always the girl who knew exactly what she wanted," I say, trying not to sound too bitter.

His eyes grow wide with shock. I really like that I can still shock him. Then it dawns on me. *He thinks that I'm talking about in the bedroom.*

"Excuse me, Caroline and Colin. I see someone who I need to say hello to," Dad says, walking away and leaving me alone with him.

As soon as my dad is out of earshot, Colin says, "Eight years and you couldn't pick up the phone and call me, Charlie? That hurt." I can see the anger in his eyes.

"Eight years and you couldn't contact me, Colin," I reply, mirroring his look. The tension is thick between us. I didn't realize how much I had wanted him to call me until this moment.

He's about to say something when another player who I recognize walks toward us. The guy is clearly checking me out. "McKinney, my man, who's the lovely lady with you? Maybe you should introduce us."

Colin is obviously annoyed. "JT Reynolds, this is Charlie Collins."

I stick my hand out. "Hello JT. I am Doctor Caroline Collins. It's a pleasure to meet you in person. I'm a big fan," I gush.

"You're a doctor?" He's surprised. "I've never met a doctor that is this hot. If I had, I might go more often," he says with a laugh.

I reach in my small purse and pull out my business card. "I'm an orthopedic surgeon who specializes in sports-related injuries. I've seen the way that you play. You might want to keep my card." I flash him my biggest grin.

"I wouldn't think of losing it," he flirts.

I can feel the heat radiating off of Colin. "If you'll excuse us one minute, JT. Charlie and I were just finishing up a conversation."

"I'll see you around, Doctor Charlie," JT says, winking at me.

Colin grabs my arm and drags me to a corner by the window, where there isn't anyone else milling around. I'm speechless. I'm not sure what I've done to make him this angry, but he is seething.

"Stay away from JT," he warns. "He's a womanizer. He's slept his way through cheerleaders, players' girlfriends, and some of their wives."

"I don't care," I spat. "Does he have bones and muscles? Then he could use me." Colin is towering over me. His six-foot, five-inch body is staring down at my five-foot, seven-inch frame. "Why is it your business, anyway?"

"You were practically throwing yourself at him, Charlie. I don't want to see you get hurt," he says. Is there jealousy in his eyes? I'm not sure.

"Look, Colin," I say as I break our staring contest. "I'm here because my dad asked me to come. Clay was an important patient of our practice, as he will tell anyone." Then in a softer tone, I add, "It's been a long time. We've got a lot of murky water under our bridge. I'm glad that we've seen each other again. Maybe it will be less awkward next time we run into each other. Let's just get through the weekend being civil to each other."

Someone else approaches, trying to get Colin's attention. I use that distraction to walk away. I can feel his eyes watching me until I exit the reception room. I flee to the restroom, needing to clear my head.

I quickly message Brad and Rachael.

Me: Colin. Fucking. McKinney. He's here. Still just as gorgeous and maddening.

I put some lip-gloss on and pinch my cheeks. I don't know what to make of his jealousy. I wish that I had time to call Brad or Rachael and analyze the conversation, but I have to get back to the reception.

I return to the other room and realize that he's gone. I briefly wonder if he left because of me. I'm a little disappointed, but also relieved. At least now I can focus on what I came here to do, which is network for our practice. I spot my dad and beeline for him.

He greets me, "Hello, Caroline. I was just looking for you …" He continues to introduce me around the room. Dad seems to know just about everyone. Either he's treated the majority of players at the reception, or he knows them through his philanthropic work, focused on preventing spinal cord injuries in youth. I didn't quite realize how well connected my dad is.

After the reception is over, Dad says that Clay called and invited us to come to his home for dinner tonight. He said that he accepted without asking me, but he offers to call back and decline on my behalf if I wish to do something else. I quickly shake my head no. I'm looking forward to meeting Clay and his family. I've certainly heard enough about them through the years.

My dad and I walk outside and are greeted by the cool Los Angeles evening. I wish that I had run back to my room and grabbed a jacket. My sleeveless lavender dress is not even close to keeping me warm.

Just as I'm contemplating waiting in the lobby for our town car, two very big hands grab my upper arms. I would know those callused hands anywhere. They belong to Colin. He runs his hands up and down my arms. It takes all my willpower not to lean back into his chest. My whole body floods with warmth remembering our times together. God, I love his touch. I realize in that second that no other person's touch has affected me even a tenth as much as his does. Once again, I'm so thankful that Brad packed for me.

"Are you going to Clay's home?" my father asks.

"Yes. I just got the invite. You?" Colin replies with a knowing chuckle.

"Yes. He invited us also. Would you be opposed to sharing a car?"

"Dad, maybe it would be better if we took separate cars. Colin might want to stay later than us. We're a bit jet-lagged," I argue. I can feel Colin's grip tighten around my biceps.

"Charlie, if I want to stay later I'll call a cab," Colin says, raising his voice just slightly. I know that tone. It's the "don't mess with me" voice that I had heard frequently when we were together.

"There. It's settled," Dad says.

When our town car arrives, Colin removes his hands from my arms. I immediately long for his touch again; I love how his touch makes me feel. But it does give me a chance to see him. He's changed into a pair of jeans that fit him nicely, a black T-shirt, and a camel-colored sports coat. He looks ravishing. I also note that he could have offered me his jacket, but he chose to rub my arms instead. He chose to touch me. *That means something, right?*

My dad offers Colin the front seat, but he politely declines. I slide in the back of the car and let out a laugh when I see Colin fold himself into the back. As the door shuts, I can feel the temperature rise in the car. His long leg falls dangerously close to mine. *Did he do that on purpose?* My body remembers how good he felt, and it is trying to convince my mind to let me move closer to him.

My father gives the driver the address. The driver says that it's approximately a thirty-minute drive, and my mind starts racing. Can I take thirty minutes in the car with him? Sharing the same oxygen? What are we supposed to talk about? I can't see myself making idle chitchat with the man who broke my heart so many years ago in front of my father, knowing that Colin must feel some sort of bitterness toward him.

My dad makes small talk. "Colin, how do you know Clay, besides the obvious football connection?"

"He was actually a mentor to me, of sorts. My second year playing professional ball was hard. I was dealing with a lot of personal turmoil," he says, shooting me a raised eyebrow. "Clay helped me put things in perspective and focus on my career. I'm the one that referred him to you, Doctor Collins," he confirms.

"Well, I certainly appreciate the referral. He became a good friend of mine. I obviously respect him a lot," Dad concludes.

We are back to silence. "Personal turmoil, huh?" I contemplate the meaning behind those words. The look Colin gave me obviously means our breakup. I get a little bit of satisfaction from knowing that it was hard on him also.

I shift in my seat, moving a fraction of an inch closer to him. When I peek up at him through my eyelashes, he's staring at me with a look on his face that makes me gasp. He's obviously checking me out.

He mouths, *You're still so beautiful.*

My eyes open wide. I feel my face heat up, I mouth back, *Thank you.*

He then moves a fraction of an inch toward me. I have a thousand thoughts racing through my mind. None of them are appropriate conversations to have in front of my father.

Fortunately, my dad and Colin start discussing football so I can be alone in my head. I wonder if he can feel the electricity passing between us? I look down, half expecting myself to be vibrating. We have a complex shared history. I'm remembering what it felt like to be in love with him and be loved that much in return. I remind myself that our shared history was eight years ago. I was a college kid. He was trying to figure out who he was professionally, and personally, for that matter. What we had was great, but he overwhelmed me and I bolted for Boston. *We can't change our past.*

We hit a bump, which jolts me out of my head, and I feel myself slide even closer to him. I long to reach out and run my hand up his thigh. I always loved how strong his legs were. I liked the feel of his incredibly hard muscles under his soft, silky leg hair. I want to touch him so badly, but I don't.

"Charlie," he says, "how long have you been practicing with your dad?"

"Umm … I guess more than two years now," I reply, snapping out of my daydream. That was a safe question for the car. *Good job, Colin.* I mentally applaud him.

"I've heard Boston is nice in May," he says.

What a strange thing to say. "Sure. Boston is a great city," I reply.

"I happen to have been in Boston in May a few years back. It rained like crazy." He shoots me that raised eyebrow look again.

He's obviously trying to tell me something. Suddenly it hits me like a Mack truck. I graduated in May six years ago, and although it didn't rain during our graduation ceremony, it rained very hard the rest of the day.

I look at him in complete shock. I mouth at him, *What?*

"I was in town seeing an old friend." He continues out loud, "Unfortunately, she wasn't available, so now I always think of Boston in May as a miserable time to visit. However I've been told that it is usually fantastic weather."

I'm blown away. He just admitted to me in a car with my father sitting here that he was at my medical school graduation. How can I ask why he didn't say hello in a way that doesn't tip my dad off to how awkward I feel?

God bless my father. He says, "Caroline, Boston usually has great weather in May, doesn't it?"

"Yes, Dad. It does," I reply.

However, I am not letting Colin off the hook this easily. "Why wasn't she available? Did you not plan ahead and call her and let her know that you were coming?"

I study his face very carefully. He's shocked that I picked up the ball he dropped and ran with it. "Her phone number must have been out of order," he says very matter-of-factly.

I know that he didn't call me. I have had the same phone number since college. I'm really getting angry. How dare he come to my medical school graduation ceremony and not say hello to me? It feels stalkerish, and I don't like it. I open my mouth to respond to his statement when I see the pleading look on his face.

Please drop it, he mouths. *I'm sorry.*

I lean back against the car seat and close my eyes, trying to process what he'd just said. Did he come to get closure? Was he stalking me to see if I had a boyfriend? Why didn't he say hello? I'm beyond curious.

When we get to Clay's beautiful home in the hills overlooking Hollywood, I practically bolt out of the vehicle. The air in the car is thick with unsaid emotions and lots of questions. The refreshing night air snaps me back to reality. I need to keep my cool and not embarrass my father, or myself, in front of his friend and most important patient.

Unfortunately, I have to walk around the car and Colin stalls enough so that he's next to me. He gently puts his hand on my lower back as if he is politely letting me go in front of him.

His touch practically sears me. It is so unexpected and my body screams for more. He whispers in my ear, "If you say that you don't feel it, you're a liar."

I let out a gentle breath of air that I didn't realize I was holding.

I nod in agreement.

"Clay is going to love meeting you," he says with a chuckle.

Chapter Three

WE'RE GREETED by a loud, booming voice that matches the man. Clay South looks like a grizzly bear with a voice that's almost a roar. He's in his late thirties and built like a brick house. His dark brown skin, chocolate eyes, and a physique make a truly imposing figure. I like him instantly.

He greets Colin first. "My man, it is you! You are fucking fantastic, you crazy motherfucker." Colin hugs Clay and slaps him on the back.

He's a little more reserved toward my father. "Doctor Collins, the best doctor in the world. Thank you for coming. I'm just so glad that I get to see you out of your office," he says, hugging my father.

Then, to my surprise, he greets me. "Doctor Collins, you're just as magnificent as I imagined. I'm Clay South, star patient of your father's and best friend to your ... well... Colin," he says, giving Colin a knowing smile.

Apparently, my reputation has preceded me. "It's a pleasure to meet you Mr. South. I'm honored to be included in your special weekend," I say in my politest voice.

"Call me Clay. Now, come in because the food is almost ready, and my house smells so damn good that I might eat it," he says laughing from deep in his gut.

I follow my dad and Colin in the front door. The house is huge. The foyer alone is the size of my living room, kitchen, and dining room combined. We follow Clay into the kitchen where there's a table that seats twelve people. I meet his lovely wife, Janis, and his four children who are particularly well-behaved. They obviously know Colin very well and start climbing on him like he's a jungle gym. Clay's only little girl, who is about four, starts asking Colin where her guitar is. Colin flashes Clay a smile and replies, "Uncle Colin will buy you a guitar this weekend, baby girl."

Clay and Janis have a look of horror on their faces. "Buy her one and you are no longer her godfather," Clay says without a hint of seriousness in his voice.

I sit back and watch the dynamic of this family. Colin is playing with the kids, and bantering with Clay. Janis and my father are engaged in a conversation near the stove. I'm a casual observer of the motley crew. I was expecting more people to be here, but it appears that Colin, my dad, and me are the only guests. I'm pondering what this all means, when Clay says, "Kids, let Uncle Colin up. He still has to throw a football in a couple of months. Colin, why don't you show Charlie my trophy room?" He gives Colin a wink.

"Clay, I go by Caroline. Charlie's a name that I haven't used for a long time," I say, smiling. Colin must have really shared some scoop about us.

They both ignore the comment about my name change.

"Clay, you're such an asshole. You're going to rub in all of your accomplishments, aren't you?" Colin teases.

"Uncle Colin, not in front of the babies' delicate ears," Clay responds in mock horror.

Colin rolls his eyes and turns to me. "Follow me. I'll show you Clay's brag room," he says, offering me his hand.

He entwines our fingers. I squeeze his hand before I can stop myself. I love how his huge hand engulfs mine. It makes me feel safe and protected, and it reminds me of a time in my life that was for the most part happy.

He leads me from the kitchen, through the foyer, and up the stairs. I don't allow myself to think about the electricity that's traveling between us. *It's in the past.*

While we're walking up the winding staircase, Colin says, "You know that this whole evening was orchestrated by Clay to get us together."

"There's obviously a lot going on that I don't know about," I reply.

He walks me to the end of hall to a set of double doors. He opens one of them and holds it for me to enter. We have to break hands. It makes me feel a little lost. I want his hand back. *You don't even know if he has a girlfriend.*

A pool table dominates the center of the room. There are jerseys, memorabilia, awards, and pictures decorating three of the walls. It takes just a quick second to see that Clay has had one hell of a career, but what fascinates me the most is the fourth wall. It's filled with pictures of his kids, wife, friends, and extended family. There are pictures drawn on construction paper wishing Daddy good luck. There's a picture of Clay kissing his wife and holding one of his sons while confetti falls around them. There's a framed letter that one of his kids wrote Clay telling him how proud he was of his daddy. It's really something special.

I turn around and see Colin watching me take it all in. I walk to the family wall and look closer at the child's letter and special drawings. I realize in an overwhelming wave of emotion that this is what every person should want most in his or her life. I could have three walls covered in my professional and athletic accomplishments, but my fourth wall, the personal accomplishment wall, would be blank. I've never seen such an obvious visual display of finding life's balance than this.

"Clay says that when he shows this trophy room to friends, if they aren't drawn to the family wall first, then he knows what kind of people they really are," Colin says from behind me. He reaches up and puts his right hand on my shoulder barely touching me, but the warmth travels throughout my body.

I see a picture of Colin and Clay together. Colin is holding a little pink blanket with just a hint of a newborn face peeking out. Clay's arm is around Colin's shoulder, and the men are staring at the little face with bloodshot eyes. It's absolutely the most emotional picture that I've ever seen.

"I was at the hospital when Janis had Marley. Clay wanted a little girl so badly. Janis had given him one more try." Colin laughs. "Clay was a man on a mission. He read books on how to have a girl. He met with a couple of different doctors to see if there was some trick."

I chuckle. I had a couple of friends from medical school that went into gynecology. They said that they had tons of patients obsessed with getting one gender over the other.

"We didn't know if Marley was going to be a boy or a girl. Clay couldn't find out. He knew that he would be disappointed if it was another boy before he met him. So he waited to find out because he knew when the baby was born, he would be crazy in love no matter what the sex. Janis asked me to be there if possible, to support Clay.

"I saw Clay win the Super Bowl. The birth of Marley made his first championship moment look like nothing. I'm Marley's godfather, and apparently, I'm buying her a guitar soon," he says, smiling at the memory.

"I'm glad that you became friends with Clay. He seems like a really good man," I reply.

"Without Clay, I don't know if I would have continued playing football. You leaving me … Well, it fucked my world, Charlie," he says with angst in his voice.

"Colin, we left each other," I say, turning around to look at him. "We left each other. Let's go back downstairs and enjoy this evening with an obviously great man. We should talk about this at a later time."

He's staring at me with such intensity that it sends a shiver down my spine. "Wait a second, Charlie. I didn't do the leaving. You ran away to Boston and left me with a shattered heart. I wanted to marry you. You wanted peace and quiet."

"Please, Colin," I beg. "We have a lot to discuss. Please don't make this evening more difficult than it has to be."

Here we stand. His six-foot, five-inches staring down at my five-foot, seven-inches. His green eyes locked with my lavender. Our bodies humming for each other. Before I can stop myself, I stand on my tiptoes and kiss his mouth. He responds instantly. At first, our lips are tentative, gently getting reacquainted with each other's lips and tongues. Once our mouths remember, the intensity increases from timid to passionate. His hands wrap themselves in my hair, gently tugging. I reach up and feel his face. His stubbly five o'clock shadow is prickly under my fingertips. I run my fingers over the short hairs, savoring the sensation. For once, my mind is blank. I'm living in the moment and feeling Colin.

He pulls away first, looking at me with such a heady expression on his face, and for a split second I think he might take me on the pool table. "We need to go back downstairs and join the family before we take each other on the pool table."

I read him correctly. We may have been separated for most of our twenties, but I know what he's thinking.

I smooth my hair and making sure that I'm put together. "That was something else," I breathe.

He fixes a piece of my hair as we walk out of Clay's trophy room. I notice the tremendous strain in his pants. I love that I still have this effect on him.

"I think that you're more beautiful now than you were in college," he whispers.

"Thank you Colin. You always made me feel so wanted," I reply with a wistful smile as we walk back down the winding staircase.

"Then what the fuck happened, Charlie? We had a life planned." The anger is back in his voice, and it takes me by surprise.

I stop in the foyer and turn to look at him with pleading eyes. "Please, let's just get through the next couple of hours."

He nods in confirmation.

I walk in the kitchen, while Colin walks into the half bath under the stairs to sort himself out.

My dad is having a glass of wine as he laughs with Janis and Clay about something that he read about in the news. All four of the South children are setting the table. It's obvious that Janis has them well trained. The three boys are in charge of the plates and silverware. Little Marley is putting the glasses on the table. I ask if I can help them. Janis says, "Thank you, Caroline, but the fearsome foursome want their weekly allowance."

She offers me a glass of red wine, which I gladly accept.

"Where's Colin?" Clay asks with a knowing chuckle.

I play dumb, but I'm very well aware of what he's insinuating. "He's in the restroom. Your trophy room's really something else." I divert the conversation.

"What did you like the best?" he asks. I know that this is Clay's test.

"The picture of you, Colin, and baby Marley. Her tiny body wrapped in a pink blanket, being cradled by two giant crying men, was one of the most beautiful things that I've ever seen."

He replies, "We weren't crying. Were we, Colin?"

I hear Colin's footsteps behind me. "No, we weren't crying. There was just something in our eyes," he says, confirming Clay's story with a laugh.

Marley says, "Mommy told me that Daddy and Uncle Colin cried like babies when I was born because they were so happy to see me. My brothers cried because they knew I was going to run their lives." She's a sassy little thing and reminds me a lot of my youngest sister.

Colin bombards Marley with lots of tickles, making her scream and laugh at the same time. My dad agrees that every man should have at least one daughter, and he winks at me.

Janis puts all the food dishes on the table, family style. The four kids obviously have assigned seats. Marley insists that Uncle Colin sit right next to her. I sit next to Colin. My dad sits across from me. Before dinner's passed, we all bow our heads and the oldest son, Marlon, leads us in prayer. I didn't realize that families still did this. It's very nice.

Then, everyone fills his or her plate, and we dig in. Janis is some kind of cook. I haven't had good southern food in years. We have mashed potatoes, green beans, corn on the cob, and fried chicken.

I'm very quiet during dinner, not because I don't have anything to say, but because I'm too busy shoveling the food in. My dad even raises his eyebrow at me.

"Colin, Doctor Collins, are you playing golf with me tomorrow?" Clay asks between mouthfuls of mash potatoes.

I'm not sure if he's talking to my dad or me. Just as I'm about to reply, Colin touches my leg under the table. "Something has come up, Clay. I'll have to catch you next time."

My dad replies, "I didn't bring my clubs, but I would love to play if I can rent some?"

Clay shoots Colin a pointed look and then turns to my father. "I'm sure that I can find you some clubs. What about you, Caroline?"

"I have a spa day scheduled." Colin squeezes my thigh under the table. I'm presuming that it's his way of urging me to cancel it. I honestly don't need much persuasion. His touch alone on my thigh is enough. Dare I even hope that I'm the something that came up?

Clay must be teaching Marlon how to play golf because he asks if he can play with them. Colin jumps in before Clay can respond, "Marlon, your daddy's such a poor excuse for a golfer that Uncle Colin will set you up with lessons. You need to learn from someone good."

This launches the four South kids into a fit of giggles, and Clay pretends to pout. He says to Colin, "You better watch it. You don't want me to embarrass you in an arm-wrestling contest."

After dinner, Janis has those four sweet kids clearing the table while she serves us apple cobbler with vanilla ice cream. I might not fit in my dress tomorrow if I have many more meals like this. I think about politely declining, but that seems rude. I take two delicious bites and announce that I'm full. Colin grabs my bowl to finish my portion while Marley starts lecturing him on how gross it is to eat after someone else.

What would she say to him if she knew that he'd put his tongue in my mouth?

After dinner, Janis sends the kids to take their showers, brush their teeth, and get ready for their night stories. Clay, Colin, and my dad head outside to look at Clay's retirement present. The word retirement associated with a thirty-eight-year-old really makes me laugh. I get the impression that it's something dangerous, because Janis shoots Clay a not-pleased look. I stay inside and help Janis with the dishes.

She loads the dishwasher, and as soon as she's sure that we're alone, she says, "I know the story of you and Colin—at least from Colin's point of view. He's a good guy, Charlie. I mean, Caroline. Sorry," she apologizes. "You've been Charlie for so long," she laughs. "Calling you Caroline will take some getting used to."

I smile at her. "Janis, I frankly don't know what Colin's side of the story is. Once we decided to separate, we didn't speak to each other again. All I do know is that we were young, crazy in love, and I was completely overwhelmed with his new life. Between fans mobbing us, and the media hounding us, I felt like I had personally lost myself, all because I was a girl who loved a boy. It was too much to take in at twenty-one. I also was dealing with my own demons." I pause for a moment to make sure that I say what I want to correctly. "At twenty-nine, I can see so much more clearly how young we really were. This is the first time that I've seen him in eight years, although tonight I learned that he has seen me. It's become evident that Colin and I have a lot we need to discuss."

"Well, I'll tell you this. Colin doesn't pass up an opportunity to play golf with Clay. Clay's an awful golf player, and Colin takes great pleasure in beating him and cleaning out his wallet. Either something really important came up, or Mr. McKinney is planning on spending some time alone with you away from the watchful eyes of Daddy," she states.

I finish rinsing the rest of the plates and think about what she just said. I hope that she's right. Colin and I apparently have a lot to say to each other. Daddy playing golf would give us five hours together. Then, I start to worry. Maybe what we have to tell each other isn't good. Surely he can see his part in our break-up. Does he think that he's blameless? Either way, I reason, I'll hopefully get the closure that I need to move on with my life.

I glance at the clock. It's only nine-thirty. I start to ponder why I'm so tired when I realize that it's really eleven-thirty at home. I try to stifle a yawn.

Janis must pick up on my clue. "Clay will keep you guys here all night. He's really infatuated with his new toys. I'll gently suggest that he drive you back to your hotel."

"Thanks, Janis. This has been a lovely evening. I adore your kids and am glad you invited me to dinner. I obviously loved my meal. You know, I have five sisters and this reminded me a lot of home."

"Well, Miss Charlie, I hope you'll not be a stranger around here," she says as she walks outside to find the men.

Chapter Four

CLAY DRIVES us back to the hotel in the "family car," as he calls it. Once again, Colin insists on sitting in the back seat with me. The difference this time is that the car is much wider, and we can't surreptitiously happen to touch each other while sitting in captain's chairs. Clay, my dad, and Colin start talking football gossip. I tune out. I would put money on the fact that football players gossip more than any group of sorority girls in the country.

This gives me an opportunity to watch the dynamic between these men. My dad, who has twenty-plus years on these guys, fits in well. He has never acted his age. I like that about him and make a mental note to tell him. Clay's giving Colin all kinds of grief over Dallas's last season. Colin's dishing it right back.

Clay has won five Super Bowls. Colin has not won any. I know from my failed attempts to not follow Colin's career that this has been a huge disappointment for him personally, and for the team. The Dallas media and fans have not abandoned Colin yet, but they're growing impatient.

Then, Colin starts asking Clay how long before he gets into coaching. This must be a sore subject because Clay gives all kinds of evasive answers. I get from the conversation that Janis is ready to have Clay home for a little while before he dives back into the football grind.

I close my eyes and lean my head back. I can always sleep in a car.

I'm startled awake by Clay saying, "Are we boring you, Doctor Collins Jr.?" His voice booms, laughing at me.

"Doctor Collins Jr.?" I ask. "I think Caroline will do."

"How about Baby Doctor Collins?"

"How about Doctor Ms. Collins?" I suggest a raised eyebrow.

"How about Charlie?"

Colin chuckles.

"Charlie hasn't been my name for eight years," I reply, a little too defensively.

"You two need to lock yourselves in a room and get your shit straight," Clay says, motioning to Colin and me while he drives. "You change your name. He hates Boston. Fucked up. That's what you two are."

I suck in a huge breath of air as Colin looks at me, waiting for my reaction. I'm hoping that he will say something, but he just sits there.

The car's quiet. I have to reply because his comment was directed at me. "Clay, thanks for your words of wisdom. You can now add therapist to your list of after-retirement jobs." It's the best that I can come up with.

Colin and my dad howl with laughter. I take it that Clay's not used to having a female to spar with.

"Janis would get a kick out of that. Doctor Clay South, Psychiatrist," Colin teases.

Fortunately we're back at the hotel, because I think Colin and Clay would have only escalated the teasing. I'm exhausted, but I would like to talk to Colin alone for a few minutes before I see him tomorrow night at the dinner. The knowledge that he turned down a game of golf also makes me curious where his head is at. Clay drops us off at the circle drive. I'm relieved when he gets back in the car. Now, I just have to ditch my dad.

"Daddy, I need to stop by the front desk and get more towels for my room," I lie.

He stops walking and turns back to me. He leans to my ear, and whispers, "You're very smart and doing so well. I love you, but please be careful."

I give him a reassuring hug back. As he walks to the bank of elevators, Colin joins me. "Care to have a drink at the bar?"

"Why? So you can drink a bottle of water, and I can get shit-faced? That sounds like a terrible plan to me," I say, half kidding.

"Okay. How about if we both drink water at the hotel bar?" He laughs.

"Fine. Don't try to get me drunk, though," I warn him.

He grabs my hand and leads me toward a corner table. There are two very comfortable-looking club chairs. The bar's very dark and feels private. The soft classical music playing in the background is just loud enough to mask conversation.

The waitress rushes to greet us and obviously recognizes the man across from me. She all but unbuttons her white blouse and offers a Sharpie marker to Colin to sign her breasts. Her high pitched giggle makes the other bar patrons turn to see what is so damn funny. I'm wondering the same thing myself.

I order a glass of Alexander Valley Cabernet. Colin orders a bottle of water. I roll my eyes at him.

The waitress gives me an appraising look as she turns and walks away from the table. The snotty side of me would love to inform her that he is all that and a bag of chips. *Now, who is the jealous one?*

All of sudden, it's the big moment when we should have the talk that we've been avoiding for eight years, and there's obvious tension in the air. This feels more like a first date than a reunion with the boyfriend I was going to marry.

He starts making idle chitchat, asking me about my practice. I tell him about Brad. He tells me about his assistant, Jenny. I instantly feel a bit uncomfortable at the mention of another woman in his life until he informs me that she's in her mid-forties.

Once my wine arrives and I've had a few sips, I feel braver. I decide to jump into the deep end and see what happens. "I know that you were married once."

"Wow! Charlie. Way to go, from assistants to divorces. Shit," he laughs shaking his head.

I don't bother to correct my name, or address the swing in conversation. "It's eaten at me for a long time."

He looks uncomfortable and shifts in his chair. A few moments of silence hang between us before he answers me. "Well, I married her after knowing her for four months. It was about a year after you broke up with me."

"You mean after we broke up with each other," I correct.

He shoots me his angry look. I ignore it and say, "Please continue."

"Anyway, we didn't know each other at all. The marriage lasted six months. The divorce took two years. I finally paid her to go away, and that's what she did. Aiden and Quinn called her Rebound Chick, and I now know that's what she was. I was in a shitty place in my life, and I thought she was what I wanted," he finishes.

"It hurt me terribly to read that you married someone so quickly after we broke up," I say, looking down and picking an imaginary piece of lint off of my lavender dress.

"That dress reminds me of the one that I bought you," he says, with hunger-filled eyes.

"Lavender has always been my best color." I smile at him.

"I didn't do it to hurt you intentionally. Although, I was hoping that you would call me when the engagement was announced," he admits.

I take a sip of wine. "No. Colin. You did do it intentionally. You poured salt in an open, gaping wound," I reply angrily. I couldn't believe it when I'd gotten the phone call from Rachael that Colin was engaged. I was devastated. Instead of doing what I normally would have done, which was go for a very long run, I called my therapist. We had an emergency appointment. She made me see that my decision to put space between Colin and I was correct. He was looking for a wedding. I wanted a life.

"Okay," he admits. "At the time I didn't think that I was using her to get back at you. I thought she was helping heal my broken heart. However, in hindsight, I wanted to prove to you that others could take your place."

His words crush me. I'm shocked that he could have wanted to inflict pain on me. I remind myself that he was twenty-three at the time, and obviously in a very angry place.

My wine's drained. I knew this would happen. I'm looking for the waitress to order another glass. I get her attention and also ask for some bar mix.

After a few minutes of silence, as if he is contemplating what to say, "Just for the record, Charlie, no one has ever taken your place." There's such a level of sadness in his eyes and voice that my heart sinks. Shit! His confession knocks me for a loop. I don't know how to respond. I drop my eyes so he can't read me.

"I love how healthy you look. I was worried that when I saw you again, you'd be skin and bones." He compliments me, but I know that it's his way of asking if I got help for my eating disorder.

I give him the answers that he needs to hear. "Thank you. I've worked really hard on myself. By the time that I started at Harvard I was painfully thin. My dad found me a great therapist in Boston. I finally dealt with a lot of the issues that I had from my parents' divorce, my fear of marriage, our break-up, and my issues with control." I pick my eyes up and look into his. "Therapy sucked, and it's still not easy. I see someone once a month in Houston for tune-ups, as she calls them. "

His face is beaming. My answer obviously pleases him. "I'm glad you decided to get healthy. I checked with Rachael frequently to make sure that you weren't slipping back into old ways. I was pleased when she said that you were seeing a therapist," he confesses.

"Funny, my dear best friend never mentioned that you were checking up on me." I'm hurt. I don't like the idea of people speaking about me behind my back.

"I asked her not to tell you. I never asked her any other questions about you. I just had to know that you weren't sick," he explains.

The waitress brings me my second glass of wine and the mixed nuts, which essentially ends that topic. She's better behaved this time.

The wine begins to talk again. "This is the craziest thing that I've experienced, Colin. In some ways it feels like we have been apart for a couple of days. I want to touch you and kiss you just like we used to do. But I don't know you anymore. I have so many questions. I don't know where you live. I don't know what your favorite color is. Do you still have Big Bertha? You were the person that I was the most comfortable with, and here I sit across from you, feeling like a stranger." *Yup! That was definitely the wine talking.*

He flashes me the half-grin. "I live in a McMansion, as you would call it, in Dallas. You'll hate it. My favorite color is still green, but I also have found that I like blue and silver. Big Bertha's a permanent member of the family. I've spent a lot of money keeping her running, but I still drive her to the stadium every game day. The offensive line tried to kidnap her and paint her burnt orange and white. I paid their hefty ransom and rescued her. You will be glad to know that she emerged unharmed. And, yes Charlie, I agree. This is the craziest experience of my life."

"Thank goodness. I would hate for Bertha to be injured." I feign horror.

Then, he says, very quietly grimacing as if he's in pain. "I also still have the maroon Cadillac Escalade that you bought for me, minus the license plates."

I try to lighten a dark mood that has all of a sudden settled over us. "See! I know how to pick out cars."

Apparently I fail, because Colin says, "Charlie, you ripped my heart out of my chest when you left. You made me feel like death was better than the pain that I was feeling. What went wrong? Why did you choose Harvard over me, knowing how much I wanted you? I would have …"

I cut him off. It's too hard for me to hear about his pain without crawling in his lap and kissing his face. I was also in pain. It's not like I walked away feeling sunshiny and happy. "You smothered me, Colin. You didn't give me space to breathe. Your success at A&M, the draft, your first season playing professional football, money, houses, cars, purses, credit cards, the media nicknaming us CharCol … it was too much for me. I had no control over my own life. I was too busy surfing the wave that was Colin. Fucking. McKinney. You asked me every day to be your wife when I was barely old enough to legally buy alcohol."

He leans forward, trying to interject, but I stop him. "Please, let me finish. This is hard enough for me, Colin." He sits back in his seat so I can continue. "My eating disorder is based on lack of control. It wasn't about my appearance. I didn't like how I looked, but I liked how I felt. Exercising until I felt in control or vomiting up my food gave me a semblance of order that I needed, being caught in your crazy vortex.

"I didn't run to Boston to get away from you. If you hadn't had the career of professional quarterback, you could have gotten a job in Boston, and we could maybe have been one of the few success stories who make it through medical school. However, you terrified me. You wanting and needing me so much was more than I could deal with at such a young age. I knew in my heart that if I went to Harvard and tried to have a long-distance relationship with you it would have killed you and your career. Although, if you remember, I was willing to try. You were the one who didn't want to." I flip my hair over my shoulder proud of myself for reminding him that he was the one who wanted all or nothing from me.

"So, you're telling me that you broke up with me because I was a professional quarterback?" His face twists in disgust, and he looks away from me as if my presence is just too painful.

"Colin, listen to what I am saying, please. We broke up with each other because I was sick, and you were obsessed with me. You asked me to marry you every single day, for God's sake. That's overwhelming." I've raised my voice enough that other bar patrons glance in our direction.

He scoots to the edge of his seat as if his proximity to me will drive him point home better. "You keep saying 'we broke up.' I don't remember it that way. When you decided to choose going to medical school in Boston over Dallas, you did the breaking. It wasn't like I was preventing you from going to medical school. Hell! I even agreed to pay the tuition." His voice has matched my volume, except his is so deep that I feel slightly embarrassed when people's glances turn to open stares.

I realize that I'm also leaning forward in my chair as if to strike. I pick up my glass of wine and drain it, and lean back in a more relaxed manner.

"Colin, I can't make you understand. If you can't accept that you overwhelmed me, and I was sick, then there's nothing more I can say. I can't change our past. I have nothing to apologize for, if that's what you're angling to hear me say," I state emphatically.

He drops into the stance that I hate. He leans forward, resting his elbows on his knees and hangs his head down. He doesn't speak. I'm compelling him in my mind to say something.

In a voice that I can barely hear, and without looking at me, "I never meant to overwhelm you. I just wanted to take care of you and share everything that I had with you. I thought I was doing it all for us. I loved you more than I loved myself, or football, or even Big Bertha," he says with a slight laugh. "I didn't know that I was making your life worse for you, or that I was making you run away from me."

My eyes fill with tears. I scramble out of my seat and drop down into a squat in front of him, not caring at all if the other bar patrons see my panties. I take his large hands in mine. "You did. You made my life better in every way. I loved you, Colin. However, in the end, I had to love myself more. I couldn't give you someone who was sick who only wanted a long-distance relationship. It wasn't fair to you."

He looks up and asks, "Would we have made it back then, if you'd married me like I wanted you to?"

I drop his hands and rest my palms on his muscular legs. I can't resist any longer. I love that I feel his muscles through his pants. "I don't think so, Colin. I needed professional help that I don't think I would have gotten. I was already heading toward a bad place before we split up. I was exercising a lot and tying to mask the weight loss with extra calories. I really think that I was only one emotional confrontation away from starting to purge. I needed to step out of the spotlight and get healthy.

"I did that. I have to admit that after all the paparazzi and media attention faded, it felt good to be anonymous again. I dealt with my parents' divorce, and we worked on the resentment that I felt toward my dad for abandoning my mom. My therapist and I spent a lot of time on you and me. There will always be a part of me that needs to feel in control, but I can manage it now," I explain.

"Charlie, do you want to know what I think?" he asks in a quiet, controlled voice. His green eyes are filled with the years of pain.

"Of course. This seems to be confession time." I gently laugh.

"I think that I would have consumed you. I could not have handled four years of a long-distance relationship. I think that I would have somehow strong-armed you into getting pregnant so you would drop out of medical school and spend all of your free time with me. You were my life, Charlie," he says with such sadness that I want to cry. However, the relief I feel that he has finally admitted he consumed me is better than all my years in counseling. He finally gets it.

He leans back, and I stand up between his strong, long legs. He puts his head against my chest, and I wrap my arms around his neck. I hold him ignoring the rest of the world. His arms wrap around me, holding me just as tightly.

"Please come up to my room," he asks while he buries his face in my abdomen. "We don't have to make love. Just let me hold you. I want to touch you without an audience."

I kiss the top of his head. "Yes." I don't even have to think about it.

He stands up and grabs my hand. We walk together to find the waitress. "Put her drinks on room 2400. Colin McKinney, please."

She yells something, but he doesn't stop to acknowledge her.

When the doors of the elevator close, he turns to me. "I can't believe that less than twelve hours ago, you were still a stranger to me. Now, you're coming back to my room. I always hoped that I would see you again. You're here," he says with wonder and awe as his fingers brush across my cheek. It's as if he is checking to see if I'm real.

I press my hand against his jaw. "We're two stubborn, proud people who lost our way. We're here together now. Let's not think too far ahead. Let's just enjoy right now."

He nods in agreement. We step off the elevator, still holding hands. I let him lead me to his room.

He slips his key in the door and opens it. I follow him in to his suite. Of course, Colin would have a suite. It's a large room with a sofa, loveseat, coffee table, dining table, and a kitchenette. The door to the bedroom is closed. He leads me through the living area to the bedroom door and opens it, revealing a lovely, large room. The bed is king-sized, next to a wall of windows looking out toward downtown Los Angeles. There's a chair in the corner. I think about the first time that we made love in my red crushed-velvet chair in my apartment in College Station.

Turndown service has come, and the big fluffy duvet is folded back. I'm instantly reminded of his bed in the fortress in Dallas. I push those thoughts out of my head and take my own advice that I gave him earlier to focus on the here and now.

He sits me down on the foot of the bed. I wonder what he's doing because he has seemed so unwilling to not touch me that I'm a little taken aback when he drops my hand and walks towards the closet. I watch him with leery eyes trying to figure out what he's doing. He starts to undress himself. I sure would like to help, but I don't dare get up. I decide this is his show. I'm just going along for the ride.

He takes off his jacket first, hanging it up. Next, he moves to his jeans. He's not wearing underwear. It's so hot. He's turned away from me so I can stare unapologetically at his fine behind. His ass is muscular and cut. God, I want to grab it. Then, to my dismay I see him find a pair of running shorts and pull them over his hips. He tugs his shirt over his head dropping it on the floor, and to my delight, he doesn't put anything else on.

I drink him in as he walks back toward me. He doesn't have a six-pack. It's more like an eight pack. He knows what a fantastic body he has. You don't model underwear by being out of shape. He walks slowly toward me, letting me admire him.

"I don't know if it's possible, but you have a better body now than you did when you were twenty-two," I exclaim.

He smiles his half-smile. "Thank you. The same can be said for you, Doctor Collins."

He reaches for my hand and pulls me up. He drops to the floor in front of me and gently removes one of my silver high-heeled sandals. I'm forced to hold on to his shoulder for support. When one shoe is off, I step down on my flat foot. He picks up my other foot and slips that shoe off. "Would you like to change into one of my shirts?"

"Yes. Thank you." My voice is raspy. There's no camouflaging my attraction to this man or that my lower stomach is filled with heat.

He walks back over to the closet and brings back a white dress shirt. "If you want to change in the bathroom, it's over there." He motions to another door without taking his eyes off me.

"Thanks," I reply, not breaking our eye contact.

"Do you need help with the zipper?" His greens become cloudy and his eyelids heavy with lust.

"Yes, please," I reply. As I turn around, I look down at his athletic shorts. His erection is tenting his shorts. He doesn't try to mask how turned on he is. I let my lavender dress fall to the floor in a puddle around my feet. I'm standing in front of him in my white lace bra and panties, just like so many years ago. He still hasn't looked down at my body. His heavy eyes are staring into mine. He undrapes the man's white dress shirt from his arm and hands it to me. I slip one of my arms in. He holds the shirt for me so I can easily slide my other arm in. The shirt is huge on me, but I button the buttons without breaking our intense stare.

He scoops me up and carries me to the king-size bed. He lays me gently on one side. He crawls over me and presses his body exactly next to mine. We lay there like that, staring at the ceiling, with electricity passing back and forth between us.

In a choked voice, he says, "Do you remember the last time that we made love?"

"Yes," I whisper.

"Please tell me about it," he begs quietly.

"We were in the fortress. We'd spent two days in agony. We both knew that in an hour, you had to drive me back to College Station, and we would not see each other again.

"I was gathering my things from your closet. You were on the phone talking to Mark about issuing a joint statement about our breakup and asking the media for privacy. I couldn't listen any longer so I closed the walk-in closet door. Just as I was putting my last dress into the bag, you came into the closet and attacked me. Our mouths found each other, and we kissed with the desperation that we both felt. Our hands touched every bit of each other, knowing that we would not have that contact again.

"Neither one of us wanted the passion to end. When it became obvious that neither of us could continue much longer, you grabbed a handful of T-shirts and threw them on the floor. You laid me down on top of them. We both came together as soon you entered me.

"We lay there, holding each other until we both knew that it was not going to get any easier. I got up first and went into the bathroom to clean myself. When I got home that night and unpacked my things, I found one of the T-shirts that we made love on inside my bag. When I pulled it out, it smelled like us. I slept in it for a long time," I whisper to him.

"Do you still have it?" He's choked up.

"Yes. I've never washed it. It's in my drawer," I say through unshed tears.

"I took my shirt and slipped it over my pillowcase. I went to bed every night smelling us until it became too painful. I still have mine, too," he whispers.

I roll over, put my head on his chest, and drape my arm over his stomach. He puts his hand on my back, running his fingers over the material of his shirt. "We're two fucked up, pathetic people," I conclude.

He rolls me off him and captures my mouth while he pins me against the bed with his hard body. Oh God! I love his mouth. I love how he tastes. His tongue gently dances with mine. We've fallen back to our perfect rhythm. He reaches up and holds my face while we continue to delight in our kiss.

I can feel his erection caught in between us. His hardness feels delicious against my stomach. I wrap my arms around his neck and trace the muscle definition in his shoulders. He's perfect. Our tongues begin such a delicious pattern. All of our emotions are in this kiss. It's passionate, sweet, lustful, and longing, all rolled up in one perfect moment.

He tenderly rolls off me and places us on our sides, facing each other, never breaking our kiss. His hand hesitantly moves under my shirt. I can tell that he's trying to gauge my reaction to him touching my breasts.

There's no doubt in my mind that I want this as much as he seems to. I touch his roaming hand, giving him the reassurance that he needs. He moans in appreciation.

He breaks our kiss to unbutton my shirt. I let him slowly undo the buttons. He's taking his time, savoring each reveal of my skin. When the last button's undone and my shirt falls open, he gasps in appreciation of my almost naked body.

"I love that you have breasts now. They're so perfect. Don't do that to your body again," he says, looking me in the eyes with desperation in his voice. "Promise me."

"I promise." I nod.

He reaches for my bra and gently slips each breast out of the cup, essentially creating a bustier. He leans down and kisses each one as if he's getting reacquainted. I'm watching him in awe. The appreciation for my body is evident in his face. I'm being admired as if I am a piece of fine art. It's such an aphrodisiac. As if he can read my mind, he reaches down and fondles my left nipple. He gasps in pleasure as it responds to his touch. He then repeats the same action on my right nipple. He smiles, obviously pleased that I'm still so responsive to him.

I hold his eye contact as he leans down and takes my right breast in his mouth. I throw my head back and moan in appreciation. His mouth is amazing. He knows just the right amount of pressure to apply to make my body move for him. He then shifts his weight so he can massage my left breast. I place my hands on his back, exploring all of his rippling muscles.

I feel myself growing very damp between my thighs. I get lost in the moment of my bucking hips and the torturous assault on my breasts. I moan as the deep pressure in my lower stomach finds the release that it's craving. He realizes that he's making me orgasm without even touching me below the waist. His perfect erection start throbbing against my stomach.

He groans in appreciation, and gently brings me down from my orgasm. "That was powerful," he exhales, smiling at me. "God, you are so fucking perfect, Charlie."

He kisses my mouth again with admiration.

I tap on his arm, indicating that I want him on his back. He gladly obliges my request. I straddle his lap, just like I did the first time that we made love. The difference is that we're ten years older, but still just as infatuated with each other. I lean down and take his mouth. I throw eight years of passion into this kiss.

His erection pokes my behind. It's hard to believe that he's still in his shorts, and I have on my bra and panties. All of a sudden, that will not do. I break our kiss and move to undress him.

I take a moment to admire his incredibly hard penis. It's lying against his stomach. It has a slight curve to the left. The throbbing veins are the most virile statement of manhood that I have ever seen.

I reach down and grab ahold of his erection. It's as perfect as I remembered. I gently slide my hand down the shaft, stopping every few strokes to catch a drip from its head and rub my finger around the tip.

He's breathing hard and moaning in pleasure. I keep this up, enjoying watching the different degrees of ecstasy that I can still bring to him. I feel powerful. He reaches down and puts his hand on mine, stopping my actions.

"I'm so close. I want to spend more time loving you before I come," he reasons with me while moving his hips and licking his lips in pleasure.

I let him roll me over on my back again. There's nothing that feels more hedonistic than an erection that I've longed for pressing against my entrance. His mouth is consuming mine in a frenzied, hungered pace. Then a fleeting thought passes through my head. "Colin … Colin …" I'm trying to get his attention, but he isn't stopping. "Do you have a condom?" I whisper.

He stops kissing me and says, "No. Do you?"

"No. I kind of haven't had sex in a long enough time to need them. I'm not on birth control, either." I'm mortified.

"Why not?" he asks.

"Oh God! This's so embarrassing." I cringe. "I haven't had sex with anyone since I moved back to Houston. I let my pills lapse."

"We're constantly tested for STDs in the NFL. I'm clean," he says, leaning back down to kiss me.

"What about pregnancy?" I ask.

"God, Charlie. You sure know how to kill get-back-together sex." He rolls his eyes. "Quit worrying about it. Get on the pill when you get back to Houston. We'll be fine."

My brain is telling me that this is irresponsible, but my body could care less about responsibility right now. I wiggle out from under him. He looks at me with a pleading/horror-stricken expression on his face. I instantly realize that he thinks that I'm leaving. I hate that look. He had the same one when I told him about Harvard.

I smile at him reassuringly and move my mouth to his erection. I take the head in my mouth and gently kiss and suck it. He falls on his back and moans in pleasure. I take the whole thing in my mouth, sucking it hard. I move my mouth up and down his erection and add my hand to the base, following each suck with a gentle stroke.

He's putty in my hands. "Fuck me. You're so fucking perfect. Slide your hot pussy on me now, baby," he commands.

I give his wonderful penis one last long suck and position my opening on top of his erection. I slide his penis inside me. When I have taken all of him, he stops my hips, and I lie down on his chest. We lie there in bliss, enjoying the feeling of being united.

He jerks inside of me. I know he is trying not to come yet. I would understand if he did. We feel so perfect together.

I gently sit back up and begin dancing on top of him. I roll my hips in circles and bounce up and down on his erection. The feeling is out of this world. He reaches up and grabs my breasts, kneading them in the same rhythm. *I'm so close.* He senses my orgasm and squeezes my nipples hard. I ride him, milking every bit of pleasure that I can from him.

"Fuck! Charlie," he yells. "You feel so fuckin' perfect. I need you. I need this." Colin grabs my hips, and pumps himself into me. His hot liquid empties inside me and I yell in delight. I have never done anything else in my life that feels this close to nirvana. Separate, Colin and I are broken. Together, we're perfect.

I collapse on his chest. He holds me tightly to him, cooing words of gratitude and appreciation to me. I don't want to move. A part of me believes that if we separate, I'll wake up alone in my hotel room, desperately sad that this wasn't real. Right here is where I want to be.

"Will you stay with me tonight?" he asks. His voice betrays his hope.

"I don't think that I can walk," I admit. "Can I sleep right here?"

"Absolutely." He strokes my hair.

After a few moments, he says, "Baby, I'm not complaining, but why haven't you had sex in a couple of years? You're ridiculously beautiful and smart. It seems guys would be fighting over you."

"I'm a workaholic, for one," I admit. I'm sure that that doesn't surprise him. "I also haven't found anyone who intrigued me enough to want to sleep with them," I mumble through my sleep-filled haze.

"I'm glad that I am intriguing to you, Doctor Collins." He gently laughs. "By the way, I really like the sound of Doctor," he says in such a lighthearted manner that it makes me feel warm inside.

"So do I," I agree. "I think that I wear doctor well."

We lay there with me on top of him. He's still inside me. He gently runs his long fingers through my hair, which lulls me to sleep. This is the happiest and most content that I've felt in eight years.

Chapter Five

THERE IS a phone ringing somewhere near me. I want it to stop.

I will it to quit ringing. It doesn't obey. I'm so warm and comfortable. Then, I remember why. I'm completely surrounded by Colin. Fucking. McKinney.

"Are you going to get that?" I mumble.

"No. Fuck 'em. They can leave a message," he says, pulling me tighter to him, if that is even possible.

I guess at some point in the middle of the night we positioned ourselves with both of us facing the wall of windows. Colin is pressed up against every bit of my skin that he can be. His arm is across of my torso, ensuring that I'm his—captured by his embrace.

The phone starts ringing again. He still makes no attempt to answer it. He kisses my hair and runs his hand over my stomach. The third time that it begins to ring he lets go of me, letting out a long string of cuss words. He gets out of bed and finds his phone in his pants pocket. He's radiating annoyance.

"I'm sorry, but I obviously need to answer this. Stay in bed. Don't move. I'll be back in a minute," he says giving his phone a very dirty look.

He walks out of the bedroom into the suite and shuts the bedroom door.

I briefly wonder why he can't talk in front of me, but I remind myself that we have only been speaking to each other for about eighteen hours.

I get up and use the restroom. I find his toothpaste in the bathroom and put a line of paste on my finger. I use my finger to brush my teeth. It's not great, but it's better than morning breath. I catch a glimpse of myself in the mirror. I look younger. My cheeks are slightly flushed. I smile at myself in the mirror. Colin. Fucking. McKinney looks good on me.

I turn around and catch him watching me. I let out a small cry of surprise.

"I didn't mean to startle you. You look radiant this morning Doctor Collins," he says as he strolls towards me. We're both naked. Colin stands behind me, looking into my eyes in the full-length mirror. He wraps his long arms around me and rests his chin on the top of head. We are stunning together. My long caramel-colored hair shines against his dark-olive complexion. My light complexion almost looks translucent in the lighting. His green eyes are piercing. My lavender eyes have never been brighter. His rock-hard body against my slightly fuller figure is the perfect contrast of soft and firm. We look like we are posing for a perfume advertisement.

Colin kisses the top of my head. "I was afraid you were going to make me get up at six-fifteen this morning to run," he says, smiling at me in the mirror.

"How do you know that I still do that?" I ask, a bit curious.

"You don't keep gorgeous legs like this," he says, running his hands down my thighs, "without doing something crazy."

"What would you have done if I'd woken you up at six-fifteen to go run ten miles?" I ask while making a sassy face.

"I would have done everything in my power to convince you to stay in my bed," he says as he presses his erection into my back.

I smile at him in the mirror. "That would have persuaded me."

He slides his feet out in a straddle position so we are now the same height. He takes my hair and throws it over one shoulder, and gently plants soft kisses on my neck. His eyes lock with mine in the mirror studying my reaction. I try not to break eye contact, but I can't stop myself. I throw my head against his shoulder, giving him better access.

"Look forward, Charlie," he instructs.

I follow his command and pick my head up, finding his eyes in the mirror again. He takes my breasts in his hands, cupping them. Each one sits nicely in his palms. "These are magnificent tits. Look how well they fit in my hands. They aren't too big. They aren't too small. They're perfect, just like you."

The underlying warning is there: *Don't slip back into old habits and have my breasts go away.*

I nod, reassuring him that I get his message. I watch him pull on my nipples, elongating them. He pinches them between his thumb and finger, causing my lower stomach to fill with such intense heat that I don't know if I can stand it. Watching and feeling the sensation is so erotic.

I reach behind me and grab his erection, watching his reaction in the mirror. His face twists into a hungered expression. We both know that we'll not last long. He takes his right hand from my breast and moves it to my clit. He checks my wetness and smiles with approval. He slowly slips two fingers inside me, pressing his palm against my clit and gently beginning to massage. I show my pleasure by matching his rhythm with my stroking of his erection.

With our eyes still locked together in the mirror, he bends me over, placing my hands on the sink, and presses his erection against my wet opening. He slowly slides inside, filling me up and allowing me to become acquainted again with the sensation. Once I feel ready, I gently move my hips back and forth. I slide forward enough to leave just the head of his penis inside me, then I slide backwards, allowing him to fill me completely, never breaking eye contact.

Watching us make love is beyond erotic. We are lost in the present. I continue this slow torture until he grabs my hips and moves me in ways that I didn't know that I could move. It's so sudden that I cry out in shock.

"Charlie, I need you. Don't leave me again," he pleads with me, staring into my eyes in the mirror.

"Don't leave me either, Colin," I reply, transfixed by his gaze.

He reaches around my hips and presses against my clit. All my willpower goes into not throwing my head back in ecstasy. We both come, staring into each other's soul.

We fall to the bathroom floor. I'm emotionally drained, yet completely sated. He leans against the wall, and I crawl into his lap like old times. He cradles me to him and whispers sweet words to me.

"Baby, are you hungry?" he asks.

"I'd kill for a cup of coffee," I mumble.

"Since when do you drink coffee?" he asks, with his eyes opening wide.

"Since medical school," I reply. "I picked up the habit, and I haven't been able to shake it."

That gets me thinking about all the stuff that we don't know about each other. If Brad heard Colin's shock over my coffee fetish, he would faint. Everyone knows that I like my three cups of coffee, black. This is a mental wake-up call. We still have a lot to learn about each other.

"What are you thinking about?" he asks while rubbing my stomach.

"How you didn't know that I like coffee." I gently drop the statement out there to see what he does with it.

"So you like coffee now. Want me to go buy you a cup?" he asks.

"In a minute," I reply. "I know that you've been married before. You also know that I have been abstinent for a while. Any other relationships that I should know about?" I ask tentatively. I really don't know if I want an honest answer, but I feel like that it's a logical question that needs a reply if we're to have a future. It's also something I should have asked last night.

"None that have compared to you," he says, leaning down and giving me a kiss on the cheek. It sounds like an evasive answer, but I choose to ignore it for now.

His phone starts ringing again. I wonder briefly why he didn't turn it off. He seemed so annoyed earlier.

"Fuck!" he says in frustration. "I have to take that."

He gently lifts me off him and walks out of the bathroom. Once again, he shuts the bedroom door. I want very badly to ask whom he's talking to, but I don't want to pry.

This gives me a minute to start the shower and think about the last day. I secretly hope that he hears the water running and decides to join me. The shower is certainly big enough for two people, and the bathtub is separate. One of the perks to upgrading to a suite, I guess.

I deliberately take my time, and rinse my hair extra well. Finally, it becomes clear that I'm not getting a visitor. I step out of the shower and dry myself. I find some great-smelling lotion left by the hotel and begin my moisturizing procedure. When I'm done, I walk back into the bedroom and look for the shirt that Colin gave me last night to wear. It's nowhere to be found. I walk back to the closet and find a T-shirt to put on. Fortunately, it's long enough that it hits me mid-thigh. I open the bedroom door and find Colin dressed and sitting on the couch with the TV on, watching sports highlights.

"Hi," I greet him. "I was hoping you would join me for a shower."

"I got you coffee." He motions to the kitchen counter, essentially ignoring me. "I didn't know what you liked in it, so I picked up some cream and sugar."

There's obviously something off. He barely looks at me when he's talking. All of his attention is on the TV. Past Colin would never have let me walk into a room without at least a smile.

"I looked for the shirt that I wore last night, but I couldn't find it. I hope you don't mind me borrowing a T-shirt," I say as I walk over to grab my cup of coffee.

"Help yourself. I dropped my shirt off at the front desk to get it laundered. I have to wear it tonight," he explains.

"Oh." It's all that I can think to say. I walk back and sit down on the love seat, which is at a right angle to the couch that Colin's sitting on.

I pretend to watch sports highlights with him, but my mind is going mad. This is feeling very much like a one-night stand brush off. I replay yesterday and today in my mind, looking for any clues as to why he is behaving like this. The only things that I can come up with are the two phone calls. Were they from another girl? Was it Clay giving him a hard time for not playing golf? This is so frustrating.

After a good ten minutes of silence, I've had enough. I walk back into the bedroom and look for my clothes. My dress is right where it fell last night. My bra was haphazardly tossed towards the windows. My panties seem to be missing. They were shredded anyway, so I'm not too concerned. I change back into my lavender dress. It is a wrinkled mess. Hopefully, I can go three floors down without anyone seeing me do the walk of shame.

My shoes are at the end of the bed where Colin removed them. I sit down and slip them on. I keep expecting him to come in here and stop me, but he doesn't.

I walk back into the suite, holding my cup of coffee and purse. He looks up from the TV, and says, "I guess I'll see you at dinner."

"Yeah. I guess you fucking will." I'm furious. As I turn and walk toward the door, I say, "Thanks for the one-night stand, Colin. You were the best." My voice is so acidic that it could melt cement.

I open the door and walk out as I hear him running toward me. I manage to get the door shut before he can grab me.

I walk to the elevators and hit the down button, trying my hardest to stop the tears that are threatening to run down my cheeks.

He yells, "You said that you wouldn't leave me again."

I spin around and glare at him. "You don't listen! I said, 'don't leave me, either'."

"How am I leaving you? I was watching sports highlights." He eyes darting around, looking for the answer.

I'm dumbfounded. Is he really this clueless? "Colin, you got a phone call and ignored me for an hour. We had mind-blowing sex, I walked out of your bedroom in your T-shirt and you didn't look up from the TV. That's not how you behave when you want to be with someone. That's how you behave when you've been married forty years."

"Charlie, can we discuss this in my room?" he pleads.

"My name isn't Charlie." I stomp my foot like a bratty three-year-old. "I'm going down to my room. I'm going to put on jeans, a T-shirt, and tennis shoes, and then I am going to find food. It's room 2118, if you care to join me."

The doors to the elevator open as if on cue, and I step in. Thankfully, he doesn't follow me. I need some time alone to think things through.

I have stopped my tears, even though I still feel like crying. What good would it do? I can't change how I feel about him, and I certainly cannot change our past. We have history that's obviously very deep. What went wrong, then? Why did we go from passionate, can't-get-enough-of-each-other sex to him virtually ignoring me? I feel used, and I don't like feeling that way.

By the time that I'm smearing makeup on my face, I've talked myself into this being a good thing. Maybe this is what I need to get Colin. Fucking. McKinney out of my system. I obviously feel more for him than he does for me. This is the closing of a book, our book. We both needed one more night of great sex. I'm now free to open my heart to someone else who I can have an actual relationship with, without the baggage.

It's been long enough that if he were joining me, he would have knocked on my door. I exhale a deep breath, grab my purse, phone—with no missed calls—and open my door with my head held high.

He's leaning on the wall opposite my hotel room. Before I can say anything, he starts spitting out words in a rapid-fire fashion, "I'm bringing a date tonight and tried to cancel. She'll not let me. I want to spend the evening with you. She's an entertainment reporter. If she finds out that CharCol has gotten the band back together, it will be all over the news. Our picture will be everywhere. You'll be hounded by the media, and you will run away from me again. Or worse, you'll get sick. I can't take you running away from me again. Worse yet, I can't take you losing your fantastic tits. Please don't freak out and leave me again, Charlie." His face is full of panic.

He's standing in front of me with pleading eyes, holding his breath and waiting for me to respond.

I let my hotel door close behind me. "I'm starving. Let's go find something to eat."

Chapter Six

HE STANDS there looking at me like I've lost my mind. I take his hand and lead him toward the elevators. I hit the down button.

"This means that you aren't running away?" he asks cautiously.

"This means that I'm starving. I need another cup of coffee, and you have some explaining to do," I reply. "We might as well do it while I am getting my coffee and food. Trust me. I deal with life much better after my third cup of coffee. Just ask Brad."

"You see, it was like this…"

I reach up and put my finger against his lips. "Shhh … Colin. Remember new Caroline. She likes three cups of coffee before she can deal with life."

We hold hands in the elevator until we reach the ground floor. I let go of his hand when the elevator doors open. He flashes me a look of confusion.

"This is Los Angeles. I'm not getting photographed holding your hand until you catch me up on your girlfriend situation," I explain.

He nods in understanding.

I'm fully aware that Clay's dinner is going to be big for the paparazzi. Not only are the top players in professional football going to be there, but sports writers and actors that are friends of his, or associated with his foundation will be there.

As we walk through the lobby my phone rings. I'm actually a little excited to get a call. Turns out it's the salon confirming my appointment in an hour. I look at Colin and tell the salon receptionist, "I have to take care of some business. Can I let you know in thirty minutes?" I end the call and slip my phone back in my purse.

Colin eyebrows draw together in confusion.

"Your answers to my questions in the next thirty minutes will determine if I spend an obscene amount of money getting ready for this dinner, or if I decide to take care of my own hair and makeup and spend the remaining day reintroducing myself to you over and over again," I explain to Colin.

His face lights up like a kid on Christmas morning. "Please choose option two."

We walk out of the hotel and turn right. Colin says that there is a great restaurant that serves breakfast all day approximately two blocks over. That gets my vote of approval.

Fortunately, it's not too crowded. When the waitress stops by our table, Colin orders for us. "She'll have coffee black. I'll have water."

I smile at him. He now knows how I take my coffee. *Score one for Mr. McKinney.* He starts trying to talk again, but I stop him. "What's my rule?"

"I know. I know. You need more coffee, but I'm on the clock," he pleads.

The waitress sets down my coffee and Colin's water. I order scrambled eggs with cheese and bacon. Colin raises his eyebrow. He orders an egg-white omelet.

I take my first sip of coffee, and say, "I'm ready." I lean back against my chair and prepare to have my heart stomped on all over again.

"Her name's Sasha Stone." I nod, indicating that I know who she is. He nervously fumbles with his silverware. "Well, anyway," he continues, "she's an entertainment reporter. She did a story on football hunks, and I was interviewed." As I look at his face, I know why. He really is just drop-dead gorgeous. "She's a very pretty girl. I'm a single guy. I asked her out to dinner after the interview. She agreed."

"And," I prompt, motioning with my hands for him to continue.

"And we hit it off. She went back to Los Angeles. I got her number and called her. We talked for about two weeks. I invited her to come to a home game. She did, and she stayed at my home," he says, dropping his eyes to the table.

I obviously can't get mad, but I would rather think Colin was as chaste as I was, even though I know that's not the case.

"Go on," I deadpan.

"We've been kind of seeing each other for about six months," he finishes.

"Are you exclusive?" I ask.

"What does that mean?" he asks.

I shoot him a disgusted look. "You know exactly what I mean. Did you and I cheat on Sasha?"

"We've never really discussed it," he replies.

This is fantastic. I just became my step-mom, Carmen. I slept with a man who's in a relationship. I'm everything that I hate. I'm furious at myself for not asking the girlfriend question before we went to his room. I'm livid at Colin for putting me in this position. He, of all people, should know how I feel about cheating.

"Okay. Colin, I am not an idiot," I cross my arms over my chest. "You didn't have condoms; you're in the city where the maybe girlfriend lives … I'm going to bet money that she thinks that you two are exclusive," I say with so little emotion that it almost scares me.

"I had condoms," he whispers, hanging his head.

Thank God the waitress brings our food at just the right moment and refills my coffee. I need a moment before I say something that I might really regret. I smile and thank her before she walks away.

I take a big drink of coffee and collect my thoughts. I contemplate killing him. I consider pouring my coffee in his lap. It's hot, and I know that it would hurt … badly.

Instead, in a low, growling voice, I spit, "Let me get this straight: you risked me getting pregnant because you didn't want to wear a raincoat. This is unbelievable."

I pick up my fork and dig in to my food. It is so good that even this conversation can't ruin my appetite. I notice that he hasn't touched his omelet.

"It's not like that—"

"Well then, how the fuck is it, Colin?" I cut him off. "You think that it would be a good idea to bring a child into this world with two parents who aren't even dating? Hell, the father is seeing an entertainment reporter." I throw my hands up in disgust. "Look, I'll own this. I should have stopped you. I should have demanded that you go purchase protection. Hell, I can take two steps back and say that I should have never gone up to your room. However, what's done is done. At least I know that if I'm pregnant you can't be too upset about it."

Then it hits me. That's what he wants. If we have a child, he knows that I'll have to be tied to him in some way forever. I drop my fork, letting it make a loud *clank* on the plate.

I look up at him. He knows what I'm thinking. The look on his face reflects the horror that I'm feeling. Charlie would have gotten up and run out of the restaurant. She would have gone up to the hotel room, changed into her running clothes and run twenty miles at that revelation that Colin wouldn't care that she was knocked up.

Instead, Caroline, who spent thousands on therapy, says, "Do you really want me that badly, Colin? You don't know me anymore. Do you want to be with the twenty-one-year-old girl you knew, or do you want to be with the twenty-nine-year-old woman who's a partner in a very successful medical practice, and doesn't need your money or your fame to be happy?"

Then he says the words that I was hoping to hear eight years ago. "I'll take you any way that I can get you."

My heart does a flip-flop. I'm waiting for bells and whistles to come out of the restaurant's ceiling and circus animals to do their tricks. This is Los Angeles, after all. Colin. Fucking. McKinney just got the right answer.

I finish the rest of my meal and coffee in silence. It's so powerful to hear someone tell you that they need to be with you enough to accept you as you are. The analytical side of me keeps questioning if this is even a healthy relationship to try to start. My therapist will have a field day with this when I see her next week.

"Look, Charlie," Colin pleads. "It's not like that. Yes, I had condoms, but I don't necessarily want you pregnant. I just didn't want to wear one. I wanted to feel all of you, no barriers between us. Please, don't be mad at me."

"I really don't care how it is. We made a huge mistake. Hopefully, it's not one that is going to change our lives forever. We were both irresponsible. I'm done discussing this. I'm sure that when I tell my therapist this story, she'll want to have a chat with both of us," I conclude.

I get on a plane back to Houston tomorrow. I decide to table this portion of the conversation until I have some distance away from him to think. I need to deal with the Sasha situation immediately.

"What did you tell Sasha this morning?" I ask, looking into his eyes. I can—used to be able to—read between the lines by meeting his gaze.

By the look on his face, I'm not sure if he would rather talk about intentionally trying to knock me up, or Sasha less.

"She asked when she could see me. I told her something came up." He laughs at his own joke.

I don't laugh and motion for him to continue.

"I said that the other guys were not bringing dates so I didn't need her to come anymore. She said that she has already bought a dress and couldn't return it. I told her that I would pay her back. She got upset with me and started complaining about how little I've seen her since the season is over. So I told her I would send a car for her," he concludes.

"Okay. Colin, I'm going to ask you a question. I want total honesty. Don't lie to me. And, please, for the love of God, don't treat me like I'm an idiot," I state.

He nods.

"If you had not run into me at the reception yesterday, would you have seen Sasha last night or this morning?" I ask, holding my breath waiting for the answer.

"If I had not seen you last night, Charlie, I still would not have gone out with Sasha. She's in to me way more than I'm in to her. As for this morning, I would be kicking Clay's ass all over the golf course right now, and making enough money off his ludicrous bets that I could fund a small third-world country." Then, he whispers very quietly, "Charlie, it was always you and always will be you."

With that, I pull out my phone and cancel my appointment at the salon.

The smile on his face while he listens to my conversation melts my heart. It's the special smile that he always seems to save for me. Even trying to stay away from his press for the last eight years, I never saw the smile that he saved for me.

"Colin, for the record, I'm furious that you put me in the position of being the other woman. I should have asked if you were seeing anyone, but you should have told me. It's not fair to Sasha or me," I say, looking directly into his eyes.

He hangs his head in shame. "I'm so sorry. I just want you to know that it's not like that. Sasha and I have never talked about a future together. If I saw on TV that she was out on a date with someone else, I wouldn't care. But, you're right. I think that she would be upset if she knew that I slept with someone else."

I let out a sigh. I'm not happy about the situation, but I can't turn back the hands of time. What's done is done.

He pays our check, and we walk back towards the hotel.

"What's next?" he asks.

"Well, I have about three hours before I need to start getting ready for the event," I reply.

"Good. That's what I was hoping you would say." He grabs my hand. "Would you like to go for a run?"

"Colin. Fucking. McKinney, are you asking me to run with you?" I tease.

"I guess I am. I'm wondering if you can still kick my ass?" he teases back.

"Care to put a wager on it?" I ask. It does occur to me that people are paid a lot of money to make sure that he's in top cardio shape.

"If I win, you come spend next weekend with me in the place of my choice," he says.

"Okay. If I win, you have to come to Houston and take me dancing at my favorite club," I propose.

I take it as a good sign that we are making plans for next weekend.

When we arrive at the hotel, we go to our separate rooms to get changed. If I had known that he was going to propose a run, I would have eaten a lot lighter meal. Maybe that was his strategy.

As I am pulling my hair into a high ponytail, he knocks on my door. I yell, "Just a minute, Colin," and finish my running 'do.

I open the door and am shocked to see my dad standing there. I shouldn't have been. He's staying three doors down from me. "Hi Dad. Sorry! I thought you were someone else. Come in."

I notice that he looks tanner. He must have picked up some sun during golf. "Headed somewhere, Caroline?"

"Yes. I was just going for a run before I have to start getting ready for tonight," I explain.

"Who are you going with?" He knows exactly whom I'm going with. He just wants to make me say it.

"Colin. Why?" I ask.

"Did you have a chance to talk last night?" Dad says, glancing at my room that doesn't look like it has been touched. He is brilliant. He knows exactly what I did. Either housekeeping is efficient, or I didn't sleep in my bed last night.

"Cut to the chase, Dad," I say, preparing myself for a trademarked Doctor Jack Collins lecture.

"He broke your heart and put you in therapy. I'm, frankly, very concerned. You aren't just my daughter; you are also my business partner." I'll give him that. He does have more of a reason to meddle than most parents.

"Dad, Colin and I separating was the catalyst that made me seek help. Our relationship was solid. I wanted to go to Harvard. We were young, and decided that we didn't want to do the long-distance thing, especially when Dallas owned him eight-plus months of the year. We're now both adults who want to see if we can have a second chance. Does that make sense?" I reason.

He gives me a kiss on my cheek and says, "It does make sense. However, I'm watching you like a hawk. I'll step in if I think that you are slipping back into bad habits, or if this relationship is hurting the practice."

"Fair enough, Daddy." I'm not sure where "Daddy" came from, but it's a rather useful term of endearment sometimes. He smiles and walks out of my room.

I wonder where Colin is and realize that I don't even have his phone number. That's sort of pathetic. As I'm contemplating going up to his room, I hear a knock on my door. I open it, and he's standing there in the same running shorts from last night and my T-shirt from this morning.

I can't help it. I launch myself at him, kissing his mouth. Our tongues begin their dance and desire passes between us. He pulls back first, breaking our kiss. "Stop this. I want to win my bet."

God, he knows me so well. He knows how competitive I am, and I will never let him win.

He kneads my breasts through my sports bra. "Say I win, and I'll spend the next two and a half hours making you scream."

Fine, two can play at this game. I drop to my knees in front of him, calling his bluff. "Say I win the bet and I'll give you my personal best, record-breaking, mind-blowing blow job."

"We are so fucking pathetic," he says. "Let's go."

I smile and follow him out the door. I hand him my phone when we're in the elevator. "It's rude to fuck someone and not even give them your phone number."

"Thank goodness I'm not a rude guy. My number is in your phone. I added your number to mine when you were in the shower," he says. "By the way, what we did was not fucking. Don't cheapen it, Caroline."

I choose to ignore his comment about my terminology. "Wow! That's a relief." I smirk. "Do you have a route mapped out for us?"

"Sure," he says, way too confidently.

I have a sneaky suspicion that I made a deal with the devil.

We step out into the beautiful Los Angeles sun. It's a glorious seventy-four degree day with low humidity. I was made to run in this weather. He gets in line for a town car.

"We're driving to run?" I ask in confusion.

He nods, flashing me his Colin half-smile. I blindly get in the town car with him, trusting that he knows what he's doing.

"How far are you running now?" he asks.

"I run between eight and ten miles every morning. On the weekends, I like to bike. I've pretty much quit swimming because my access to a pool is limited," I explain.

"I have a pool at the McMansion," he says with a smirk.

"Of course you do. Any McMansion comes equipped with a pool," I reply sweetly.

"Clay suggested Malibu Creek State Park," he says. "They're supposed to have great running trails."

"Are we running for speed, then?" I ask. I need to know exactly what I need to do to beat him.

"I think we're going for endurance," he says with a huge smile on his face.

We turn into the park, and I see why Colin said that we were running for endurance. We are running in the mountains, although they are probably hills to people who grew up in the rest of the country. I have run on nothing but the flat plains of Texas for the last two years. I'm hoping that my biking will help me with the incline.

Colin asks the driver to wait for us. He just shrugs. What does he care? He's on the clock.

Colin and I begin to stretch, and Colin starts his trash talking. "Say that I win our bet, and instead of punishing ourselves we can find a secluded spot and have crazy outdoor sex," he says, smiling at me.

I hate being taunted. "Great idea. You admit that you're scared of me and crazy outdoor sex is yours."

"Charlie, I am fucking terrified of you." He is all of sudden serious, and I know that we aren't talking about our run. His face becomes so pained that I stand up and walk over to him.

I kneel down beside him and wrap my arms around his neck. He grabs me and pulls me into his lap. "I never again want to feel the kind of pain that I felt when I drove away from your apartment. My mom kept telling me that with time it would get easier. You know what, Charlie? It didn't. My heart just became calloused, but the hurt stayed. Seeing you again and knowing that you still have strong feelings for me has given me hope. You can't leave me. I don't know if I can survive it again," he pleads.

The tears are streaming down my face. All I can do is nod in agreement. I understand completely because that's how I feel about him.

"I don't know if I can let you get on the plane tomorrow," he continues. "I'm afraid that you'll forget how good it feels to be together, and you won't let me back in your life."

Confession time is killing me. I can't believe that he feels this way about me after all these years. I keep feeling like I'm in a movie. This doesn't happen in real life.

My heart aches seeing him like this. I suffered when we broke up, but I went through therapy. I realize in that moment that I might have gotten the easier of the two roads. "I'll break one of my biggest rules and let you win your bet. I'll go wherever you want me to go next weekend. Hell, you can even come back to Houston with me tomorrow if you want. I will not forget, Colin. I promise," I say as I plant small kisses on his forehead and down his face, paying extra special attention to his crooked nose.

He holds on to me so tightly that it is almost painful. "If I tell you that I still love you, will you feel overwhelmed?" he asks me very seriously.

My heart swells. I know that I still love him, and I always have. As crazy as our future will be, it's a future that I can't live without. "I love you too, Colin. I never stopped."

We sit like this for a long time. I know that he's not going to let me go. I have to be the one to break our moment.

"So, I may have let you win the bet, but now we run for bragging rights," I state emphatically.

"Charlie, it kills me that you're just as competitive as me. Fine. Let's go torture ourselves." He laughs.

We stand and start running up a trail. He falls into position on my right side, just like he had so many times before.

The trail is grueling. It never levels out so you get a break. Running ten miles on flat ground is nothing compared to this. I keep looking over at Colin to see if he's showing any signs of fatigue. Just my luck; he has barely broken a sweat.

I can't believe that I'm struggling. I hate feeling weak. My upper thighs and hips are burning. I'm sweating profusely and my lungs are craving oxygen. I keep thinking about the dress and ridiculously high heels that I have to wear in a couple of hours.

It is absurd that I'm doing this to myself. I talk my legs into one more mile. Colin keeps glancing at me. Suddenly, I notice that he has a worried look his face. He motions for me to remove my earphones.

"You okay? Your face is white." He stops running and looks at me.

"I better turn around. I'm not sure if it's the altitude or what, but I'm not feeling very well," I explain.

"We're walking back," he says.

Fortunately, when we turn around it's all downhill. The longer we walk, the better I feel. I'm able to take a full lungful of air and I begin to cool down.

"I'm sorry I flaked out," I say. "I grant you your bragging rights." This is physically painful to say.

"To tell you the truth, Charlie, I couldn't have gone much farther," he admits with his half-smile. "I just couldn't let you beat me."

I punch him in the arm.

"By the way, I think that this is the first time that I've beaten you," he taunts.

"I'll make sure that it doesn't happen again," I tease back. "Hey! I need to talk to you about my name and you calling me Charlie."

"Yes?" he says, raising his eyebrow.

"If you want to call me Charlie when it's just the two of us, I'm okay with that. However, please don't introduce me as Charlie or call me Charlie in public. I really feel strongly about going by Caroline," I say, hoping not to hurt his feelings.

"The media will be so disappointed if they can't call us CharCol," he prods me.

"Like I care. They will just have to get more creative," I state, taking his hand in mine.

I'm relieved to see the town car is still there, and even more relieved when the driver hands us bottled water.

Colin sits in the back of the car with me. My eyelids become droopy, and I relax into his side. He must notice because he pats his leg for me to lie down on. I put my head on his thigh and curl into the fetal position. He strokes my hair, lulling me into a great nap.

Chapter Seven

"WAKE UP, beautiful girl. We're back at the hotel," he murmurs.

I open my eyes, a bit surprised that I fell asleep. I sit up and yawn. "I'm sorry that I was such boring company."

He laughs. "I got to stare at you as long as I wanted without feeling like I was overwhelming you. You have nothing to apologize for."

He used the phrase "overwhelming you" again. I'm going to have to make a point to explain my feelings better. I don't want him to worry that I might be scared away every time he expresses himself to me. If I didn't bolt when he purposely didn't use a condom, I'm here for the long haul.

I check the time. We're a bit late getting back. I'm going to have to get dressed more quickly than I'd wished.

As we step on the elevator, he asks, "Can I come to your room for a few minutes?"

"Sure. I have to start getting dressed, though," I remind him.

We walk off the elevator together and enter my room. When the door is safely closed, Colin says, "We need to talk about tonight."

"What about it?" I ask while I start the shower water.

I can tell that this is not a pleasant conversation for him to have with me. He looks uncomfortable and is fidgeting with the hem of his shirt. I'm not used to nervous Colin.

"I told you Sasha is going to be at the dinner," he says as if this is the whole explanation.

"Yes?" I prompt him.

"I'm going to have to be attentive to her," he says, showing me his angst-filled eyes.

"Okay. So this is what this conversation is about," I say, stripping off my clothes and standing in front of him completely naked. I watch as his erection grows and makes his running shorts tent. That has to be the hottest sight on earth. I feel powerful knowing that just my nakedness has this effect on him.

I slide the shower curtain back and step under the running water. He follows and opens the curtain enough so that he can watch me. The non-suite rooms in the hotel don't have separate showers and bathtubs.

"Colin, I'm an adult. I understand that she is your date, and you can't leave her high and dry. I also understand that she's a member of the media, and that if we hope to have any privacy we need to keep the two of us under wraps; therefore, you need to be her date. I'm assuming that you're making it clear to her that whatever semblance of a relationship that you two have is over?" I raise my eyebrow.

He nods. "I'll let her know tomorrow."

"Fine. Then we keep our distance from each other tonight," I state, matter-of-factly.

I put soap on my hands and start washing my body. Then, I get a brilliant idea. I maybe do it a little more sensually than I would if I didn't have an audience.

When I get to my breasts, I gently pull on my nipples elongating them into hard erasers. His face becomes dark and lustful. I know that his erection is rock hard.

"What if I can't stay away from you?" he says in a gravelly voice. *Oh! This is very fun.*

"You don't have a choice. Sasha is your date. It would be rude to show me attention," I reply as I start massaging my breasts, paying close attention to my nipples.

"But suppose that I want to touch you?" He is a man on fire. I am so secretly pleased with myself.

I run my hands over my flat stomach and start toward my clit, when he says, "You're driving me crazy, Charlie. You know that, don't you?"

"I'm just teaching you that you can show restraint," I reply in a very innocent voice.

My finger finds my hard clit, and I begin to tease myself, reaching up with the other hand and massaging my breast. It feels so erotic. I would rather have Colin doing this to me, but I love how crazy this is making him. Getting myself off in front of him is so intoxicating.

"Are you going to make yourself come?" he chokes out in a husky voice.

I'm at the point where I can't stop. My lower stomach is filled with heat. I'm dripping wet, and I know that it's not because of what I'm doing to myself. I'm responding to how turned on he is.

He pulls back the curtain and shows me his erection, gripping it through his shorts with his hand. "This is all because of you, Charlie."

It sends me over the edge. I have to stop touching my breast and brace myself on the wall of the shower so I don't collapse.

That was so hot!

I grab the shampoo and start lathering my hair. He's standing there with a raging erection, looking at me as if he might attack me, and I'm going on about my business.

"Are you going to leave me like this?" he asks, surprise written all over his face.

I start rinsing my hair. "Of course not, baby. After Miss Sasha goes home I'm going to make love to you all night long. I want to be so sore when I get on the plane tomorrow that I'm walking funny."

He gives me a rueful grin. He now has figured out my game. He shakes his head and says, "You drive me crazy. You always have."

He turns to leave the bathroom and I yell out, "Don't sort yourself out either, Colin. That's all for me."

He turns around, flashing me his half-smile. "All for you, Charlie."

***

My hair is styled in loose curls hanging down my back. My makeup is natural and soft. I message Brad a picture of myself to get his opinion before I slip my dress on. I sort of wish that I had kept the salon appointment, but then I would have missed out on Colin's confession run.

I know who Sasha Stone is, and she's gorgeous. I'm quite certain that she's had a team of people working on her all day, in contrast to me, who's a complete idiot when it comes to fixing my hair and makeup. I have an overwhelming feeling of dread that she is going to look like a superstar, and I'm going to look like the ugly duckling. I also secretly worry that Colin is going to be so knocked out by Sasha's California golden hair, clear blue eyes, and killer curves that he forgets about me all together.

While I wait to hear back from Brad, I send Colin a message.

Me: I am looking forward to later …

He replies quickly.

Colin: Me too. Sasha is on her way up. Remember, Charlie: All for you.

My stomach drops. The idea of Sasha and Colin together is quite different than knowing that she's on the way to his room to be alone with him in the same place where we recommitted our relationship mere hours ago.

Me: I love you.

Colin: Those words from you take my breath away. I love you too.

Oh, my!

Brad messages me back, scolding me for canceling my salon appointment and suggesting that I add more makeup. He reminds me that I am going to a formal dinner and not the local pizza joint. What would I do without Brad?

I go back in the bathroom and add more makeup. All the orgasms that I've had over the last day look really great on me. My cheeks are rosy and my eyes sparkle. Loving Colin is good for my overall appearance.

When my dad calls to say that he will be down in five minutes, I finally step into my aqua dress. I slip my high-heeled shoes on and start fussing with my jewelry.

I hear a knock on the door and assume that it's my dad. I walk as fast as I can in these ridiculous shoes and open the door. To my surprise, an employee of the hotel is standing there with a blue Tiffany's bag.

"Ma'am, one of our guests asked me to deliver this to you," he says, holding out the bag.

I take it and turn around to look for my purse so I can tip him.

"Ma'am the guest took care of the tip. Thank you."

"No. Thank you," I reply, dumbfounded.

I open the bag and see a small blue Tiffany's box. I open it, and there's a silver necklace. Two chains hold the symbol for infinity, the sideways eight. It's simple and stunning. I love it.

Then I open the card. It's written in Colin's terrible penmanship. *Charlie, please wear this tonight. It's my football number, 8, turned on its side, and it's the amount of years that I went without you.*

It is also much more than that. It's the symbol for infinity. Infinity is how long that I will love you. Infinity measures the depths of my feelings for you. Infinity is the amount of time that I will spend making up the last eight lost years to you.

Yours for infinity,

Colin. Fucking. McKinney.

"Oh God," I say as I sink to my bed. My eyes fill up with tears. I look up at the ceiling, hoping that I can keep the tears from falling and ruining my makeup.

I quickly remove the necklace that I purchased to wear with the aqua dress and replace it with the infinity necklace. I walk into the bathroom and grab a tissue to blot my eyes. The necklace looks perfect. It's a statement. It's a statement from my Statement.

The note is so beautiful and the necklace is the symbol of the note. I know instantly that I'll never take the necklace off. I love it, and it's absolutely perfect. I put the note back inside the Tiffany's bag and place it in my suitcase.

My dad knocks on the door. I do one last check in the mirror. I no longer care about Sasha and her beauty team. I'm wearing the most powerful statement that a man can give. His infinity.

I hold my head up high and take my dad's arm as he escorts me to the elevators. He's stunning in his perfectly-tailored tux. I laugh a little when I wonder if people will think that we're a couple, Doctor and Doctor Collins.

"Caroline, I'm proud to be your escort tonight. You look beautiful and classy. Remind me to compliment Brad," he says with a grin.

"I will let Brad know that you approve." I grin back.

"There is a red carpet that we've been asked to walk, and have our pictures taken on," he states.

I let out a sigh. I knew that this would be the case, but I don't understand why we have to do it. No one cares about Doctor and Doctor Collins.

"Let's hope that I don't trip." It's all that I can think to say.

As the elevator doors open, I wonder where Colin and Sasha are. I'm hoping that they have already walked the red carpet, and are inside the ballroom. I get anxious thinking about them alone in Colin's suite. I end that train of thought. There's nothing that I can do about the situation at this point.

A lady from the hotel is waiting for us. She directs us to a long hallway that leads to the ballroom. I know we're close because the sound of snapping cameras becomes louder and louder. I can hear the voices of photographers yelling questions at the guests. I know that this will be me in a few short minutes.

Another employee of the hotel stops me. "It will be just a minute. Sasha Stone and her fine quarterback are on the red carpet now. The photographers love them," she says conspiratorially.

At the mention of them together, my stomach becomes sour, and I feel my blood pressure rising. I hate that they're being photographed together. It confirms to the world that they're a couple, and it makes me feel like a great big cheater.

One of the photographers yells, "Colin, give Sasha a kiss."

I hear his loud, jovial voice say, "I don't want to mess up her makeup." He says it in such an *aw shucks* kind of way.

Then I hear Sasha coax his on, "Come on, Colin. Give the people what they want."

I hate her. I have no reason to hate her, but I hate her. I will never watch her show again. I'm green with jealousy.

Then, I literally gasp as I hear the photographers going crazy, snapping pictures and hooting and hollering. I know that he kissed her. That picture will appear all over the world.

My dad notices my reaction and whispers, "Get it together, Caroline. You know that this is part of his world."

To my horror, it's now our turn in front of the media. The lady from the hotel motions for me to walk on the red carpet. I do as I'm told and stop on the silver *X*. One photographer says, "And who are you?"

"Doctor Caroline Collins, friend of Clay South," I reply.

I swear there are only two photos snapped. This is so humiliating.

I walk off the red carpet, and listen as my dad gets as warm a reception as I did.

He walks over to me when he's done and says, "Glad we aren't too famous."

I smile at him in agreement.

"Ready to go in?" he asks with concern in his voice.

I flash him my best plastered on grin and reply, "As ready as I'll ever be."

Chapter Eight

THE SHEER number of people and their voices, as well as the lights, noise and chaos assault my senses. What I expected to be a distinguished event is the jock version of a cocktail party. The music is loud and the place looks more like a dance club with passed drinks and appetizers. My dad and I check in at a table that is set up just inside the room. Our I.D.s are rechecked and verified.

The two ladies working the table are admiring my dad. He's a very good-looking man, and carries himself with supreme confidence.

One of the ladies hands us a card. "Doctor and Doctor Collins, you're seated at table one."

"Thank you, and have a lovely evening," my dad replies.

I lean over to Dad and whisper, "They think that we're sleeping together."

The look on his face is priceless. He's mortified and disgusted all at the same time.

I smile at him and say, "At least you look good in a tux."

He escorts me into the room where I'm quickly recognized by JT, the player that Colin warned me about. He approaches me with a swagger. "It's lovely to see you again, Doctor Charlie."

"It's nice to see you again also. This is my father, Doctor Jack Collins." I introduce Dad into the conversation.

We make small talk for a moment until, thankfully, the wine server walks by. I help myself to a glass of white.

I've made a point to not look for Colin. I'm not overly excited to see him and Sasha together.

"Caroline, I have your business card. I've seen a lot of doctors and not one of them has been as gorgeous as you," JT compliments me with a very cheesy line.

I respond without missing a beat, "Or as smart."

He raises an eyebrow and laughs. "You're cocky. I like that."

"I noticed that you practice in Houston," JT says. "How do you know Clay?"

That launches my dad and JT in a long conversation about sports injuries. I mostly listen and interject when something interests me. JT might be a womanizer, but he seems like a nice guy. He's much smarter than he comes off from his initial impression.

Suddenly, I spot Colin across the room. Our eyes lock: his green to my lavender. Sasha is standing next to him. She looks Hollywood-beautiful. She's charming the guy that she's talking to. He's laughing, and obviously thinks that she is fabulous.

Colin isn't engaged in the conversation at all. He looks distracted, bordering on annoyed. He's looking everywhere but at Sasha or the gentleman that she's charming. When JT reaches out and touches my arm, I see Colin excuse himself from Sasha and the other man and walk toward me with heat in his eyes.

I finally have a chance to check him out. Colin in a tuxedo is quite a sight to behold. It fits him so perfectly that I'm sure that it was made for him. He has on the white shirt that I wore last night. God! That's so sexy. The black jacket makes his eyes look like green glass. I subconsciously bite my lower lip, knowing that I get to remove it later tonight. Colin. Fucking. McKinney is making a statement tonight.

He joins our conversation by standing between JT and me, forcing JT to remove his hand from my arm. "Good evening, Doctor Collins," he says, shaking my father's hand. My father smiles at Colin, knowing exactly what he's doing.

"Caroline, or should I say, Doctor Collins, you wear that dress well. And by the way, that necklace is stunning," he says, turning just enough towards me that he can compliment me and turn his back to JT without overt rudeness. Just the close proximity of our bodies is almost too much. I'm vibrating with need for him. It takes every bit of willpower that I have not to reach out and grab his hand. I crave his touch in a primal way.

Although I do hope that he doesn't plan on crashing every conversation that I have tonight, I need distance from him if we're going to attempt to get through this evening without alerting Sasha. I have to keep reminding myself that she did nothing wrong. She's just a girl who also happened to fall for the Statement. It's easy to do.

"Thank you, Colin. If you'll excuse me," I say to the group. "I need another glass of wine."

As I turn to leave, not bothering to wait for their response, Colin says from behind me, "I'll join you."

Well, so much for trying to avoid each other tonight.

"What are you doing?" I hiss when we are just out of earshot of JT and my father.

"Taking care of what's mine," he says as if it's perfectly logical.

"JT just put his hand on my arm. He wasn't trying to rape me. You're here with a date, Colin. I thought you were going to stay away from me," I say with a smile on my face, feeling anything but happy.

I place my order at the bar, another glass of white wine. Then, to my complete surprise, Colin orders two fingers of scotch on the rocks.

I look at him with complete shock. He grabs his drink and shoves a couple of dollars in the tip jar. He takes my arm and leads me to a somewhat quiet corner. "I'm having one, maybe two of these, to help get me through the night," he says, holding up his glass. "I can't fucking stand that every guy in the room watched you walk in and are hoping that they get to be the one to fuck you tonight. You look beyond hot in that dress. Did you try it on before you bought it? The slit's obscenely high. I'll have to mention to Brad that I like you completely dressed in public," he says while scanning me from head to toe. "Sasha's here, and I can't touch you and that feels like not breathing. So, for my sanity, I would appreciate you not letting anyone else touch you, because it makes me crazy."

"Deal," I agree. "But I would appreciate you not kissing her in front of me. Think that's fair, champ?"

"You know that I had to do that," he seethes.

"All I know is that we have to stay away from each other for three more hours. Please, for the love of God, Colin, just go back to Sasha's side and leave me alone. This is hard enough on me without your jealousy," I plead.

He looks down at my chest and fingers the infinity necklace. "You're mine for infinity."

"I love it, Colin. And I love your note even more," I say, looking into his green lustful eyes. "I love you. I'm yours for infinity."

He smiles his half-smile.

"Please go back to Sasha's side and not make this night, or the next few months, any harder on her or me than it has to be," I plead.

With that, he turns and walks away from me toward her. I walk in the opposite direction, begging my eyes to not find his for the rest of the night. I didn't touch him for eight years. I can avoid him for three more hours.

I, fortunately, spot my dad visiting with a group of players, and I recognize the majority of them. Two of the players I know are on Dad's waiting list. I slide my business face on and walk over to the group.

All of a sudden, I'm very greatly relieved that Brad went with the more conservative dress over the racy ivory one, because the group of players stop talking and watch me with appreciation in their eyes as I walk toward them.

My dad greets me, "Hey Caroline. Gentlemen, this is my daughter that I was telling you about. Doctor Caroline Collins. Her specialty is sports injuries also, and she graduated from Harvard Medical School."

I smile politely at my admirers. The guys one by one introduce themselves. I then spend the rest of cocktail hour chatting with the group. I pass out my business card, and the two players that are on my dad's waiting list tell me discreetly that they'll be scheduling an appointment to see me. This really is great networking.

When the doors to the dining room open, everyone begins making their way to their assigned tables. My dad offers me his arm, and I gladly accept it. I mentally decide to slip my shoes off during dinner and give my aching feet a rest.

There's a stage at the head of the room with a podium and a very large screen. The room is filled with fifty tables, each seating ten people. Each table has a floral centerpiece with black and silver accents—the team colors that Clay wore most of his career.

Table One is front and center. My dad and I are the first to arrive and find that our names are printed on cards indicating where we should sit. I notice that I will be seated next to Brandon Booth. Brandon played center, protecting Clay for the last years of his career. Then it dawns on me: if Brandon is sitting at our table, will Colin be also? I say a quick prayer that Colin and Sasha are at a different table.

Apparently, God does not like cheaters, because Colin and Sasha find their chairs, directly across the table from ours.

Sasha gives us her million-dollar smile when she sits down. She really is prettier in person than she is on TV, and I didn't think that was possible.

"Hi, I'm Sasha Stone," she greets us.

I speak first. I decide to go ahead and introduce Dad also, and drop our doctor titles. "Nice to meet you, Sasha. I'm Caroline Collins, and this is my father, Jack Collins."

Colin has the blandest look on his face. I quickly wonder how many more two-finger scotch-on-the-rocks that he's had.

"Oh, Colin said that we would be sitting with you." She beams. "Doctor Collins, Colin," she stops and laughs at the sound of both of the names together before she continues, "Colin said that you did the surgery on his ankle when he was in college."

So Colin knew that we would be sitting together? How convenient that he forgot to mention it. Sasha also knows our specialty, so Colin must have told her a little bit about us.

All my father says is, "Yes. That's how I met Colin." I mentally thank him for not elaborating on the two years that he spent at holiday dinners.

I quickly change the subject and start asking Sasha about her show business job. Just like everyone in the industry, she likes to talk about herself. I'm thankful that I can just listen to her ramble about herself and politely nod or throw an occasional question in to make her think that I'm interested. I glance at Colin. He's still stone-faced. I reach up and gently finger my necklace. When he sees me touch it, he gives me a wink.

As Sasha is winding down, the other couples join us at our table. Brandon introduces himself and his lovely wife, Bree. Brandon and Colin obviously know each other well because Brandon starts giving Colin a hard time about missing the golf outing this morning. Sasha's lips form an "O" in surprise, but she quickly pastes the smile back on. Colin must have forgotten to tell her that "something came up." *I know that look well, Sasha.* I'm reminded of the first team party that I went to with Colin at Quinn and Jennifer's home. Everyone knew me, and I knew no one. Colin does a great job of forgetting to mention things. I make a mental note to remind him to knock it off if we have chance of making this work again.

The other couple is Clay and Janis's minister and his wife. They seem to be a little out of sorts. I can tell that they are relieved when Clay and Janis take their seats at the table.

At the table directly next to us are Clay and Janis's parents and the four kids that I met last night. All three boys are in tuxedos, and little Marley is in a silver party dress. She keeps looking at Colin, trying her best to get his attention without getting in trouble. Just seeing their family interaction last night, I'm sure that all four kids have been well lectured about their behavior tonight.

"Colin," I say. He looks at me, very surprised that I'm speaking to him. "There's a little girl at the next table that is dying for your attention."

"Thank you, Doctor Collins," he says as he turns toward Marley.

Janis is watching like a lioness ready to pounce on Marley if she's out of line. Fortunately, Colin is able to pacify her and keep her out of trouble.

He says to Janis when he joins us back at the table, "Apparently, I owe Miss Marley a dance, and she reminded me about the guitar."

Janis smiles and shakes her head. "Colin, that girl is crazy over you."

Then, he looks my way and says, "In her defense, who isn't crazy about me?"

My lower stomach floods with warmth. Apparently, I am. As Sasha is talking to the minister and his wife, she reaches over and places a hand affectionately on Colin's arm. It's such an innocent gesture, one you make with someone you are intimately comfortable with.

Colin eyes dilate as he shoots me a panicked look. I know that he can't brush her hand off, but it literally makes me sick to my stomach to see her touch him. I take a big chug of my wine and pray it will help calm me down. To my relief, she lets go of him when the servers come to place our salads.

I barely eat mine, and it's not because it tastes bad. Actually, it's rather good for banquet food. Seeing Colin with someone else has ruined my appetite. When I couldn't avoid seeing him play football or on a billboard, at least he wasn't with another woman. I made sure to not click on any link that said, "See who Colin McKinney was dining with last night." Here he is in front of me with someone who knows his body as well as I do. It's killing me.

Fortunately, my salad plate is removed quickly so I don't have to see the green lettuce for long. In synchronized service, our dinner plates are set down in front of us. I talk myself into eating. I've had three glasses of wine. I know that I need something in my stomach so I can slow down the effects of the alcohol. I vow not to look up from my plate until I have taken two bites of everything.

Unfortunately, I look up as Sasha begins chatting privately with Colin, and her hand falls under the tablecloth. Is she touching his knee? His thigh? Higher up? He's interacting with her although I can tell that he's only giving her enough of himself to not make a scene.

I stare at my plate of food. There's no way that I can eat. My appetite has been replaced by a dull ache in my stomach. My dad glances at me and in a very low voice, whispers, "Is everything alright?"

"I suddenly don't feel well," I explain. "I'm going to the restroom."

His face betrays his obvious concern.

"I'm okay. I just need a minute," I reassure him.

He nods and stands up, pulling out my chair for me. I grab my purse and excuse myself from the table. I can feel Colin's eyes bore into my back as I walk out of the ballroom. I don't turn around, but I do reach up and gently touch my necklace. I hope he gets the message that I am okay.

I find an open balcony door and step outside in the cool Los Angeles night air. I lean against the railing and take deep cleansing breaths. I hate that I feel this way. Sasha's a nice person. Her body language says that she has strong feelings for Colin. I hate myself for being the other woman. I hate knowing that she is about to have her heart broken because of me, but my selfishness wants Colin more. A part of me wishes that he would have followed me out, but it would have been too obvious.

My phone indicates that I have a message. I grab it hoping that it's from him.

Colin: *Are you okay? I'm losing my mind in here.*
Me: *I needed some fresh air. I'll be back in a minute.*
Colin: *I traded spots with Bree so Sasha and her could visit.*
Me: *Thank you.*

I feel much better. I can do this. The evening is halfway over. I can deal with my guilty cheating conscience on the plane ride home tomorrow. Tonight, I get to have my cake and eat it too.

I walk back into the ballroom and take my seat. Thankfully, the dinner plates have been removed and my wine glass has been refilled.

"Everything okay?" my dad whispers.

"Yes. I'm feeling much better," I reassure him.

When dessert is served, the commissioner of the NFL stands up and approaches the podium. The room grows quiet in anticipation of his remarks. Brandon and Colin stop visiting and look ahead, giving him their full attention.

"We are here tonight to honor the long and distinguished career of Clay South …" he begins. He goes through Clay's impressive statistics, his awards, and accomplishments. I glance at Colin while the commissioner is speaking. Colin's so focused. I know that look. He only has the look when he's playing football, or trying to convince me that his way is the right way. I love the intensity of his eyes. I love when that intensity is directed at me.

"In conclusion," he says, "we have put together a fifteen-minute highlight reel of Clay's career. Then there are a couple of people that I've asked to speak. Finally, the man of the hour will regale us with his own words."

The room laughs. I just met Clay for a couple of hours yesterday, and I know that he's a real character.

Before the room darkens, Brandon asks Colin to swap seats because he wants to sit by Bree. Instead of Colin swapping with Bree, he swaps with Brandon. Over the course of a dinner, Colin has managed to play musical chairs around the table to get to the prize: me. He's also managed to do it without raising any eyebrows.

When the lights go down, Colin's hand is underneath the tablecloth and separating my dress at the slit so he can touch my bare skin and, well, everything else.

He shifts slightly in his chair, giving him better access to his goal. He stares forward impassively at the screen while he rubs and massages my thigh, working his way to my panties. This feels so wrong. His maybe-girlfriend and my dad are mere inches from us as he begins to massage my clit through my lace panties. I would love to squeeze my legs together and prevent his contact, but I crave his touch. And frankly, I want him just as badly as he wants me.

I spread my legs open a little further, allowing him to slide his fingers inside my panties. I feel how wet he's making me, and the fact that me being this wet for him drives me crazy. I'm working hard at concentrating on the video and not throwing my head back and screaming his name. I glance up at him. He's focused on the screen with his poker face on. He speeds up his assault on my clit just as they show the picture of him, Clay, and baby Marley when she was born. Sasha turns and smiles at Colin. I bite the inside of my lip to keep my face from contorting as I come all over his hand. He slides two fingers inside me, allowing me to pulse on them. When I'm done, he slides his fingers out, pulls my panties back into place and returns his hand to my thigh. I peek at his face. His mouth is turned up into his half-smile.

I don't want the video to end. I want his hand to stay right where it is for the rest of the evening, but alas, the screen goes dark and the lights come on, and everyone begins to clap. He reluctantly removes his palm from my bare thigh and joins in the clapping.

He leans over close enough for me to hear him whisper, "That was fucking hot."

I smile.

The commissioner stands back up at the podium, and to my surprise, introduces Colin to speak. I know for a fact that Colin must be as hard as a rock. This is going to be interesting. I sit back and wait to see what he does. He adjusts himself as he stands to walk up on stage. I don't know how he does it, but he just looks like he has a big package, not a raging hard-on.

I look over at Sasha, and she's beaming with pride at him. I feel like a guilty home-wrecker for all of two seconds before he absentmindedly uses the two fingers that were just inside me to scratch his nose. The heat immediately returns to my lower stomach.

"Clay South and I met many times on the football field. I respect him tremendously as player, but that's not what I'm here to speak to you about tonight. I'm here to talk about Clay South the man, the father, and the husband.

"My coach in Dallas was friends with Clay from his previous coaching job. I had just suffered an extreme personal loss, and couldn't find my place in football anymore. My coach called Clay and told him that I needed my head set straight. Clay invited me to his lovely home, opened his guest bedroom to me and spent the next month helping me cope with my loss. It's because of Clay South that I found my way back to football again, and ultimately to what I want most in my life."

He doesn't elaborate on what that is, but I know that he's talking about me. Our eyes lock for just a moment, and it's magical.

The rest of Colin's speech is about Clay's relationship with his wife Janis and his four kids. He also tells the story of Marley's birth and how they both got a little dust in their eyes. Everyone laughs. By the end of Colin's talk, I'm ready to crown Clay a saint.

"Now, I would like to introduce you to Doctor Jack Collins," Colin says.

I pat my dad on the back as he stands up to take the podium. My dad walks up to the podium with the grace of an athlete. Even though he's not as big of a man as Colin, he still commands the stage.

Colin casually brushes his hand along my back as he takes Brandon's still abandoned seat. I reach over under the tablecloth and rest my hand on his knee.

My dad begins to speak. "I'm Doctor Jack Collins. I have a practice in Houston that is dedicated to extending the professional life of athletes while focusing on their quality of life after their careers are over. Clay came to me with a neck injury that was preventing him from getting the kind of power that he needed to maintain his status as an elite quarterback. Every doctor had recommended surgery, but he was anxious. The first thing that he said to me was, 'I've got to still be able to pick my kids up when I am done playing ball.'

"Every decision that we made together went back to that goal. Ultimately I recommended that we avoid surgery and he spent the off-season in my practice, under my watchful eye, and we rehabbed the injury like crazy. His family moved into an apartment nearby, and every single day, I watched him work harder to get better than anyone else I have ever seen. He brought his family to watch every couple of days and cheer him on. Devotion is not a word that I throw around lightly, but devotion is what he showed to the game of football and to his family."

Finally, everyone stands up and gives Clay a standing ovation as he takes the podium. Clay's speech is memorable because he jokes that he didn't get the memo there wasn't a roast before he prepared his remarks.

He proceeds to deliver zingers and one-liners at everyone's expense. However, at the end of his remarks he profusely thanks my dad for saving his career and allowing him to be able to still wrestle with his kids. He lets Colin know how much his friendship means to him, and then teases that one day maybe Colin will have some jewels like his, and flashes his championship ring at our table. He then threatens to break both of Colin's kneecaps if he buys Marley a guitar. He concludes by thanking Janis for following him all over the country to support his career, for going to the kids' school plays, games, and recitals when he couldn't because he was chasing his dream, and most of all for being his biggest fan and toughest critic.

I don't think that there was a dry eye in the house when he was done.

The doors from the ballroom open and lead toward the reception room that has been turned into a dance club. The music is loud and the bass is thumping. My dad gives me a look. I know that this isn't his scene, and he'll be heading out shortly. Sasha and Colin are in front of us. She grabs Colin's hand and drags him excitedly toward the room.

Damn! I know that he's a good dancer, and so does she. She's going to occupy him all night.

By the time that we make it to the club, the dance floor is filling up. Sasha leads Colin to the center, and I watch the two of them begin to dance. It feels the same way as watching him make love to someone else. It sucks! As long as Colin and I were together, he never danced with anyone but me.

I decide that I can spend the rest of the evening miserably watching them simulate their bedroom moves on the dance floor, or I can take off my shoes and join in the masses. I go to the bar and order a gin and tonic, and then head to the dance floor.

I start dancing by myself, but I'm quickly spotted by JT. He walks toward me, falls in with my moves. He's a damn good dancer. *This might not be so bad after all.*

I pointedly don't look for Colin and Sasha. There's nothing that I can do about it, and I know that ultimately he's mine, so right now I'm just having fun. By the end of the second song, I've drained my gin and tonic. JT offers to refill it, and I let him. As soon as he walks off, another guy that I'd met earlier but whose name I can't remember joins me. He's not as coordinated as JT, but I give him one dance.

I sit out the next song and take a moment to check my phone. There is a message from Colin.

Colin: Meet me by the restrooms in five minutes.

I check the time that it was sent and realize the five minutes is now. I throw my phone in my purse and head out of the converted club to the restrooms.

I spot him standing by a water fountain. He's leaning against the wall and looks all kinds of sexy. His face is a little red. He must have gotten some sun on our confession run. It looks good on him. He really is a walking mission statement.

He flashes me his half-smile when he sees me. I walk to him, and he plants a chaste kiss on my lips. When he does, I catch a whiff of scotch on his breath. He's had a few.

"Colin, how many drinks have you had?" I ask accusingly.

"Charlie, shut up and listen to me," he orders. I'm shocked. He has never talked to me like this.

"I had the scotch so that one, I could better deal with tonight, and two, so that I would have an excuse for not sleeping with Sasha."

"I guess that's good, Colin?" I ask, completely confused.

"Sasha knows that I do not drink—ever. She was quite shocked when she saw me have a few glasses of scotch," he confesses.

I cut him off. "And frankly, so was I."

"Just listen," he pleads. "I told her while we were dancing that I think I had a bit too much to drink and excused myself to the restroom. I'm going to go back in there and tell her that the scotch has made me not feel well, and I'm going to my room to sleep it off. I'll tell her to enjoy the rest of the night, take a town car back to her place, and I'll see her tomorrow. As much as this disgusts me, go dance three or four more songs with JT, and then come to my room. Do not change first," he orders with a wicked glint in his eye.

"Sounds like you have this well planned," I respond as I turn around to walk back into the club.

"Charlie," he calls after me. "Don't let him touch you."

Chapter Nine

I WATCH as Colin delivers the news to Sasha. She looks worried. I can tell that she wants to leave with him. He shakes his head no. She rubs his arm and grabs his hands. He shakes his head no again. I guess she finally gets the message because she throws her hands down by her side in a giving-up motion. He gives her a peck on the cheek. She tries to take his mouth, but he makes a motion, warning her off. After he leaves and I'm sure that she doesn't follow, I find JT on the dance floor again.

I explain that I was in the restroom and thank him for my drink. We dance four more songs together. I'm really having a great time. He's good and hasn't tried anything inappropriate. I begin to wonder if Colin's description of JT is incorrect.

After the fifth song, I thank him for some great dancing but explain that I have an early flight out tomorrow, and I'm exhausted.

He gives me a hug and tells me that he'll call on Monday to make an appointment. I smile and tell him that I look forward to seeing him again, which I strangely really do.

Before I leave, I spot Sasha. She's picked up a new dance partner. He's a very single, very hot defensive lineman who plays for Chicago. It makes my conscience feel better knowing that she didn't run home when Colin left her. Maybe she doesn't have as strong of feelings for Colin as I had thought.

Once in the elevator, I eagerly select Colin's floor and lean against the wall as the elevator doors close. I hope that I can talk him into a foot massage before the night is over because my feet are screaming at me.

I gently knock on Colin's door. When he opens it, the sexiest sight ever greets me. My Statement is in his tuxedo pants, no shirt, and barefoot. I can't stop myself. I greedily launch myself at him. He catches me and picks me up. I wrap my legs around his waist and attack his mouth. All of our frustrations at spending the night pretending we didn't care are wrapped in this kiss.

"God, I love your mouth," I say as he starts nibbling on the special place on my neck. He shuts the door with his foot and carries me into the bedroom tossing me on the bed. He pulls my dress up over my hips and rips my panties off in one fluid move. The look on his face makes me want to explode. He is looking at my body with appreciation and lust. He reaches down and runs two fingers over my slick opening. "This is mine," he says.

"It's all for you until infinity," I breathe my reassurance.

He undoes the button on his pants and pulls down the zipper. He doesn't even bother to pull the trousers down. Suddenly, he slams inside me. I cry out in shock, pleasure, and pain. He only gives me a quick moment to adjust to his presence before he starts thrusting into me.

"Charlie, this is how you make me feel when you pleasure yourself and don't let me touch you," he says, hammering into me.

"This is how you left me when I watched you come, but was denied what was mine," he says with heat and passion in his voice.

I moan in pleasure rolling my head from side to side. The assault feels perfect. This is what I had been craving all day. I've needed this level of rawness.

"I've been denied eight years with you. Don't deny me again," he orders.

"You have all of me, Colin. Remember? To infinity," I promise while I writhe and groan in ecstasy.

That pushes him over the edge. We come together, both stealing each other's pleasure.

When we're done, he pulls out of me very gently and walks into the bathroom, shutting the door behind him, leaving me in a messed-up state.

I lie there for a few minutes, waiting for him to return. When he doesn't, I stand up, reach around and undo my zipper, letting my dress fall to the floor. I pick it up and throw it over the chair in the room. It really is a gorgeous dress. I don't want it ruined.

I sit on the edge of the bed and remove my shoes. It feels almost orgasmic removing them from my poor abused feet.

I take off my strapless bra and feel gloriously naked. I walk into the suite and open the refrigerator. Just as I expected, it's well stocked with bottled water. I open a bottle and walk to the bathroom to see what's taking Colin so long. The door is closed and locked.

That's odd.

I knock. "Everything okay?" I ask.

"Give me a second," he groans.

What's wrong with him? "Colin, open this door. There's something not right. Let me in," I demand.

I wait a moment and nothing happens. "Colin, I'm freaking out. Open this door or tell me what's wrong," I raise my voice.

I hear the door lock click, and I quickly turn the knob and rush in. He's positioned over the toilet, losing everything in his stomach. I rush to him and kneel down on the cold tiles next him, rubbing his back. "What's wrong, baby?" I plead.

He can't answer me, so I just stay next to him, doing what I can. His face is bright red. I check his pulse. It's normal, thank God. I soak a washcloth in cold water and use it to mop his brow, then I lay it across his back. When he breaks into shivers, I remove the cold washcloth and cover him with a bathrobe from the behind the door.

When he's finished dry heaving, I hand him my water bottle and encourage him to drink. This reminds me of so many years ago when I took care of him in a similar manner.

"What's going on? You didn't drink near enough to be this ill." I'm beyond worried about him.

"I have an alcohol intolerance," he explains. His voice is raw from being sick.

"What? I heard of it in medical school, but it's usually a reaction to mixing medication with alcohol."

"Well, I'm one of the lucky few whose body can't break down the grains in alcohol," he says ruefully.

His face is still so red that he looks sunburned.

"I'll drink about half this water and throw it up again. Then I'll be perfectly fine with slightly pink cheeks." He sounds so pitiful. His voice is raspy and weak. His face is twisted in a look of disgust. I know that this is not how Colin planned tonight going … or is it?

"Is there anything that I can do, or that you need?" I ask.

"You. I need you," he says, looking at me with pleading eyes.

I watch the man that has consumed my life for ten years position himself back over the toilet and lose the remaining bit of scotch in his body, and all the water that he just drank.

I run a bath for him in the giant whirlpool tub while he finishes. *There really are benefits to upgrading to a suite.* The tub is awesome.

I grab him another bottle of water, and place it by the tub, then I get a fresh towel. Kneeling down in front of him, I clean around his mouth, then bring him his toothbrush and toothpaste so he can get the taste of sick out of his mouth.

He stands up and walks to the bathtub. I unwrap the bathrobe from around him and help him remove his tuxedo pants and underwear. Even after getting sick, he has a semi-firm erection. *Amazing!* I encourage him to get into the bath.

I open his bottle of water and hand it to him.

"Will you join me?" he asks, running his eyes up and down my naked body.

I nod and slide in the warm water, lying against his front. My body instantly responds to our contact.

His erection grows against my back.

He laughs in his raspy voice. "My dick doesn't realize that you just watched me puke my guts up, which puts a wet blanket on anyone's libido."

He is sounding more like his old self. That makes me happy. "Oh, Colin! I think my libido is already back in business," I reassure him.

I can tell that he's still weak so I change the subject from sex. "Tell me how you discovered your intolerance."

"Well, you see, Doctor Collins," he says, playing with the chain of my infinity necklace. "You know that I rarely drank because I seemed to be so affected by it. Like, even in high school, a few beers would make me sick. After you left, I decided that Jack Daniels was my best friend. I was drinking shots of Jack one night with Clay, and he's the one who pointed out that my reaction was far from normal. I wound up mentioning it to a doctor, and they confirmed the diagnosis. To my body, alcohol is toxic. The guys on the team love it, because I am always the designated driver."

"I bet they do." I laugh.

"So why did you drink tonight?" I ask, knowing the answer but wanting to hear him say it.

"I did it so there would be no chance that I would have to have sex with Sasha," he says sheepishly.

"That was really dumb. You purposely poisoned yourself. You have to deal with your relationship with her tomorrow, right?"

"Right," he confirms.

"By the way, she danced after you left with the defensive lineman from Chicago." I just toss that little grenade out there. He can do what he wishes with it. "Also, I want you to promise me that you aren't going to drink again. No matter how convenient it might be to avoid a bad situation."

"Trust me, Charlie. The decision was not made lightly. No one likes to puke less than me. After I kissed her on the red carpet, I knew that I had to do it, or she would have made a beeline for my hotel room."

The thought of him sleeping with her disgusts me, but I choose not to harp on it.

"By the way, that's the last time that I have unprotected sex with you. We temporarily lost our minds. Let's hope we don't have a baby to show for it in nine months," I state, matter-of-factly.

"Would that really be so bad?" he asks with a hint of sadness in his voice.

"Yes. It would, Colin." The water gets a little cold. I reach up with my foot and turn on the faucet, adding more hot to the tub. "We have a lot of shit that we need to figure out. It would be nice to figure it out before we start trying to keep another human being alive."

"Gosh, Charlie. I had forgotten what a romantic you are," he teases, tickling me lightly on my sides.

I roll over on my stomach so I can see his face. He looks so much better. "Can I order you up some food?" I ask. "Anything sound good?"

"You. Naked. On my bed." he says, flashing me his half-smile.

"I'll be naked on your bed with a box of condoms on the bedside table. How does that sound?" I ask in my best seductive voice.

"I'll agree to you naked on my bed with a cheeseburger," he counters.

"I will agree to the cheeseburger, but I'm not negotiating on the condoms. However, I promise to make an appointment with my doctor as soon as I get home to go on the pill." I smile sweetly and stand up to get out of the tub.

"Fine," he says with a pout as he watches me dry myself off. I take an extra second or two to make sure my breasts are dry. His eyes grow dark with lust. "Charlie, don't do that me again," he warns.

"What, baby?" I fake innocence. "You don't want me getting water everywhere, do you?"

I drop my towel, and I do my best model walk out of the bathroom. I can feel him fucking me with his eyes, and it is so exhilarating.

He runs some fresh water as I exit the bathroom. I walk over to the hotel phone on the bedside table. I call room service and order Colin a cheeseburger, fries, and a Diet Coke. The Diet Coke is for me. I hang up the phone and yell at Colin, "Food will be here in forty-five minutes; whatever shall we do while we wait?"

"Give me five minutes, baby, and I'll show you how we can occupy our time." He's done pouting, and back to jovial Colin.

I hear the water draining out of the tub and the bathroom sink running. Soon enough he emerges in nothing but his birthday suit, and a mighty fine suit it is. He starts walking to the bed like he's stalking his prey.

I sit up and point toward the bathroom. "Go find them. You aren't touching me until they are on the bedside table."

"Come on, Charlie," he pleads. "The damage is already done."

I'm not giving in on this. "I don't care, even if it's too late. However, you're wasting precious minutes by arguing with me when you could be enjoying some of this," I say as I reach down and begin to touch myself.

"Not cool," he says as the stomps back into the bathroom.

About thirty seconds later, he emerges with the golden tickets for the rest of the night and tomorrow morning. He's in full sulk mode. He puts them on the table and flops down on the bed next to me.

Oh, this is ridiculous! I scoot next to him and start playing with his semi-erection. He quickly responds to me. "See! Isn't this better than pouting?" I ask while I pump him up and down.

"Yes, I guess," he acquiesces.

"Well, let's see if you think this is better than pouting," I say as I take his erection in my mouth. I take all of it in and suck as hard as I can.

"God, that feels good, Charlie. Much better than pouting," he confirms.

I sheath my teeth in my lips and gently nibble and bite the head, and then lick it tenderly, catching the liquid on my tongue as it runs out.

He groans and grabs my hair in appreciation.

Then we hear a knock on the door. "Fuck!" he says, completely ruining the mood.

He grabs his bathrobe and throws it on, tying it around his waist. He closes the bedroom door behind him so that I don't have to cover up.

I lay there, frustrated by room service's timing when I hear his voice, "Sasha, right now's not a good time. You can't stay. Can I call you a car?"

Her voice is muffled, but he responds loudly with, "You know that I'm allergic to alcohol. I've just spent the last two hours puking. I was already in bed. Please go home, and I'll talk to you tomorrow."

Her muffled voice is starting to sound hysterical. I contemplate whether or not I should put on clothes. I reason that naked is just as incriminating as a bathrobe so I opt to do nothing. This might be Colin's put up or shut up time.

"Seriously, Sasha! This is not the time that I care to have a deep conversation about our relationship." He's reasoning with her, but he sounds so harsh. I don't recognize this tone.

I clearly hear her yell, "Why won't you just say that you love me?"

He yells back, "What part of *I feel like shit and want you to leave* don't you understand? You're drunk and horny. I'm sure that there are fifty football players downstairs who would give their right ball to fuck you. Go throw yourself at one of them."

Dear God. I inwardly cringe. I had no idea he had this in him. He's being a real bastard.

Then I hear another knock on the door. *Please, don't let that be another girlfriend*, I silently pray.

Prayers are answered. It's room service delivering his cheeseburger, fries, and Diet Coke.

Apparently, when she sees his food order, she really flips out. "You're so sick that you can't fuck me, but you can eat a cheeseburger?" she screams.

I actually have to laugh at that one. She's very correct in her reasoning.

Colin yells, "I'm fucking hungry. Not fucking horny! Look, Sasha, you want to have a conversation about our relationship? Let's do it. I don't want to see you anymore. Don't call me. Don't message me. Go!" he orders.

I hear him pick up the phone and ask the front desk to arrange a car to take Sasha home. As Brad would say, "This shit just got real."

She cries loudly and begs him not to do this. Poor thing is drunk. She would have much more dignity if she weren't, I can only assume.

Much more civilly, Colin says, "Look, we had a good run. You're a very sweet girl. I just don't think that we have a future, so why keep doing this to ourselves?"

She starts begging him. This is really getting pathetic. "Colin, please, just fuck me. You'll remember how good we are together. You just need a reminder …" she says, using a seductive voice.

"Sasha, your car is already downstairs. I'll come by your house tomorrow and collect the few things that are there, when you're sober, and we'll talk about this," he soothes.

Then she says in her best *reporter has a whiff of a juicy story* voice, "Who is she?"

"What?" he asks feigning shock.

"You didn't order this food for yourself. You don't drink anything but bottled water. Your cheeseburger has a bun. You don't eat any grains." She's just getting revved up. Sasha Stone smells a story. "Is she in your bedroom now? Is that why the door's shut?"

"Sasha, I've asked you politely to leave. Please don't make me call security." His voice is so cold that I shiver.

"Open the bedroom door, Colin," she screams at him.

"No," he states, without an ounce of emotion.

"Fine. I'll leave. But let's be clear: this is not over. I expect you at my house tomorrow."

A few seconds later, the door slams shut.

I wait a few minutes to make sure that she isn't coming back before I open the bedroom door and walk out. He's in his infamous Colin pose. He's seated on the couch with his elbows resting on his knees and his head hanging. I walk over to him and join him on the couch wrapping my arm around his back.

"Who knew that you no longer eat bread?" I say breaking the silence.

He looks up at me and flashes me his gorgeous half-smile. "Yeah. How can I be this in love with you, and you don't even know how I take my burger?" He laughs.

"Look. That really sucked. I'm sorry."

"Don't be. You probably saved me a lot of unhappy years with her."

"Please eat a little something and we'll go to bed," I coax.

"What little appetite I had is gone," he says. "Let's just go to bed."

He stands up and offers me his hand. I take it and allow him to lead me into the bedroom. He shuts the bedroom door while I fold back the covers. We snuggle into each other. Our naked bodies spoon together.

"Colin, will you tell me a bedtime story?" I ask sheepishly.

"What kind of story would you like to hear?" he asks.

"I want you to tell me about football."

"What would you like to hear about?" he replies warily.

"Everything," I say. "I feel like when we were together I didn't try hard enough to understand your passion. While I fall asleep I want you to tell me why you love football so much."

He gently giggles and pulls me to him. Then he begins, "There was once a little boy who had a wonderful dad who would take him outside and toss the ball with him after school ..."

Chapter Ten

I AM awakened by the smell of bacon. There's no better smell to wake up to except the aroma that is Colin.

"Wake up, baby. Breakfast is here," he coos in my ear.

I roll over and reply, "You really know how to wake a girl up." I stretch out like a cat on the bed and look at his chiseled face. I still can't believe that this is real, and he's here with me. His face is buoyant. He's like a little kid on Christmas morning. I had been a bit worried that since I'm flying back to Houston today he would be grouchy and sulk all morning. Instead, I get the opposite. I get the Colin that I adore. The one who's mischievous, and silly, and fun.

"Your breakfast is getting cold. Come eat with me," he says, smiling.

"You ordered us room service?"

"I don't want to waste a minute of the next five hours that I have with you," he says. He leans down and kisses my nose. "I love you, Doctor Collins."

I smile back at him. "I love you too, Colin. Fucking. McKinney."

All of sudden, he gets a glint in his eye that makes me panic. *What is he going to do?* Before I know it, he picks me up and throws me over his shoulder and carries me to the dining table while I scream with laughter. He sits me down in a chair.

"You know, I could have walked," I say, trying to be angry but failing miserably.

"What fun would that have been?" he asks as he sits down beside me at the table and uncovers our plates. We're both still gloriously naked.

Ordinarily, dining in the nude would gross me out. I make a huge mental gasp at my audacity, and I mentally give myself a pep talk. I want to do nothing that will ruin this morning.

He ordered me pancakes with bacon and coffee. He has his same egg-white omelet. "Do you eat egg-white omelets every morning for breakfast?"

"Mostly," he replies. "Why?"

"It's just funny to me how well I still know you, yet I don't know things like you don't eat hamburger buns, or that you have egg-white omelets every morning for breakfast," I reply. "I'm looking forward to learning all those little things about you again."

He smiles a goofy grin at me and says, "Me too, Charlie." Then his face gets wary. "I would like to talk to you about something, but I don't want to overwhelm you. Look, I need for you to tell me if I am overwhelming you, okay?"

"I promise that I will tell you, but I also want you to be Colin. That's what I love the most about you is that you are the Statement: Colin. Fucking. McKinney. I'm not a twenty-one year-old girl anymore." Then I pause for effect. "Plus, after years of therapy, I'm better equipped to deal with your overwhelming tendencies." I smile at him, hoping that he can read that I'm only half kidding. His forehead creases so I reach out and hold his hand on top of the table, giving it a little squeeze.

"Overwhelming tendencies," he says, trying the words out. "I have to say, Charlie, that no one but you has ever accused me of overwhelming tendencies."

I rub his arm and say in a patronizing manner, "Honey, that's because you only have overwhelming tendencies when it comes to your three loves: football, Big Bertha, and me."

He throws his head back and laughs. "You might be right about that. But, in all seriousness, you have to tell me if I'm overwhelming you. I want this to work more than I have ever wanted anything. Okay?"

"That's a deal, Colin," I reply. I let go of his hand and pick up my fork, continuing to inhale my breakfast and drink some much needed coffee.

"Well, I got up early this morning and called my assistant, Jenny. She was very pleased to hear from me so early on Sunday morning," he says, smiling at the thought.

"I bet she was. I can't wait to meet her" I shovel in a bite of pancakes.

"She'll love you," he assures me with his half-smile. "Anyway, I asked her to start working on clearing out my calendar and paring down my schedule to the commitments that I have to keep. I told her my goal is to spend as much time as possible in Houston over the next two months."

He cuts his eyes and gives me an anxious smile, waiting to see my reaction. I nod and take a big drink of coffee. "That would be wonderful."

He continues, looking very relieved by my reaction, "I also asked her to find a trainer in Houston for me to work out with."

"You know, Colin, my practice has two of the top professional trainers in the world on staff. I'm sure that, for the right price," I say, winking at him, "they could either work you out or know someone who's good."

"Right price, huh? That could be negotiated," he says.

"If you're asking me if I want you to stay with me and spend as much time as possible with me, the answer is yes," I say, beaming. "However, you have to remember that I've got responsibilities to my patients, staff, and father. I sometimes don't get home until after eight o'clock at night. If that's the case, you can't make me feel guilty about not spending more time with you. Okay?" I warn.

"I know, Charlie. Right now, I'll take the time that I can get. But, when I have to be back in Dallas, I hope that you'll make time to see me," he says with a hint of desperation in his eyes.

I put my fork down and finish off my coffee, and pour myself another cup. After I've downed half the second mug, I walk to him, pulling his chair out from the table and straddling his lap. I reach up and touch my necklace while I stare into his green eyes. "We're getting a second chance at happily ever after. I want you, Colin. I want you in my bed. I want you to run with me in the mornings. I want to fix you dinner at night. I want to lay on the couch with you and watch terrible rerun TV. I want to worry that you aren't taking your vitamins. I want to talk to you on my way to work and my way home. I want a real and honest life with you. I'm not settling for anything less."

He leans forward, resting his head against my chest, and wraps his arms around me. "I want every bit of that, too."

"It's settled then. We're not going to mess it up this time. What shall we spend the next four and half hours doing?" I ask.

"Oh! I think you know Doctor Collins," he says, poking me with his erection. "I believe a goal was set for you to be so sore by the time you get on the plane that you walk funny. I have four hours to make that happen."

He picks me up and lays me on the table, pushing our plates to the floor. They crash to the ground, making loud, jangling noises. I mentally think of the dollar-cost associated with broken plates. *I hate being practical!*

He crawls onto the table, positioning himself over me, staring into my eyes. "You're my dessert. I'm going to start at your forehead and explore every single bit of you."

He begins by planting soft kisses on my forehead, and moving sweetly over my cheeks, nose, and jawline. When he gets to my chin, he works his way back up to my mouth. He gently kisses me, using his tongue to make reverent, tender love to me. This isn't a side of Colin that I'm familiar with. He's passionate, athletic, and domineering in his lovemaking.

I like this. I feel like the most beautiful and desired woman in the world. He's making me feel this way … my Statement.

I reach up and touch his face to make sure that he's real and that this is really happening to me. All of a sudden, the wall of protection that I've built up around my heart crumbles. I know in that instant that the horrible breakup and eight-year separation was worth it for this moment. I meant every word that I just said to him. I want him and all his baggage. I want him, even if I have to share him for nine months of the year with the football world. It's okay if we can't go grocery shopping or eat at restaurants like a normal couple because I'll get to wake up every morning with this man. In this instant, my world shifts on its axis, and I succumb to my wants. I want to be with Colin more than I want anything else in this world.

I stop his descending hands and grab his face so that he can look me in my eyes. I feel the tears running down my cheeks.

"Charlie! What's wrong?" he asks, panicked.

"I love you," I whisper.

"I know, baby. You told me," he says, confused as he uses a thumb to wipe away a tear. "Why are you crying?"

"No, Colin. You don't understand. For the first time in my whole life there are no nagging doubts in my mind about us, and if we can make this work. I love you. I love you enough to put you first," I confess through my tentative sobs.

He picks me up and cradles me to him. He scoots us off the dining table and carries me into the bedroom, placing me gently on the bed while he holds me. I'm turned away from him so I can't see his face. Colin is completely silent. I keep waiting for him to respond. I start to feel a little panicky. Maybe my confession was too soon. *Did I just scare him away?*

The seconds crawl by. Finally, I can't take it any longer. I change positions so I can see his face. Colin's eyes are wet with unshed tears.

"Baby, what's wrong?" I ask. "I didn't mean to upset you."

I crawl on my knees and wrap my arms around his neck. If it's possible, my six-foot, five-inch man looks like a scared little boy. I hold him in a hug while he embraces me around my waist, pulling me tightly to him.

"Colin, please talk to me," I implore. My head is nuzzled into his neck. I feel dampness on my cheek. It could be my tears or Colin's. I am really not sure.

Through his choked voice, he says, "I've waited ten years to hear that you love me enough to put me first."

I didn't realize until this moment the depth of his feelings for me. When we were together I'd thought Colin would get bored of me and find someone else that was prettier or sexier. I never felt worthy of his devotion. I now understand just what it means to be loved by Colin McKinney, and it's powerful.

He pulls me away from him and takes my face in his large hands. His green eyes and long, black eyelashes are wet. I feel my soul being probed by him.

"I love you, Charlie," he says with such conviction that there is not a doubt in my mind that he believes what he is saying. He leans into me, placing a short but passionate kiss on my lips. "I will love you until infinity."

Epilogue

FIVE DAYS later …

Once again, I'm alone. I'm more alone now than I ever have been before. I just knew that Colin was the one. We were a perfect match. Everyone said how great that we looked together. He's the David Beckham of professional football. I could totally have been his Posh Spice.

I was prepared to relocate to Dallas for him. I had even talked to the powers that be about flying back and forth for my job. Giuliana Rancic does it. Why couldn't I?

Now, here I sit in my beautiful bungalow in the Hollywood Hills, waiting to bare my soul. The reporter will be here in thirty minutes. I've gone back and forth over if I want to do this. Our breakup is just one more bump in the road to me getting married.

I keep telling myself that I'm not doing this to hurt Colin, but I know that's not true. The focus of the interview is supposed to be about finding love in the Hollywood spotlight. My relationships have been chronicled in the tabloids for the last five years. Sometimes, I'm even shocked at who I'm supposedly dating.

I'd thought my relationship with Colin was real. I had been so sure that he was going to propose that I put the wedding planner to the stars on notice. *God, I feel like the biggest fool.*

I was so furious with Colin that when I got home early Sunday morning after learning that there was another woman in his hotel room that I shredded what belongings he had at my house and put them in black garbage bags. In all honesty, it made me feel better for about ten minutes. Then, I collapsed on my bed and cried until I fell asleep.

Just thinking about it again makes me realize that I'm making the right decision. Everyone needs to know that Colin McKinney, underwear model, spokesperson, all-American boy, and football stud is a cheater who has no respect for women.

I want the world to know that Colin left me. Colin cheated on me. I want him and his new piece of ass to hurt like they've made me hurt.

I walk into my closet and choose a thin, black sweater and designer jeans. I pair my ensemble with brown boots. I put on a minimum of makeup and pull my hair into a loose braid. I look at myself in the mirror, and I'm pleased with the results. I look demure and somber. This is the impression that I want to give. I know that this is as important as the words that will come out of my mouth.

The knock on my front door causes my stomach to jump into my chest. *Oh my God! I'm actually going to do this.*

I answer the door, and the reporter greets me. She gives me a careful hug. I thank her for her sympathy. I know this game. I know how it's played. I've been the best in my field for years now. I can turn on the sympathy like water from a fountain.

"Come in, Amber," I greet her, opening my door wider for her to enter. As we walk into my living room, I offer her a drink.

She's good. Amber knows to accept a drink from me. It makes the interviewee feel more comfortable to offer hospitality, and it puts me more at ease and open to her questions. I fix her a glass of Zen green tea. I put her drink in a Ralph Lauren glass and grab a Papyrus Stationery napkin. As my momma would say, "Always put your best foot forward."

Amber has made herself at home on my black-and-white striped wingback chair. I hand her the glass of tea and settle into my black-and-white flowered sofa.

"Great place you have here, Sasha," she compliments. That's another rule of interviewing someone. Make them like you by paying them a compliment.

"Thank you, Amber. It's my little sanctuary," I reply, remembering to be extra solemn. "How's *Talk* magazine?" I ask, to make sure that she knows that this interview is friendly.

"*Talk* is great. As you know, print journalism seems to be a fading art, but I love our readers. They're loyal to me and follow the blog religiously," she replies.

"That's wonderful," I say sweetly. Amber's not pretty enough for television. Even if she loses twenty pounds and drops $100,000 on plastic surgery, the television camera will never love her.

Then, Amber shifts in the wingback chair and shows me her recorder. "You know the drill, Sasha. I'm going to record this interview and then write the story using a combination of my notes and this recording. I'll give you the opportunity to fact-check the story before it runs."

I nod in confirmation and begin to tell Amber about how Colin and I met. It's an old-fashioned love story. I interviewed him. He swept me off my feet. I went to all of his games. He made me feel like the only girl in the world. Then, I tell her that the whole time he was seeing me he was screwing Doctor Caroline Collins. I tear up when I tell Amber about the last night at the hotel where she was waiting for him in the other room. I describe in detail how cold Colin was to me. I leave out the part where I begged Colin to have sex with me, but I really play up how I asked him over and over again to tell me that he loved me. Amber shivers as I recount how he ordered me out of the suite.

I pause for a moment to dab my eyes with the tissues that I placed conveniently on the coffee table before Amber arrived. Thinking about the night that Colin was such a bastard does make me cry, but I might be hamming it up just a wee bit for Amber.

When I tell Amber about Jenna, and how Colin had been stringing her along since she was eighteen, Amber's mouth falls open. I go into detail about how he keeps her as a mistress and pays for her living expenses. I don't exactly accuse Colin of having sex with her, but I certainly plant doubts in Amber's mind.

To further ruin Colin, I drop the bombshell that he and Jenna had a child together when they were in high school. Amber is shocked. She asks follow-up questions, and I do my best to answer them.

After we move away from Colin, she quizzes me about previous boyfriends. I make sure to keep the answers very short. I want the majority of the article to be about Colin and Caroline.

The article will drop a week from Friday. I'll be granting my news station an on-air interview to follow it up. Colin's going to hate me, and I don't care. He'll regret ever screwing me over.

Charlie and Colin's story continues in From Now Until Infinity …

Dear reader,

Thank you for hanging around to the end of the book/beginning of Colin and Charlie's story. They've been a part of my life for as long as I can remember. I named Caroline "Charlie" Jane Collins when I was in seventh grade, if that gives you an idea. I've loved sharing them with you.

There are three more books in the Infinity Series.

Love or hate a scene or quote from *Falling Into Infinity*? Please share it with me at layne@layneharper.com. I would also appreciate you leaving a review on the retailer's website. Good or bad, it helps all of us authors do a better job for you, the reader.

Thanks!

Layne Harper

Acknowledgements:

First of all, I would like to thank my college sweetheart and very supportive husband. In the eighteen years that we have been together he has been my cheerleader through numerous creative endeavors, without once questioning my sanity. He has also tirelessly listened to me rattle on about Charlie and Colin. He even told me we could name our son Colin. I'm so thankful that we didn't, because now it would just be creepy. He's my safety net, allowing me to soar while knowing that there is a soft place to land. I told you, baby, that marrying me would be a good idea. I love you enough!

To my children, I owe you everything. Just know that being your mom has been the greatest pleasure of my life.

Here's an odd one. I'd like to thank Jim Rome, host of the *Jim Rome Show* on *CBS Radio*. When I graduated from college and started life in the real world, I was lonely being away from my friends and family. Jim Rome's sports-talk radio show came on at eleven o'clock, daily. I would eat lunch in my car, listening to his sports rants and interviews. He made me laugh as he regaled me with stories about the on- and off-the-field lives of the players that I enjoyed watching. I've been a proud clone since 1998.

I would like to thank the girls in my life. I'm blessed to be surrounded with the best girlfriends in the world. You sharing your hopes, dreams, dating disasters, mistakes, successes, and love stories with me have made this book. I hope that all of you see bits and pieces of our friendship in it. I also thank you for drinking wine with me, never judging, and always finding a babysitter when it's time for a G.N.O. It's still my ultimate goal that when our children are adults they will be as close as we are, and toast their crazy moms.

Huge thanks goes to the girls who read *Falling Into Infinity* before publication. Their probing questions, story suggestions and late-night texts have made this book the best that it can be. I owe you all much more than a glass of wine.

I have two wonderful editors who helped me with *Falling Into Infinity*. Special thanks goes to Kristi Zeller (klzeller99@gmail.com). Any errors in the book are mine.

Most of all, I would like to thank my parents—who will hopefully never read this because I would just die if I my dad knew that I write sex scenes for a living—for sacrificing to pay for all four years of college at Texas A&M. The greatest gifts that they gave me were a superb education and being debt-free when I graduated. I was able to take a job at a technology start-up, making peanuts but gaining the best real-world education around.

Oh! I also should thank my mom, who taught elementary school kids to read for thirty years, for developing my love of reading. She didn't care what I read as long as I was reading. When I was in fifth grade, she didn't bat an eyelash at my choice of authors like Stephen King or V.C. Andrews. She happily checked their books out of the library for me when the librarian said I was too young to read them. I remind myself of that story frequently, and I hope that I will encourage and support my children like she did for me.

About Layne:

Layne Harper is a mom, wife, book junkie, and sports fanatic. However, when the kids and husband are safely ensconced at school and work, she slips into her office with her three rescue dogs and writes until it's time to drive carpool. Her children have no idea about her secret life (and they hopefully never will), and the dogs won't tell. She's always writing in her mind though and making notes on whatever is close by: envelopes, napkins, and kid's homework ...

There's nothing that makes an author happier than to hear from their readers. Follow Layne on Twitter or on Facebook. She checks her email frequently. Her address is layne@layneharper.com. Follow her blog at www.LayneHarper.com.

www.ingramcontent.com/pod-product-compliance
Lightning Source LLC
Chambersburg PA
CBHW050024180626
46810CB00002B/558